Dear Reader,

I have four great *Scarlet* books to get you in the holiday mood this month! To start with, Judy Jackson's Canadian heroine suddenly finds her life whirling *Out of Control*. Then Stella Whitelaw takes *her* heroine to Barbados where nothing (and no one) is quite as it seems! In Kay Gregory's novel, Iain and Phaedra play out their involving story against a dramatic Cornish backdrop. And, last (but by no means least!) *will* Jocasta be *Betrayed* in Angela Drake's latest *Scarlet* romance?

You will notice that each of these authors has been published in *Scarlet* before and we are delighted to see their names back on our list. One of the things that makes *Scarlet* so special, I believe, is the very individual style each of our authors brings to her writing. And, of course, they also offer us a wonderful variety of settings for their books. It's lovely, isn't it, to be able to enjoy visiting a different country without having to leave home?

So, whether you're reading this book on a train, a bus or a plane, sitting at home or having a well earned vacation – I hope you'll enjoy *all* the *Scarlet* titles I have chosen for you this month.

Till next month,

Sally Cooper

SALLY COOPER,
Editor-in-Chief – *Scarlet*

About the Author

Stella Whitelaw began her working life as the youngest female chief reporter in London. She has had nearly 30 novels and 208 short stories published and has won various national prizes for her short stories. In 1995, she was shortlisted for the highly prestigious Catherine Cookson Fiction award.

In her (very limited) leisure time, Stella enjoys walking around Britain's coastal and scenic routes and caring for her six beautiful cats.

The author is a talented amateur actress whose stage roles have included Eliza Doolittle, Kate and Miss Prism.

Stella's first book for *Scarlet* was *No Darker Heaven* and we are delighted to welcome her back to our list with *Revenge Is Sweet*.

Other *Scarlet* titles available this month:

HIS FATHER'S WIFE – Kay Gregory
BETRAYED – Angela Drake
OUT OF CONTROL – Judy Jackson

STELLA WHITELAW

SWEET SEDUCTION

Enquiries to:
Robinson Publishing Ltd
7 Kensington Church Court
London W8 4SP

First published in the UK by Scarlet, 1997

A copy of the British Library Cataloguing in
Publication data is available from the British Library

ISBN 1-85487-958-8

Printed and bound in the EC

10 9 8 7 6 5 4 3 2 1

CHAPTER 1

She had this persistent feeling that someone was staring at her. She didn't like it. The hot trade wind blowing across the wild, mountainous island of St Lucia combed through her unruly chestnut hair and covered her face with strands of fire.

Kira turned slowly on one heel, her lame leg resting against the gate that confined passengers to the transit lounge. The muscles were aching and she was disconcerted by the eyes that felt as if they were burning into her back.

Head and shoulders above the crowd, far across on the other side of the crowded lounge, stood a tall man in an expensively tailored business suit, the jacket unbuttoned. He wore a wide-brimmed hat pulled low on his forehead. Kira could feel the magnetism of his eyes, forcing her to look at him.

1

She caught the glint of a gold watch-chain worn across a double-breasted waistcoat. How could he wear a waistcoat in this heat? He touched the brim of his hat in mock salute.

Damn him, she thought; she didn't need or seek a pick-up. It was the last thing she wanted, now or ever. She deliberately turned her back. But she could feel the man moving towards her. It was uncanny, something perhaps to do with the long flight, the sultry darkness and the unaccustomed heat of the velvety Caribbean night.

A quiver of apprehension ran through her body in those moments, a sudden eruption of the past as the man's stride slowed into the slow motion of a dream.

Before she'd turned away he had thrown her a long, challenging look that was almost overpowering. Memories she had tried to suppress were surging back through her mind. Why had this man's glinting eyes begun to peel back layers which she had successfully kept hidden from the world?

Three men had nearly destroyed her life: grandfather Benjamin Reed, ex-fiancé Bruce, and Percival Connor MP. They had sent her reeling into a corner. Now at last, rid of them all,

Kira Reed was back on an even keel, about to be herself, live out her own life.

A smile touched her lips, deepening the small dimple at the corner of her mouth. Salvation was in her own hands. She would make sure it happened. She would become a different woman, leave that other, damaged person behind in London.

'Is the heat getting to you, ma'am?' he asked, stopping by her side. His eyes were a piercing blue, the clearest blue of the ocean, startling in their purity. 'It's a hot night and this cattle-pen is no place for a lady to be kept standing.'

His gravelly voice bored through her thoughts. She wanted to get away from him, sensed he was dangerous, but somehow she was rooted to the spot. She didn't answer.

'I guess London is still cold,' he went on. 'This heat will take some getting used to.'

'Yes,' said Kira, turning away. 'It's been a cold winter.'

London, that winter, had been a synonym for rain, sleet, plunging temperatures and slushy snow underfoot. But hurricanes were not part of its grey scene. Instead, cold northeasterly winds regularly whipped wavelets along the murky mud-water of the Thames, blew umbrellas inside-out, sent junk-food wrappers skittering along gutters. Winter moved sluggishly into the wettest spring for years.

Her mind went back to her accident. It had not been the fault of the wind, nor had the motorbike been out of control. *She* had been out of control. Her mind had been teetering on the edge of sanity, her mouth constantly full of ashes.

She had met Bruce when he'd come to the House of Commons to install a new computer system in the Members' Library. Kira met him while having a quick coffee in the cafeteria. He stayed to steal her heart.

Bruce had been impressed by her job and she had been smitten by his fair good looks. He had had a cheerful and casual outlook on life which lightened her more serious attitude. He'd charmed Kira out of her quiet, reserved ways and showed her that there was more to life than security and a pay cheque. Her orderly life went into a spin from the moment she met him.

She had fallen in love with him, thinking in her innocence that their romance would certainly lead to marriage. She began saving for a wedding and a home. Bruce had a way of agreeing with everything she said. Everything was wonderful. He was younger than her but it was no problem.

'Did you get any Valentine cards?' she'd asked that evening in February. She should have noticed the strain on his handsome face but she was too blinkered with her own happiness to notice.

'Cards?' he replied vaguely.

'Oh, dear, perhaps you're not so popular this year,' she teased. 'Don't you know what day it is?'

His face was a mask. He didn't meet her eyes. Kira sensed a distance that she did not understand.

'I haven't been home yet. Kira, I must tell you something. I'm sorry, it's been wonderful, you and me . . . but now – well, there's someone else,' he said, his voice full of genuine misery.

It was like a pan of ice-cold water thrown in her face. The shock hit her, his words echoing darkly in her mind. Someone else. Someone else. She tried to find the solidness of something, anything, to hold on to so that she would not fall.

'I sent you a Valentine's card,' she said, as if that made any difference.

5

'I've met this girl,' Bruce went on relentlessly, his face stiff and unapproachable. 'We didn't mean it to happen. I was in love with you and wanted to be, but this was too strong for me. Please try to understand.'

It was all meaningless. 'But I thought you loved me. I love *you*. What about our plans? I thought we were getting married . . .'

'Jenny and I are very much in love. You and I . . . well, it was wonderful but it's all over. I'm really sorry.'

'We'd talked about marriage. Made plans . . .'

'Only talked,' Bruce corrected her. 'Nothing more. If you thought it was more serious, then you imagined it. It's never been more than . . . a lot of fun.'

Kira felt the colour drain from her face as if she were bleeding. The sharp easterly wind cut through her coat like a knife.

'Fun? *Fun?*' Her breath caught in her throat. She struggled on. 'You can't mean it. What we have is special. You'll get over her, this Jenny.'

'It's not so simple. Jenny is going to have a baby. She's pregnant.'

The world shattered into a thousand pieces and lay around her feet like so much broken glass. She did not move. She could not move.

'A baby . . .' she repeated, dazed, her mind flashing over the intimacy.

'Jenny is my secretary,' he went on, just for the sake of talking. 'She joined the firm last October.'

'And pregnant by February?' Kira exploded. 'You move fast, don't you? Was it at the firm's Christmas party? Remember, I couldn't come? Mr Connor had work to be finished before the Christmas recess. So when is the baby due?'

'September.'

'Perhaps Jenny would like some of the things I've bought for our home and housing details from the estate agents? Anything else of mine she'd like?'

'I've already moved into *her* house.'

Kira hit rock-bottom.

She did not see him to speak to again. But she caught sight of him once in the furniture department of the Army & Navy Stores in Victoria Street. She hid behind a sturdy walnut bookcase, like a fugitive, desperate for an escape route down the stairs.

It was a similar chilling wind that had Kira hanging on to her calf-length skirt as she came out of Great Smith Street and turned into Parliament Square some weeks later. It threatened to wrap the skirt round her waist, revealing long shapely legs in sheer black tights and the useless modesty of a brief silk slip.

'Drat this wind,' Kira gasped, struggling with her skirt, shoulder-bag, clutch of library books and splitting brown paper bag of fruit from Strutton Ground market. She was in a hurry. Mr Connor had a question down for Prime Minister's Question Time and that always made him nervous. He was afraid of the braying pack on the other side of the House.

Parliament Square was snarled up with traffic: red double-decker buses, slogan-painted tour buses, black beetle-like taxis in droves, huge container lorries, coachloads of tourists gaping at Big Ben and the newly cleaned stone face of the ancient Westminster Abbey. The traffic lights at the north end of Victoria Street were working normally but a vast number of vehicles had jammed Parliament Square, choking, clogging, barely moving, and the tailback grew impatient.

Mr Connor was a junior minister at the Ministry of Defence, and regarded his embryo career as being of the utmost importance. He expected his secretary to be there when he needed her, day and halfway through the

night. Late sittings and his erratic work schedule gave Kira little or no social life. It was a
wonder she had ever had time to meet and
romance Bruce. Mr Connor thought nothing
of dictating a pile of letters to his constituents
just as she was packing up for the day.

'You don't mind staying late, do you, Kira?'
he'd say, pacing his office, not waiting for an
answer.

Kira did not mind hard work. Being at the
heart of Parliament and working in a historic
building never failed to give her a thrill every
morning as she slotted her identity pass in the
electronic entrance gate. The cloisters of New
Palace Yard had witnessed so much history.
Guy Fawkes had been hung, drawn and quar-
tered in the Yard.

Kira worked long hours in cramped conditions. Mr Connor shared one of the old minis-
terial rooms but Kira had a desk in a crowded
secretarial area in a semi-basement. The secretaries positioned filing cabinets and plants as
screening to give themselves some privacy.
There were windows along one wall, high up,
but all they saw were legs walking through Star
Court. Occasionally a friendly face peered down
and smiled.

Kira stood on the pavement and checked her watch. She was running out of time. Revving engines spewed out dirty exhaust fumes. The wind billowed her skirt as if she were a dancer and momentarily she wished she had known her father, Aaronovitch, the famous Russian dancer. She was sure he wouldn't have minded a few inches of thigh showing.

'Keep down, you dratted skirt.' She glared at the whirling material. 'This could cause an international situation.'

It was at that moment that the flimsy bag of shopping chose to split. Apples and pears scattered across the pavement. The culprit was a juicy over-ripe pear which the market vendor had slipped in. Kira raced after the rolling fruit. She was not aware how close she was to the kerbstone, nor that an express delivery rider, helmeted and goggled, on a heavy black Honda 750cc motorbike was roaring through gaps in the stationary traffic.

For a second Kira saw the shiny black helmet. Then her skirt caught in the front mudguard of the bike and she was jerked off balance. The bike dragged her into the roadway. The sky spun, buildings towered, colours flashed. Pain stabbed her leg, shot through her shoulder.

Kira heard the screech of brakes and the hoarse cry of the motorcyclist as the big machine skidded out of control. Patches of sky swam scarlet with the pain; windows in her head shattered with strobes of light.

She lay in the grey no-man's-land of unconsciousness. Kira surfaced briefly, found herself plugged into the complicated wires and tubes of the intensive care machinery. She did not move. She hurt all over.

'Miss Reed? Kira . . . can you hear me? Grip my hand if you can.'

The voice was calm but comforting. Grip whose hand . . . what hand? Kira thought vaguely.

'I'm Dr Armstrong. You've been hurt in a road accident. But you are going to be all right.'

Kira tried a polite smile but her face wouldn't work. She drifted back into the dim sleep where she wasn't required to do anything but float in pain.

When she surfaced again, she became aware that something tight was constricting her arm and one of her legs felt like a ton weight.

'What's happened . . . to me?' she managed to ask this time. She did not recognize the croak as her voice.

'You've a cracked collarbone, a broken leg and some concussion. Nothing that won't heal perfectly well in time. We had to shave off some of your hair to stitch a head cut but it'll soon grow,' said Dr Armstrong.

'Save me . . . going to the hairdresser's,' Kira said weakly. The nurse was swabbing her arm for an injection.

'Miss Reed, have you any family? We looked in your bag and found your Commons pass. We've been trying to trace relatives.'

The doctor's voice was far away as waves of healing sleep engulfed the pain. Kira sank into cotton-wool darkness, longing for the hurt to go. She had work to do; she ought to be getting on with it. How would Mr Connor manage without her?

'I've a grandfather,' she managed to murmur. 'In Barbados. Fitt's House. It's a castle . . .'

'What did she say, Nurse?'

'Something about a castle in Barbados,' said the nurse primly, as if Barbados were one stop along from Clapham Common on the Northern Line.

'Ask her again when she comes round.' Dr Armstrong folded up his stethoscope and put it in his top pocket. 'Perhaps you could catch

12

that MP she works for and ask him, though he seems more worried about getting a replacement than about his secretary's injuries.

'One of those dedicated career-women,' he grunted. 'No family, no relations, no real friends. A little flat in Pimlico, conveniently close to work. Who's going to take care of her when she comes out of hospital?'

'Not you or me,' said the nurse curtly, adjusting the height of the drip. Dr Armstrong did go on.

'That's what I mean. We shall do a good job on Miss Reed, then throw her out into the community to get on as best she can.'

'She could go to Barbados,' sniffed the nurse.

'She probably meant Barnstaple. And grand-fathers are usually old men, not up to nursing an accident victim with a lame leg.'

'Won't her leg ever be right?'

'Hard to say. I don't know. It was a tricky break with a stress fracture. She fell at an odd angle. It might be possible to re-set it again at a later date. The stress fracture might give her a lot of pain.'

Three days later Kira was moved out of intensive care into a side room on the orthopae-dic ward. A large, ostentatious bouquet of stiff-headed flowers arrived via Interflora from Mr Connor. Kira wondered which of the other secretaries had telephoned the order for him. Perhaps he had organized a temp by now.

Kira was on painkillers and sleepy most of the time. The collarbone injury was painful and the bruised ribs were not amusing. Every movement, breath, cough, was an agony in her chest. But she was young and healthy and her body began to heal.

'Do you enjoy your work?' asked Dr Armstrong.

'Very much,' she said. 'It's so interesting. I don't write Mr Connor's speeches, of course. He insists on doing that himself.' Yes, she thought ruefully, and they were uniformly dreadful and usually delivered to an audience of six, seven on a good day. The House had a way of emptying when Percival Connor got to his feet.

Kira had expected some kind of get-well note from Mr Connor but it came sooner than she thought. It was typed immaculately on top-quality House of Commons notepaper, cream-laid, portcullised.

'Dear Kira,' he had dictated. 'I understand that you will not be back before the start of the summer recess so I have had to engage a replacement. She is very thorough and will probably want to stay. I therefore enclose your due sick pay and a little extra to tide you over. Do contact me again when you are fully recovered and perhaps we can work something out. All the best. Yours sincerely, Percival Connor MP.'

Kira was stunned. How like the man. He had always seemed to value her but he had no intention of waiting until she was a fully recovered working machine. She had been nothing to him. There was already another little robot sitting at her desk, typing his speeches and coping with the constituents' daily avalanche of domestic problems. It was all very well — there would probably be a job found for her somewhere — but she would have to start earning the approval of a new boss all over again.

'A big sigh, Miss Reed. Yet you're improving daily. Is the hospital food getting you down?'

Dr Armstrong leaned over the end of the bed. He was captivated by the fragility of this young woman. There were sad secrets behind those clear hazel eyes that he wished he had the means to heal.

She smiled at him ruefully. The doctor had been consistently kind and attentive.

'I've just been dispensed with,' she said. 'My boss has already replaced me.'

'It could be a blessing in disguise,' said Dr Armstrong. 'You'd only go racing back to work when you need several months' convalescence. At least three months.'

'That's quite out of the question.' Kira wriggled further down the bed as if to shut away the world. 'I have a living to earn and a career to pick up again. There's a by-election soon . . . perhaps the victor would be glad of my Parliamentary know-how.'

'Forget it,' the doctor persisted. 'What about this grandfather? Can't you go and stay with him?'

'My grandfather?' Kira looked surprised and confused. How did Dr Armstrong know about her grandfather? He was someone she never mentioned to anyone, never, ever. He was buried in the past. He could be dead for all she knew.

'You said you had a grandfather, living in Barbados, I think.'

Kira sank back against the pillows and a cloud settled on her ashen face. 'I think you must be mistaken, Doctor.'

'No, my nurse heard you mention your grandfather quite plainly.'

'I was probably delirious.'

Dr Armstrong did not push her. For some reason Kira was refusing to talk. He patted her good foot.

'You can try getting up tomorrow,' he said. 'See how you manage with the crutches. They take some getting used to.'

'I can get used to anything,' said Kira firmly.

She had not thought of her grandfather for years, pushing him completely from her life. It had not been difficult, when he had made no contact with her or her mother. Why had her mind suddenly dragged him out of the shadows? Had she subconsciously been calling for help again, as she had when her mother had died?

'Go and visit him? Never!' said Kira grimly to herself.

He was a vague, shadowy figure with no face. Tamara's father. Kira had never met him. But she remembered, only too clearly, her mother's distress as letter after letter was returned to her, unopened.

Tamara had been a widow with a young daughter to bring up in a strange country, her

17

eyesight failing. It was only natural that she should turn to her father for help but it seemed he could not forgive his daughter for leaving Barbados and her inheritance.

Tamara's eyesight got worse. She was in poor health and died one winter in a severe influenza epidemic. Kira was taken into care, placed with a series of foster parents, eventually boarded at a convent for disadvantaged children, funded by the Government.

It was during those suspended years that Kira had resolved that nothing so disastrous was ever going to happen to her again. She was going to be self-supporting. She was going to have a career. Her mother's pale face haunted her.

But Tamara had had no regrets about falling in love with Aaronovitch and said many times that their brief time together had been magic.

Kira grew into a tall, reserved girl, nurturing a fierce ambition and independence. From an early age she realized that everything depended on her own efforts. Even her chestnut hair seemed to be alive with electricity, bouncing in all directions, her green-flecked eyes kindling energy. When she ran, her long legs carried her like the wind. The nuns liked Kira winning races but they did not approve of the legs that took her past the winning post. They were far too shapely.

Kira took a secretarial course, determined that this would be her passport to an executive post somewhere in the world. She would not be taking dictation for ever. One day people would take orders from her. She was going to make it happen.

'Still not eating, miss?' The hospital orderly looked at Kira's untouched tray. 'You gotta build up your strength. Broken bones don't mend by themselves. I'm not surprised you were knocked over by the wind. There's nothing of you.'

'It was a motorbike,' said Kira.

'I'll get you a cup of tea and a biscuit.'

Kira had no appetite. It was not simply the road accident. She had not eaten properly for weeks. She could cope with a broken leg, the hospital stay, the unexpected lack of purpose. It wasn't anything to do with having a grandfather who had disowned her for years.

The numbness crept over her again and Kira closed her eyes against the grey daylight filtering through the high windows. She did not want to face the day.

She still ached from Bruce's below-the-belt body-blow. The road accident hardly mattered. It was merely another event in the chain of blows dealt to her over the years. The abrupt letter from Mr Connor was almost a relief. It was liberating. Now she was free of them all.

'One day at a time,' said Kira to herself, easing her good leg over the side of the hospital bed. 'Don't go and break the other leg.'

She was no longer wearing the foam collar and cuff to support the cracked collarbone. She longed to leave the antiseptic hospital atmosphere and was keen to go home to everything that was familiar. As she no longer had a job, she could do whatever she liked. Go anywhere, be anyone. There was nothing in the world to stop her.

She looked out of the window at the drizzle of rain running down the glass. It was the worst spring for years. She wouldn't be missing anything if she left London. She would avoid meeting pregnant secretaries and having to hide from men buying furniture.

'Soon be time for you to go home,' said Dr Armstrong on his next ward visit. 'We can't keep you here forever, even if you do decorate the ward. Have you any plans?'

'I think I'm going to learn about the sugar industry,' she said without thinking, surprising herself too. 'Or something like that. And go somewhere that's warm.'

Dr Armstrong was taken aback. It was the last thing he'd expected to hear. Still, it showed that Kira was emerging from her lethargy.

'I hope it doesn't involve anything too strenuous. You must take care of that leg.'

'Nothing more strenuous than a phone call to my former employer, who owes me a big favour. There was a trade delegation at Westminster recently, to promote the sugar industry. Mr Connor went to a luncheon, a conference and a reception on the Terrace. He ought to remember at least one contact name that would be useful to me.'

Dr Armstrong gave a low chuckle. 'I'm glad to see you're better. I don't know what Sister was getting worried about.' But he did know, intuitively. Her leg was on the mend, but he wasn't sure about her heart. Someone had hurt her badly, and there wasn't a plaster yet invented that would heal those feelings.

Kira had flown club class on a British Airways 747 out to Bridgetown, Barbados. The ticket

21

was an extravagance but she had been saving to get married and it seemed a good way of spending the money. She had almost no information about her grandfather except that his name was Benjamin Reed and that he grew sugar on the island. Tamara had reverted to her own surname after her husband, Aaronovitch, died, tired of always having to spell it out to people. Now another name, Fitt's House, kept coming into Kira's mind, though she had no idea why.

She planned to meet her grandfather but without letting him know who she was. And it was important that she was out of the country and a long way away when Bruce's baby was born.

It was a challenge . . . to arrive as an unknown on Barbados and see if by sheer force of personality she could become someone. Not Kira Reed, out of work, lame, jilted and rejected. There was a word for her hope. 'Hype'. A self-generated publicity stunt.

It was velvety dark when the plane made an unexpected landing on the Caribbean island of St Lucia. The captain invited passengers to stretch their legs and Kira followed the exodus from the plane with relief. It had been a nine-hour flight and the knotted muscles in her leg hurt. She kneaded away the pain, glad to be moving at last. The island was only a shadowy dark shape but she could smell the volcanic dust. Kira walked slowly to the perimeter of the airfield, the landing lights twinkling in the darkness, the dramatic hills a backdrop to the sultry night sky.

It was then that she had the strangest feeling that someone was watching her and caught sight of a tall man in the airport lounge. She did not know him. No one knew her on St Lucia or on Barbados.

She tried not to look in his direction but he was compelling. He was like no other man she had ever seen before. He was strangely different, with such confidence and assurance. She felt it, like an invisible power, winging towards her over the heat of the space between them.

Hannah sang no songs, nor danced, nor whispered enticing words of love. Her hair was a whisper, not long, blown strands of ripe corn or dark waves as blue-black as a humming bird's wing. She did not twist a man round her little finger nor beckon him into the soft, warm hollow of her arms.

Yet she held a fragrant promise of pleasure and her elusive scent was disturbing; her secrets lay hidden in the invisible depths of her dark eye. Some men panicked and went mad. For most people she had no face, no body, no eyes, and the only certainty of closeness in her arms was death.

Hannah did not yet exist. Hannah . . . capricious, powerful, terrifying . . . was the name of a hurricane being seeded a thousand miles away by the fluttering wings of a single checkerspot butterfly high in a mountain.

CHAPTER 2

The St Lucia airport officials were dismayed by the sudden number of passengers strolling around the airfield. A harassed woman official in a creased uniform began handing out transit cards.

'I'm not in transit,' said Kira. 'I'd rather go back on the plane and sit in the air-conditioning if I can't walk about.'

'You wait here, please. Passengers are not allowed to walk anywhere.' The woman was at a loss. 'You wait in the transit lounge, please.'

'Then why let us get off the plane in the first place?'

The woman was adamant. She refused to allow Kira to return to the plane without first waiting in the transit lounge.

The transit lounge was crowded to the point of suffocation. There were no seats left and the noisy air-conditioning was overworked. Kira looked round in despair.

The crowded area was a heaving mixture of tanned tourists and island-hopping locals with bags and bundles. Babies cried, skins sweated. Brightly coloured Caribbean clothes and head-dresses and straw hats painted the scene. Voices were loud and distracting. Kira listened to the West Indian accent. It was a strange mixture of dialects from Wales, England and France strangled with their own particular clipped intonation.

She turned slowly on one heel, her lame leg resting against the barred gate again. She was going to faint if she didn't get somewhere to sit down.

Kira's physical discomfort was heightened by the tall man's steady and relentless gaze. She was jostled by another angry passenger demanding to be allowed back on the BA flight and the intensity of his eyes was broken. She turned her back on the stranger but the silhouette of the man in a brimmed hat stayed in her mind.

She became aware that the man was moving through the mass of people. She could feel her pulse quickening for no reason at all. She knew she did not want to look into those powerful eyes or be confronted by such an aggressively masculine man.

It was strange that he should be even remotely interested in her. She looked a mess and was too tired to be civil. Perhaps it was merely politeness to a visitor.

'Shall I get you a chair, ma'am?' He raised his hand and snapped his fingers at an airport guard. 'Please find this lady a chair.'

'Certainly, Mr Earl, but I can't leave my post.'

'Then get someone else to find a chair. Now, and be quick about it.'

His voice was gravelly and confident, touched with a trace of impatience. She did not speak to him. She looked down and saw long legs in well cut trousers, polished light brown shoes. The slimness of his legs and the expertly tailored trousers that encased them make Kira avert her eyes.

She was shaken by the intensity of the feelings stirred by this stranger; longed for release from the disturbing encounter by some flight announcement. She felt desperate to get away from him and yet something deeper made her stay. Perhaps it was the chair. It arrived and he placed it for her.

'Thank you,' she murmured, sitting down, pressing her skirt over her knees.

He was looked straight at her, critically taking in Kira's creased linen suit and tousled hair. His mouth had a curved upper lip that held a hint of a sardonic smile. Under the brim of his hat Kira saw a fringe of crisp black hair. His skin was deeply tanned and slightly rough in texture. There was a fresh scar on his cheek and she wondered how he had got it. His eyes dared Kira to ask him about the scar. But she did not care or want to speak. She did not want to say anything to this unnerving man.

'We have to wait for the Caribbean Airways flight to take off and then they will allow you to reboard your plane to Barbados,' he said.

'They could have said,' Kira remarked.

'They have problems. St Lucia is not Heathrow, London, with sophisticated equipment and highly trained staff. They were overwhelmed by the number of people who suddenly began to walk all over the airfield. It was for your own safety that they herded you into this building,' he went on.

'Herded is the right word.' Kira didn't like the sharp way she sounded. It was a foreign tone for her.

'You will soon be in Barbados. It's only a twenty-minute flight from St Lucia. Hardly time to fasten your seat belt.'

'But why stop here at all? I thought it was a direct flight to Bridgetown.'

'We use planes like buses,' he explained with a wry smile. 'Some passengers have got off at St Lucia and the plane will fill up with people just wanting to make the short flight to Barbados. Like myself,' he added. 'I've been to St Lucia on business and now I wish to return home with all speed.'

Kira found the force of her anger draining away. The stranger had reassured her that the plane would not take off without her. He was looking deeply into her eyes as if he wanted to know much more.

'Don't I know you?' he said curiously.

'I don't think so,' said Kira, prim and remote.

'There's something familiar about your face.'

'Impossible. I've never been to Barbados before. This is my first visit.'

He was several inches over six feet tall, rangy and loose-limbed. His white shirt was unbuttoned at the neck showing a strong throat gleaming with the heat. He had dispensed with his tie and it was draped over his briefcase.

A young man in a brown uniform shirt strolled over to the gate, opened it and began to collect in the transit cards. There was a surge of people behind Kira, almost sweeping her off her feet, in spite of the chair.

A steady hand gripped her elbow and the man lifted her, then shouldered a way through the crowd for Kira, protecting her with his body, creating a clear path through the milling mob of people with bags and babies and baskets. The new passengers broke into a run across the tarmac to the waiting plane. Kira had never seen anything like it.

He steered her towards the front section and the steps which led into first class, assuming control of her travel arrangements.

'Everyone is a little over-anxious about getting a seat, despite being booked in. It's still like a bus to the locals. But don't worry, they will not take off without me.'

The warm breeze was wonderful after the stifling airport building. Kira felt a wave of relief to be moving and stiffly climbing the steps into the plane. The tall man was right behind her, not allowing anyone to jostle her.

Once in the cool cabin, Kira turned to thank him.

'Thank you,' she said. 'I'm all right now. I'm very grateful.'

He took off his hat, holding it by the brim in lean brown hands in front of him. His blue eyes were startlingly clear now, darkly lashed unclear dark brows, their expression unswerving.

'My pleasure, ma'am.'

As Kira moved away to find her seat in the forward section, she heard an air hostess greeting the dark stranger.

'Good evening, Mr Earl,' said the air hostess with a smile. 'Nice to have you travelling with us again. Your usual seat, sir?'

'No, thank you. I think I'll see what there is further back.'

He was following her again. Kira was half afraid, yet half wanting him to sit in the empty seat beside her.

She busied herself fastening the seat-belt, stowing her bag, marking territory, looking out of the window. She was being incredibly foolish. Her heart was racing. This was no way to behave after all she had gone through. What did it matter whether the man sat next to her or not?

'I believe this seat is free?' he asked, stopping in the aisle. 'May I join you for the flight?'

'Please do,' said Kira, but she did not look at him.

He eased himself into the seat, stretching out his long legs. She could not help liking everything she saw about him . . . the capable brown hands fastening the clasp, the old gold of the watch-chain, the sharp crease in the trousers, the faintly aromatic smell of a spicy cologne, the darkly glistening hair crisply cut into the nape of his neck. He was all man, and a magnificent man at that. But she wanted nothing to do with him.

'Do you always travel first class for a twenty-minute flight?' Kira asked.

'You may have noticed that I need the legroom.'

His arm brushed against her as he moved sideways to stow a wallet in an inside pocket. It was like an electric shock. It took a physical effort to stay still in her seat and let the feeling wash away.

'Allow me to introduce myself. My name is Giles Earl. I own Sugar Hill Plantation in the Parish of St John,' he said.

Kira took a steadying breath and smiled briefly. 'My name is Kira . . .'

'That's a very pretty name.'

Kira was hardly listening as Giles Earl continued talking. Sugar Hill Plantation. In the briefcase at her feet was a letter of introduction written by Percival Connor to the owner of Sugar Hill Plantation.

And Benjamin Reed's business colleague had been Reuben Earl. Reed and Earl. The name had been famous in the sugar industry before they quarrelled. They had set up a partnership in the late forties, harnessing the power of both their plantations and refineries. Her mother had often told her how Benjamin and Reuben had planned a brilliant future for Barbados, intending to work towards Independence.

It would have been the easiest thing in the world to open her briefcase and bring out the letter to start things going. But somehow she could not. Her hands lay frozen in her lap, despite the comfortable cabin temperature. This was not the time to say that she was Benjamin Reed's granddaughter.

The short flight had a mystical quality that Kira found hard to pin down. They did not talk much but simply sat in a companionable silence, occasionally exchanging a few words. Giles pointed out the approaching lights of Bridgetown. The dark shape of the island was dotted with lights and Kira could feel his pride in his homeland.

'It is a beautiful island,' he said. 'Maybe you will never leave it. Where are you staying?'

'Sandy Lane Hotel,' she said, not mentioning that it would only be for a few days.

'Then maybe I shall see you around. It's a small island.'

'Maybe.'

'The hotel was built on the site of an old sugar plantation called Sandy Lane, in a small bay on the west coast of St James,' Giles went on. 'It's the island's most elegant and luxurious hotel.'

Sandy Lane, he explained, was the dream and inspiration of an English Member of Parliament, Ronald Tree, who bought the site in 1957 and spared no expense in putting the finest materials and workmanship into his paradise hotel, making it world-famous.

Giles chuckled. 'Ronald Tree even took a shovel himself to dig down into the black sand, a relic from two hundred years of settling ash from the nearby sugar refinery. Happily, two feet down he struck the pure golden sand that now makes the island's most beautiful bay. Where you'll go swimming tomorrow, no doubt.'

'I'm not here just for a holiday,' she said, but he was already moving out into the aisle as the plane came to halt on the runway. A man in a hurry to get back to his plantation.

So it was fitting that Kira should stay at the Sandy Lane Hotel for a few days. The English parliamentary connection was the right place to polish up her new image.

As she had expected, Giles Earl left her abruptly at Grantley Adams International Airport. He had no luggage to collect and a car was waiting outside. He bade her goodbye, tipped his hat and strode off through the crowds. She saw him wave to some youngsters hanging over the rail of the visitors' gallery which spanned the upper part of the curved building. They grinned back. The gallery was packed with sightseers. It was obviously part of their regular evening entertainment.

There was a loud argument among the porters over who should trundle her luggage. Kira was surprised when the victor was a tough-looking girl of about twenty in tight jeans and a skimpy T-shirt. She swung Kira's case on to her trolley, still shouting at her male colleagues.

'This is my customer,' she insisted. 'Clear off, you jerks.'

Kira followed her out into the warm night air. Even though she was now incredibly tired, her interest revived as she took her first look at Barbados. There was not much to see outside the airport; the land was flat with few buildings, tall palms swaying against the tropical black sky. The balmy air was full of pungent scents . . . sugar cane, flowers, tobacco, the sea . . . all mixed into the sweet and spicy aroma that she was soon to recognize as being pure Barbados.

She tipped the girl porter well and was rewarded with a flashing smile. 'We w'men should stick together,' she said.

'Sandy Lane Hotel, please,' Kira said to the owner of a large, dilapidated American Ford. All the taxis looked old and in need of a re-spray.

'Yes, ma'am,' said the driver jauntily, opening the door for her. 'Sandy Lane it is!'

It was Kira's first experience of the Barbadians' friendliness and inborn politeness. They were gentle, polite and smiling. From young beach vendors to old women selling fruit from their doorways, each had the same kindly manner. It was a new and pleasant attitude after the surliness and indifference so often encountered in England.

The taxi driver took her through rolling countryside in the diluted darkness away from the airfield. Winding lanes meandered between hedgerows and fields full of pale green sugar cane, the breeze rustling through the tall stalks and long waving leaves. Their music stirred through the fields, sighing and rising like an unseen choir, a long note of song carrying out to the sea.

Rows of small wooden houses, bleached and decaying, clustered along the new ABC road, little more than huts but each with an air of tidiness, with neat curtains and plants. The roads were a hub of nightlife: people sat on steps outside their houses playing dominoes, listening to music from transistors, eating fruit, drinking local rum, sleeping. The taxi driver hit the horn to break up a game of road cricket. The young players whipped up the stumps and stood aside, grinning.

Kira had never seen so many faces of mixed African and European origin. It was a predominantly black island, although the English had settled and developed the land from 1627 onwards. But it was the English who discovered the thick dark soil that grew tobacco and sugar so well and made the island one of the richest of the Empire's outposts.

The Elysian trade wind touched her face from across the oceans. It was as fresh as a morning wind, its coolness taking away the residue of the day's heat. Already Kira felt herself relaxing in the warmth and newness of the island. If only she could simply enjoy having a holiday here; she knew her health would improve. But she had to confront her grandfather, avenge the injustice suffered by her mother. Or did she? She didn't really know what she was doing. Perhaps she would find out tomorrow.

They left behind the street lamps and the road ran through pitch darkness; a weak glow came from fishermen's houses scattered along the shore. Sudden headlights from an oncoming vehicle lit up the swaying palm trees and rustling sourgrass.

'And we got pirates, you know,' the taxi driver told her cheerfully. 'You watch out for their ships, ma'am. Big black sails, you can't miss 'em.'

'Real pirates?'

'Sure. There's a lot of piracy goes on. Not just a tourist attraction and day trips, but real piracy.'

Arriving at Sandy Lane was something else. Surrounded by lush green countryside, it was an elegant Spanish hacienda-style building constructed out of expensive coral and designed to follow the natural curve of the bay. From the moment the taxi turned into the driveway, Kira knew she had been right to stay here for the first few nights. She needed to be kind to herself.

'Have a pleasant holiday,' said the driver, smartly taking in her luggage before the bell-boys could put their hands on it. Kira was impressed. She had never been surrounded by so many people wanting to be of service. It was a heady feeling.

She paid the fare and tipped the helpful driver. He gave her his card and told her did private work. Early Bird Services, he called himself.

The reception lobby was cool and spacious, stone and marble, displays of exotic flowers everywhere

Her room was in the new wing, an elegant room in pastel colours, only a little less expensive than the rooms and suites in the original building. She had to remember that she had not won the Lottery even if it felt like it.

She went out on to the balcony to take a first real look at the Caribbean. The sea was a deep blue, dark and mysterious, tipped with phosphorescence. She leaned on the balcony rail, letting the wind take her hair out of its careful styling. No more hairdressers. It could go wild. She breathed in the warm, aromatic scents of flamboyant flowers that tumbled over the walls of the hotel gardens.

It had been a strange day. Leaving a cold, chilly London at dawn; the long flight; meeting Giles Earl on St Lucia and now installed in a beautiful hotel in St James, waiting to be healed by its peace and tranquillity. It was a whole world away from the fumes of Parliament Square, the demanding Mr Connor and a 750cc Honda motorbike.

A waiter brought her a late supper on a trolley laid with a linen cloth and silver cutlery. There was cold chicken, cold salmon, salad, a selection of fruit and cheeses. She was not really hungry, but after a shower Kira sat on her balcony in a wrap, enjoying the delicious food and sipping fresh juice. She was here. She could hardly believe it.

It was some time before she fell asleep. She was thinking of the tall man in the wide-brimmed hat. It was ridiculous to think that anything could come out of their brief meeting, especially with the troubled background of Reed and Earl. She should concentrate on storming the sugar community with some research papers and meeting her crusty and unforgiving grandfather. She would put the handsome stranger right out of her mind. She still hurt too much to risk getting to know another man.

Any research was still only a hazy idea in her mind. She switched on a lamp, found some hotel notepaper and began to set her ideas down, making something constructive of her thoughts. But she kept seeing Giles Earl's face, hearing his voice. It was disconcerting.

Something dark and winged flew against the window, hitting the glass. Kira jerked backwards, her throat dry with fear. She switched off the lamp and burrowed under the sheet. The hotel might be beautiful but it was still a strange island, with animals and insects she had never seen before.

Kira woke early, disorientated by the time difference. She had had very little sleep, tossing restlessly under the single sheet, listening to a tropical dawn chorus of birdsong that was truly glorious. She pulled on a black one-piece swimsuit and a baggy black T-shirt and hurried down a floor and through the gardens to the beach. The hotel grounds were full of trees: royal palms, mahogany, breadfruit, avocado and the bearded fig trees. Legend had it that the oddly ragged fig tree was the origin of the island's name. The early Portuguese sailors had called the tree '*los Barbudos*': the bearded ones.

The white sand was cool to her feet, powder-fine and tickly. Trees and flowering shrubs swept down from the gardens to the wide shore of the curving bay. A few painted boats bobbed on the gentle waves. The sea was a glittering blue and inviting. It was perfection. No wonder they called it a paradise. Kira stretched her arms upwards. She had it all to herself.

She stripped off the shirt and waded into the sea, letting the cool waves wash against her legs. The surgery scar on her thigh stood out, fierce and angry. She ducked under the waves and swam out to one of the boats.

She hung on to a rope and turned to admire the coastline. For as far as she could see in both directions, it was bay after curving bay of sandy shores lined with sweeping trees and flowering bushes. Between some of the trees, she glimpsed the white and pink coral stonework of private houses built on the Sandy Lane Estate. Film

stars and pop stars and millionaires guarded
their privacy on this stretch of the coast.

The water was transparently clear and Kira
could see down to the sandy bottom. A shoal of
tiny white patterned fish swam past, darting off
at an angle when they sensed her presence.

How could her mother had left such a hea-
venly place? Kira remembered their cold and
drab life in North London, often moving from
flat to flat as the rents went up. Tamara's pride
had been as unrelenting as her grandfather's.

But Kira was here now and she knew without a doubt that she had done the right thing.
Bless that persuasive Dr Armstrong. She must
send him a card. Wish you were here . . . She
would need a mask and air pipe if she was to
watch the exotic fish life among the reefs. And
her frothy trousseau nightdress was too hot for
comfort. She needed a plain cotton one. A
shopping trip to Bridgetown was definitely
on the agenda.

She wondered if she could get some visiting
cards printed so that she existed, even if only on
cardboard. Kira Reed, Research Consultant . . .
that was vague enough. And she would invent a
string of phone numbers, fax number, e-mail
number. After all, they weren't going to bother

to fax or ring her 'London office' while she was actually here. Reception might be able to recommend a local printer.

As the rising sun began to warm the beach, Kira came out of the sea and walked along the shore line to dry off. Her skin felt smooth and cool. The morning was calm and peaceful, so unlike the bustle of London and the crowded airport. She felt truly alone and yet not at all lonely.

Life was stirring. Fishermen were bringing in their catches. A burly man was sweeping the sand outside his wooden beach bar. He nodded and called out a greeting.

'Good morning, miss. You want a coffee? Coke?'

'Good morning,' Kira smiled back. 'Later, thank you.'

She was surprised at the mixture of seaside dwellings. Next to another luxury hotel with flamboyant gardens was a cluster of old wooden houses, lithe children swinging on a tree that dipped down to the sand. There were well-kept private houses next to shacks made of corrugated iron. Another was a ruin, burnt out and derelict. There did not seem to be any planning policy.

The sea was not always clear. Some of the beaches were strewn with rocks and a lighter green showed a sandy channel towards the deeper water.

Kira climbed round a rocky headland and heard a deal of splashing. She couldn't imagine what was happening.

'Now, boy, now, boy. Good boy. Good fella.'

A man was pulling a goat into the sea. He had a big scrubbing brush and was scrubbing the goat's behind. The goat was making a vigorous attempt to escape, leaping and tugging on the rope.

He lifted the goat up by one leg and dunked the animal into the waves. There were furious protests from the goat but the grizzle-haired owner was determined to get the animal clean.

'Drat it, boy. You's getting me as wet as a bathtub. Give over. You's nearly done.'

Kira laughed at the spectacle and made a note not to swim at Goat Bay, as she would call it. 'You've got a reluctant bathing beauty there,' she said.

'It's like this every time. You'd think he'd know I ain't gonna hurt him. Just cussed awkward.'

By now she was not alone on the beach as she turned back. Jogging had reached the Caribbean. Figures were running along the water's edge. Several young men came in sight, swarthy chests gleaming, towelling sweat bands round their foreheads, slim hips in bright running shorts. It was very Western.

One of the joggers wheeled on a heel, spurting up sand, and slowed down to a trot beside Kira. She took no notice of him, hoping to shake him off.

'Good morning. You're up early, Kira. Did you find it too hot to sleep? It does take some getting used to.'

Kira felt dizzy with a weakness that flooded through her at the sound of his voice. She had not expected to see him again so soon. He was one of the rag-bag pack of joggers in cut-off jeans, his tanned skin so dark that she had mistaken him for a local. Sweat was trickling down his chest to a slim waist.

'Mr Earl, what a surprise. Er . . . yes, it is hot.'

She felt the colour rising in her face as she tore her eyes away from his body. No man had ever aroused such exciting sensations in her before. She had hardly ever thought of Bruce as having a male body she wanted to touch . . . she had only dreamed of his handsome face, his charm, her own love for him.

'Please call me Giles.'

He was looking at Kira at intently, as he had at the airport. She wished her one-piece swimsuit were not so high-cut on the thighs, nor so low-cut at the back. It had seemed modest enough in the store but now it revealed too much bare flesh for her liking. Her skin was ivory and the scar on her leg was raw and ugly. She felt a flash of anger and humiliation that he should be looking at her so intimately.

'Don't look at my leg,' she breathed. 'I'm not a freak-show.'

'I haven't got as far as your legs,' said Giles. 'I'm still absorbing your face. I could spend at least another week just looking into your eyes.'

She gasped at his nerve and swung away. But he caught hold of her arm and turned her back to face him.

There was the merest twinkle in the electric blue of his eyes which went a small way to calming her jangling nerves.

'Your eyes are quite the most beautiful green I have ever seen,' he went on. 'Is it very wrong to say that?'

'Hazel,' she corrected. 'They're hazel.'

'This morning, I assure you, they are green with golden flecks, luminous and shining. And your lashes are so dark and long. My sister Lace would be consumed with envy if she saw them. She wears false things, sticks them on with glue, along with a few other false bits and pieces, I'm sure.'

'Good for her,' said Kira. 'Fortunately women don't have to ask permission to wear false eyelashes or any other bits and pieces, as you put it. Or is it different in Barbados? Is there still male dominance here?'

He threw back his head and laughed, showing strong and even teeth, startlingly white against his tanned face.

Kira attempted to hurry ahead but it wasn't going to happen. Cramp attacked her leg, making her hop and hobble. She screwed up her face with pain.

'Damned bike,' she groaned.

'Kira, what's the matter? Is your leg hurting? What have you done to it? Have you got cramp?'

'Damned leg. I'm so angry,' she muttered, clutching at the contracted muscle. Giles went down on a knee in the sand and pushed his fingers deeply into her calf, kneading and massaging the taut flesh. The fingers were expert, easing the pain, bringing relief.

'Oh . . . that's better. Thank you.' She sighed as she flexed her leg and tested her weight on her foot, pushing on the ball. 'You seem to know what you're doing.'

'I've got horses,' he grinned.

She pulled on the baggy T-shirt she'd left on the beach and turned towards the Sandy Lane Hotel. Giles was brushing the sand off his knees.

'Have breakfast with me?' he said. 'They'll serve us at the Sandy Beach restaurant, out in the garden. We don't have to dress. They're used to people in swimsuits.'

'Sorry. I've several things to do.'

'You have to eat.'

But not with you, Kira wanted to say. Not with you or any man. I breakfast alone these days. The sun was climbing the sky and suddenly she was quite hungry.

'I have some business arrangements to make in Bridgetown.'

'They can wait. You're on Barbados now. Take your time. Nobody hurries unless there's a hurricane on the way. Then, believe me, you move.'

'Thank you for the warning. How shall I know when a hurricane is coming?'

'You'll smell it in the air. It's unmistakable, like rotting fruit, like fermenting alcohol, like dust from a century ago.' Giles was mocking her now. He knew full well that she would not have the slightest idea what a hurricane smelt like. But he knew only too well.

Kira suddenly felt insecure. Hurricanes were a foreign word. Everything was foreign. This man was born on this island, in a culture so different from hers. He had money, position. They had nothing in common.

'My work comes first,' she said boldly. 'I've wasted enough time already. Goodbye.'

'I approve of the work ethic but you need nourishment like any machine. Besides, I might be able to help,' he added.

'I doubt it,' said Kira, wishing she could turn smartly. There would be nothing dignified in hopping away on one foot.

'Then we'll have breakfast together. That's settled.'

Giles steered her across the sand. There was nothing she could do about it.

CHAPTER 3

Giles gripped her arm and took her into the gardens of Sandy Lane towards the open-air restaurant. He stopped only to wash the sand off his bare feet at a tap embellished with ornamental tiles. Kira could not avert her eyes from the sight of the water splashing off his brown feet and straight toes.

'What sort of work did you say you do? And what position do you hold in this company?'

Kira thought quickly. What had she said on the plane in those suspended minutes? 'Consultant,' she said. Now she would have to decide what a consultant did. 'I'm in charge of political and industrial research for the sugar industry.' It came out in one long rush. She knew a lot about political research. Hadn't she been doing research for Mr Connor for years?

51

'Then you should know that the first rule for any executive is being in good health. You don't look in good shape to me and I'm not asking anything about your leg. You've had a long flight and you should give yourself at least a day to get over the jet-lag.' He ran his hand through his hair. Despite the cut-off jeans, he still had that air of arrogance and breeding.

Kira felt herself wilt. She didn't look in good shape. That was all he had to say to her. It was enough to make any woman feel worse. She plucked at the hem on her T-shirt, dragging it down over her scar. She didn't like being taken to pieces, dissected like a specimen.

'Are you ready to serve breakfast?' he asked a waiter, choosing a table with a view of the ocean.

'Yes, of course, Mr Earl. Good morning, Miss Reed. Do you wish to order or shall I bring a selection?' It was the same waiter who had brought the supper to her room.

Kira felt she was just awakening from a dream of being bullied by this tall, dominant man. The growing warmth of the morning and scent of the hibiscus, the shaded oleander, were making her relaxed and half asleep. Sun was streaking across the table, picking up glints on the silvery cutlery and the dew-washed flowers in the small vase.

She could hear the sea, see it sparkling. Gardeners were silently rearranging pots of flowers and scooping up luckless leaves from the ground. Friendly little sparrows hopped on the tables, cheekily helping themselves to crumbs and sugar. She was jet-lagged, for sure.

'Does everyone know you?'

'Of course. It's a small island and I've lived here all my life. My father, Reuben Earl, inherited Sugar Hill Plantation from his father, and he from his father before then. We've always grown sugar, long before Benjamin and Reuben became partners and started Reed and Earl.' He stopped and stared at her. 'Miss Reed? Did he call you Miss Reed?'

She knew what he was thinking. 'The telephone directory here has a whole page of Reeds,' she pointed out hastily. It was the first thing she had done in her room last night: look up Benjamin's address. It had been no surprise to find that he lived at Fitt's House. 'And back in London there are half a dozen pages devoted to Reed. It's hardly a unique name.'

The breakfast selection arrived on a trolley which the waiter put by their table. It was like an illustration out of a colour magazine. Tea and coffee in silver pots, fruit of every kind, sliced in dishes and fresh in baskets, bread and rolls, cheese, cold meats and fish, honey, jam, marmalade, cereals and yogurt, juices. The choice was alerting her taste-buds. The waiter served Kira with tea and slices of paw-paw, mango and pineapple. Giles helped himself to coffee.

'Would you or madam like some cooked eggs, fried, poached, scrambled . . .?'

'Kira?'

'No, thank you. This is lovely. I'm quite hungry after all.'

Giles ordered scrambled eggs and took a glass of blueberry juice. 'It's a pity you're not into interior decorating. Sugar Hill has been neglected for years, ever since my father died and my mother became ill. Lace has no interest in anything except parties and dances.'

'Are there lots of parties and dances?'

'All the time.' He stopped abruptly, thinking perhaps that she couldn't dance. 'But lots of other things go on. Cricket, fishing, sailing . . . going to church. Now, going to church is one of the chief occupations of good Barbadians. There are more churches than shops.'

'And what do bad Barbadians do?' she grinned.

'Fight, drink, indulge in a little piracy.'

'Are there real pirates?' She remembered her Early Bird taxi driver's warning. 'Sailing schooners?'

'Oh, yes, it's almost respectable. They smuggle contraband and hijack a ship or two. If you want an introduction, I know quite a few.'

Kira began to laugh. This was unreal, having breakfast in the sunshine with a handsome man, talking about pirates. Any moment now she would wake up and find herself staggering to the narrow kitchen counter in her Pimlico flat, putting on the kettle, hugging her dressing gown round her for warmth.

'That's better,' said Giles. 'A real laugh. It makes you look quite different.'

He had noted that Kira did not like personal comments so he did not mention the dimple that appeared at the corner of her mouth. It was a touch of magic. The waiter arrived with the scrambled egg and Giles tore his eyes away from her moist mouth.

'Want some?' He offered his plate across the table.

Kira took a forkful. It was delicious, creamy and light, cooked to the moment of perfection and not a second more. 'That's a gift. Knowing how to cook scrambled eggs.'

'Lace makes mountains of yellow rubber,' he said.

'Don't you have a cook?' She stopped, not wanting to probe. 'Sugar Hill sounds like a big house.'

'Yes, we have some staff. Housekeeper-cook, general maid, gardener, but Lace comes in so late most mornings, she has to make her own breakfast. I insist on it. Dolores has enough to do looking after my mother.'

Trouble, thought Kira. This sister sounded like a problem. It would be interesting to meet her. But that would mean seeing Giles again and that was not on the agenda. Once this pleasant meal was over, she would make sure that their paths did not cross. Mr Connor's letter of introduction could stay in her case.

Kira watched the guests arriving for breakfast. The women were wearing fabulous beach outfits, matching hats and wraps and accessories. She had nothing so glamorous.

'Shouldn't you be wearing a shirt?' she said nervously. 'All the men are wearing shirts.'

'Does my chest offend you? I'll borrow a shirt from a waiter if you like. I'm sure one of them would oblige.'

'No . . . no . . . I didn't mean that. I just thought we both looked a bit casual. Everyone is so dressed up.'

'You wear what you like here. It's what's underneath that matters. Get yourself a sarong from one of the beach girls and you'll have everything you need.'

'A sarong?'

'A most useful garment. You can wear it, lie on it, even use it to dry yourself after a swim. They'll show you how to put it on so it doesn't fall off.'

'Oh, dear.'

'Don't look so alarmed. A knotted sarong is iron-clad safe and I should know. In my youth, I tried to get a fair number of them off their delectable wearers.'

Kira blushed. It was hopeless. The colour flooded her face. She did not know where to look. She pushed the newly grown fringe out of her eyes. She did not know how to cope with this man. Her years in dusty, musty tradition-bound Parliament and the ordinary, English-style courtship with Bruce had not prepared her for the maelstrom of emotion this islander was arousing in her.

'Sorry, I'm a little jumpy. Ravages of London life,' she explained. 'It's been hectic.'

Clearing out her desk had been hectic. Not that there was much left to clear. Her replacement, a stunning blonde temp, had merely dumped her stuff into boxes and put them into a cupboard.

'I'm sorry, but the electric kettle is also mine,' Kira had said firmly, unplugging it. 'You'll have to get a new one.'

'No problem,' the blonde had replied. 'I'll charge it to Mr Connor. Office expenses.'

'You need to slow down,' said Giles, breaking into her thoughts. 'A few weeks at Sandy Lane and you won't recognize yourself.'

Kira did not say that she could not afford to stay at Sandy Lane more than a few days. But her morning walk had given her an idea. There were lots of small apartment buildings right on the coast, their gardens sloping down to the beach. A studio apartment was a tempting idea. She would enjoy shopping locally and eating sliced paw-paw on her own balcony, a drink and a book at her side.

'So you have a sugar plantation and a sugar-refining factory,' observed Kira, changing the subject. 'That's very impressive. And an old house that needs restoring.'

'The plantation has belonged to the Earls for several generations. It's in a lovely part of the island, rolling hills and fields. Very English-looking. But not far from the rugged east coast where the Atlantic rollers are so different from the placid west. You must go and see it. But don't swim in the sea, it isn't safe. Too rough and rocky.'

'Can I get a bus there?'

'A bus is slow and bumpy. Goes all round the island. Hire a moke. Or better still, let me lend you a moke. I have a spare vehicle. They're the only way to travel.'

Kira did not take up his offer. 'And you refine your own sugar?' she persisted.

'We have a factory out past the airport. But it wouldn't be working to full capacity if we only refined our own crop. We take in cane from a lot of smaller growers. The cane is brought in by lorry, though the access road is poor. No money for a new road. It's quite a problem for the small man to get his sugar ground.'

'No money for a road?' Giles did not look as if he had financial problems.

'My father's partner, Benjamin Reed, filtered off a lot of the firm's capital in order to build a house, Fitt's House, a pink castle with battlements and turrets, totally out of keeping with its surroundings. It was to impress his new bride. My father didn't find out till long afterwards that Benjamin had borrowed money from the firm. Meanwhile he'd borrowed money from every bank to finance a new plant. They had a blazing row. And then there was the problem of Dolly. She was the real spanner in the works, little minx.'

Kira had not heard the name Dolly mentioned before – or had she? She wished she could remember.

'And how do you get along with Benjamin Reed now? Is he still your partner?'

'I speak to him only when I have to. He's not an easy man to work with.' Giles slammed down his knife and fork abruptly. He pushed away the plate and poured himself half a cup of black coffee. His breakfast was obviously reaching its final stage. He looked at his watch.

'I have to go,' he said. His voice had cooled unexpectedly. 'I have an appointment. It's been nice meeting you again. Have a good holiday.'

The polite phrases were dismissive. Kira did not know whether to be relieved or disappointed. So Giles Earl had decided he was wasting his time with a thin, jumpy woman who was obviously mentally a mess. Well, it was what she wanted. She did not want to see him again.

He scraped back the chair and stood up. The ragged jeans had dried, clung to his thighs. 'Don't walk in the cane fields,' he said, signalling to the waiter.

'Why not?'

'Monkeys. Vicious little devils. The fields are overrun with monkeys.' He touched the scar on his face. 'This is what one did to me. Don't take a chance. They bite. Growing sugar isn't all sweetness. Monkeys, cane fires, hurricanes, the small growers' problems, the shortfall in the Caribbean quota. Think of all that when you buy a packet of sugar lumps down at your local supermarket.'

Kira grasped the opportunity. She did know something about their problems. The trade delegation at Westminster had been concerned for the industry worldwide and she had read many of the documents. Sugar consumption in the world was falling despite a growing population. They had to find alternative crops or sources of income.

'Why not let me research that?' she said boldly. 'There must be areas where accurate information would be useful. And I'd like to meet the President of the Sugar Growers' Association.'

His face darkened. A waiter appeared with a bill, which Giles signed before answering.

'He's the same Benjamin Reed. The man who had done more to ruin the sugar trade than anyone else on the island. We've been trying to oust him for years but he has his supporters. He's been here too long.'

The way he spoke made Kira shiver. It also made her pull herself together sharply. She, too, had reason to dislike, even hate her grandfather. But Giles was not to know.

'I'll make up my own mind whether I want to see him or not,' she said levelly. 'He may be a big fish here, but Barbados is only twenty-one miles around the coast and that makes it a pretty small pond.'

She didn't care about the mixed-up speech. It conveyed her meaning.

'So what does that make me?' he asked.

'A shark,' she said.

'Sharks can bite too. Think of those teeth.'

'I shall keep well away from any.'

Giles took a step towards her. He seemed to be tightly sprung with what might be unleashed anger, although she could see no reason for it. But when he put out his hand, it was only to tilt her chin with a finger. Then he brushed his thumb lightly down her slim neck to the hollow of her throat, touched a tendril of hair. It produced a sensation that left Kira powerless to move or speak.

'Such pretty eyes,' he said abruptly. 'But a hard heart.'

With a curt nod he dropped his hand and strode away towards the beach and the sea, back rigid as a ramrod. Tissues of cloud fluttered in the now azure blue of the sky. Boats bobbed at anchor; sailing yachts loomed on the horizon like coloured rags.

Kira watched his departing figure in a turmoil of emotion, waiting for the thudding of her pulse to calm down. She was relieved to see him go. Giles was too much of a threat. Yet her body longed for him to touch her again. She wanted to be touched by a man . . . even the offer of a comradely arm would be nice. She tried to suppress her wanton thoughts.

It must be the sun, the jet-lag, the relaxing charm of a natural and beautiful island, she told herself. It was destroying her protective armour. But she knew that was not the complete truth. If she had met Giles on a crowded underground train on the coldest, dampest day in London, her reaction to him would have been exactly the same.

'I could even sort of love him one day,' she said, half aloud, with a sudden amazing elation. A smile broke across her face. It was like a burst of sunshine on a wintry morning.

The waiter, coming to clear the table, thought the smile was for him.

'Have a nice day, Miss Reed,' he said, beaming. 'Don't worry, be happy.'

Kira did have a nice day. The unhurried pace of the island took hold of her, held her fast in its magic. She found the morning gone, and all she had done was make a couple of phone calls.

Next to cricket, telephoning was the second most popular pastime on the island. Perhaps there was another, but it wasn't logged. Local calls were free and this meant that half the population were on the phone to the other half most of the day. If a Barbadian home did not have a telephone, then the place of work provided one and here it was that waiters, shop assistants, hotel staff made their social calls. No one seemed to mind much if it kept everyone else waiting. Mobile phones were mushrooming like a third ear. They hadn't heard of the cancer scare.

She discovered that bus fares were a uniform sum regardless of distance and that the buses into Bridgetown stopped right outside the drive of Sandy Lane. She would have no trouble getting round the island if she could get on one of the crowded vehicles.

She ordered visiting cards from a firm of local printers, plain and simple. They would be ready in twenty-four hours and she arranged to collect them the following day. She would be fit to face Bridgetown after a day of sunbathing, leisurely swims and an early night.

Kira could not help noticing the British ways and traditions that had survived and blended so well with the distinctive Bajan character. British place names – Worthing, Hastings, Christchurch – but so different from those resorts at home. Three hundred years of British occupation had left an aura of old-world courtesy and industry which was a surprise and delight to jaded visitors from abroad. Traces of elegant colonial days were everywhere.

It was the rainy season, so Kira found that the beaches were not crowded. She could easily find a quiet, tranquil spot all to herself. She had only to walk northwards, away from the line of hotels whose guests did not seem to wander far from the pool.

The beaches had a life of their own. The vendors trudged the sand, flat-footed, plying their various trades with infinite patience and good humour. Melon-women carried trays of fruit on their heads.

Kira was apprehensive when approached by a young man with a Western-style briefcase. He had a red rag tied round his arm. Was he selling insurance? He went down on his haunches on the sand beside her and opened the case. The base and lid were a display unit with coral necklaces and bracelets in every possible colour and size.

'No charge to look, miss,' said the young man. 'My name is Moonshine. Today I have special bargains.'

He draped the pretty necklaces from his fingers, dangled them in front of Kira. He wore opaque mirrored sunglasses which reflected her own face, oddly curved like mirrors at a funfair.

'Fifty dollars this one,' said Moonshine, picking out a string of delicate pink and white coral. 'But thirty to you.'

Kira sighed. She hated saying no.

'They are all very pretty,' she agreed. 'But this is the first day of my holiday and I don't want to buy anything yet.'

'Your first day? So how do you like Barbados so far,' said Moonshine, taking off his glasses. It was obviously a signal that ended his selling patter. He was a handsome young man with smooth skin and crisp, glistening hair.

'I think I'm going to like it very much,' said Kira, putting Giles to the back of her mind. 'I haven't had much chance to look round but everyone is so nice.'

'You must go to the East Coast, to the Scotland district. The sea is magnificent – rollers this high. I surf there but it is very dangerous. You should not swim there.'

'You have a very unusual name.'

'Moonshine is my nickname. Everyone has nicknames on the island.'

'How did you get it?'

He threw back his head and laughed. 'Now that would be telling. Perhaps it's the sunglasses.'

He closed his case and stood up, grinning. 'Now you have a good day and don't get yourself burnt in the sun, lady. It's very strong. And when you want to buy a necklace, remember Moonshine. I see you on the beach. So long.'

He moved off to the next potential customer. Time was money and he had to make the day's quota of sales before he could relax.

During the day Kira was also offered, at various times, sarongs, fresh pineapples, carved figures and the opportunity to have her hair braided. There were no long faces when she did not buy. The vendors were happy to have a chat and then leave her alone. She did buy a sarong, a cheerful yellow number splashed with riotous flowers. She wrapped it over her black swimsuit and saw the sense of it.

'It's lovely,' said Kira.

'You want two?' said the woman, quickly on to a second sale.

Kira shook her head. It had been simple last night to find her grandfather's name in the telephone directory: Benjamin Reed, Fitt's House, Fitt's Village, St James. It was not far from where she was now, apparently. She could probably walk it if she had any sense of direction. But it needed a lot of courage to face the man who had left his daughter to starve.

There was a balmy trade wind blowing off the sea, taking the oppressive heat out of the sun.

But Kira was careful to put a shirt over her shoulders. Barbados was the most windward of the Windward Islands group and Kira realized why it was possible to live there without air-conditioning. The first British settlers were quick to note the cooling winds, built their houses to face them and built windmills to harness the power for their sugar mills. They used the same winds to carry their fleets back to England with their rich harvest of sugar and tobacco.

Kira found the beach bar she had noticed on her morning walk. If the owner took time to sweep the sand in front of his wooden bar, she reckoned he would have the same pride in the food he served.

The place was packed, mostly with people drinking rum punch at the bar. But the barman recognized her.

'So you've come back.'

'I said I would.'

'What would you like? A drink? Some food?'

'Yes, please. Can I have some sort of sandwich and a long, cool drink? Lemonade or something?'

'Yes, ma'am. Coming up. Take a seat and I'll bring it out to you.'

She sat on a bench facing the sea, watching a catamaran with colourful striped sails skimming the waves, waterskiers being towed by speedboats, windsurfers, a Jolly Roger pirate ship taking tourists on a cruise up the coast. Its red sails were full of wind, billowing, the faint sound of Bajan pop music floating to the shore.

The sandwich was inches high with sliced cold chicken and salad, the fresh lime drink clinking with ice. Kira decided not to worry about the purity of the ice water, feeling sure it came from a deep island well.

'Thank you. This looks lovely.'

'Best sandwiches on the West coast.'

Later in the afternoon she changed into a simple black cotton skirt and striped top, tying her hair back with a scrunchie scarf, and set out to find Fitt's House. She looked casual and smart even if her clothes were bought from a London chainstore. Tendrils of unruly chestnut hair escaped the scarf, tugged by the wind, framing a face which after only a few hours in the sun looked rested and glowing.

There were no pavements so Kira walked carefully, side-stepping over the deep ditch along the roadside each time she heard a vehicle approaching. Cars, buses, carts, bicycles passed her, all rattling and noisy, stereos blaring. She felt safer standing still till they had gone by. Rows of black faces stared and grinned at her from the bus windows, the pop music from the in-bus stereo deafening; they were interested in visitors, particularly those who chose to walk.

The traditional chattel houses were fascinating: so small, doll-like, with neat curtains at their windows and flowers by the centre door; and each one was different in some architectural aspect. As the family grew, they built a similar unit on to the back. In some homes the roof stretched back several units, going up and down at odd slopes.

She paused by a ramshackle house built of wooden planks with wide shutters and a red corrugated iron roof, a tottering veranda all round. It had been built on a rise of ground and a well-swept path led to the open front door. There seemed to be something special about the house because a woman in a brightly coloured dress and straw hat was sitting outside and showing people in. Surely such a tumbledown place was not a tourist attraction? Kira went closer and read a notice nailed to a wall.

THIS IS THE HOME OF ANDRE LE PLANTE, FAMOUS ARTIST. 1908–1960. ALL VISITORS ARE WELCOME.

Kira went in, glad to be out of the heat for five minutes. She stood in the darkened hallway and realized that everything had been kept as it once was, as if it were still lived in by this André Le Plante. The house was a capsule frozen in time.

She wandered through the rooms, looking at the ornaments and photographs and old copies of newspapers strewn on tables. His pipe was still by his chair, a faded patchwork cushion dented as if by the weight of his back. It was uncanny, and Kira shivered for no reason.

The lean-to kitchen was almost primitive with a earthenware sink and a single cold water tap. Mrs Le Plante, if there had been one, had had to cook on a kerosene stove and her pots and pans were battered and ancient. Kira looked with interest at the contents of the larder, the packaging outdated and brown-stained.

She went out into a back yard and followed other visitors into another open-sided wooden building. This was the artist's studio and the walls were hung with his paintings. An easel stood in the sunlit doorway, a half-finished painting on display, his paints and brushes still on a high table at the side.

Kira took a closer look at the paintings. They were vibrant and full of colour and light; mostly native pictures . . . every aspect of the island and its people. One canvas in particular caught her attention. It was of a young girl, about sixteen or seventeen, running through the waves, her hair flying. He had caught the enthusiasm for life on her radiant face.

'That was his daughter,' said another house custodian, from her rocking chair by the entrance to the studio. 'Dolly Le Plante, when she was a young 'un. André was always painting her. Pretty thing but a headstrong handful of trouble, I've been told.'

The woman grinned, her teeth large and berry-stained. She went on talking, gossiping, glad to have an audience, but Kira was hardly listening, her attention transfixed on the painting of Dolly Le Plante.

Dolly ran along the beach, kicking up the powdery white sand with her bare feet. Her hair was flying, her loose cotton dress falling from one shoulder. She clambered over a rocky peninsula into the next bay, which was quieter and had not yet been developed.

She'd heard there were plans to build hotels all along this part of the coast. A tourist boom was predicted for Barbados, now that the war was over and there were more flights from Europe and America. She did not like the idea of the privacy of the beaches being invaded by foreigners, but on the other hand they might buy her father's paintings. They were always short of money and a few sales could mean a new stove. She was sick of cooking on that old thing.

Not that it mattered, being poor white on Barbados. It was warm, there was plenty of cheap food in the market, and although their house was old and desperately needed repairs, it could withstand the rainy season with a few strategically placed buckets and that useful new stuff, plastic sheeting, stretched across the leaking roof.

But Dolly dreaded another hurricane. Even now the wind rattled the doors and windows and sometimes lifted the red corrugated iron roof. Her father's studio would not survive the first onslaught of a big wind. The wooden outbuilding would collapse card-like on its non-existent foundations.

She searched the sweeping palms, shading her eyes, but there was no one there. Perhaps she was early. She never wore a watch, did not possess one.

'It's either getting-up time or going-to-bed time. I'm either hungry or not hungry. I don't need a clock-watch,' she would say. She used the Bajan double-nouns all the time. It was her way. She had been born on the island.

Dolly's eyes sparkled. She had an enormous zest for life and being poor did not diminish her joy. She was never more than seven miles from the sea and she lived in a climate of perpetual summer. It was a paradise.

She did not work. She was too busy to work. André made just enough money from his paintings to feed them and buy new paints and brushes. People often gave him old canvases to paint over. She was wearing one of her mother's cut-down frocks, a floral cotton. Dolly had stitched it on the large side in case she grew some more.

But at seventeen Dolly was not likely to grow any more. She was a slim sprite of a girl, figure unformed, hair wild, green eyes always full of merriment and laughter.

She saw a tall figure striding through the coconut palms and ran towards him, pushing her hair from her eyes. She flung herself into his arms, her head pressed close to his chest, breathing in the scent of his skin.

'I thought you weren't coming,' she gasped. 'I've been here ages.'

'Liar. I saw you climbing over the rocks.'

'Why weren't you here?'

'Some of us have to work. We don't all laze about like social débutantes.'

'Your father is a monster. I hate him. He makes you work too hard.'

Reuben Earl shook her shoulders and laughed. He had strong facial bones that made him appear almost handsome, a thick thatch of dark hair, eyes as blue as the Caribbean ocean.

'Don't be daft, Dolly. We have a big plantation and refinery to run. It doesn't run itself, and the monkeys would soon take over if we weren't vigilant. You'll be glad too, one day, when I'm a big success – factory owner, planter. Now stop talking, you minx, and let me kiss you.'

They sank on to the sand, arms entwined, half in the shade of a sweeping palm, shielded by the big leaves from any curious eyes that might pass by. Reuben cradled her in his arms and took her sweet lips, offered so generously and warmly.

His hands moved to her small breasts, pert against the thin material of the cotton frock, and he felt his groin contract with desire. He could not resist her softness and the scent of her flesh. He kissed her face, her neck, moving down to the silken skin of her exposed shoulder, pressing his lips close to the almost revealed shadowed valley. He groaned. He would have to stop. This was killing him as usual.

Reuben rolled over and stared up at the flawless sky between the branches. He had been in love with Dolly since they were at school together. For years they had just walked and talked, teased each other, swum in the sea, played cricket, gone to a few parties. Everything had been light and easy until the day he'd kissed her. Now he could barely leave her alone. His love changed into a monster invading his veins, urging him to take her, possess her, make this wilful creature his own. His dreams were full of her soft body, of crushing her beneath his weight, of penetrating her secret places.

'Why have you stopped?' said Dolly, leaning up on one elbow, tickling his face with a stem of dry grass. 'Please kiss-kiss me some more.'

'I can't. You know what it does to me. Drives me crazy. We shouldn't keep meeting like this, secretly.'

Her hand went down to the hardened shape between his legs, curious what it meant. Reuben pushed her away, rough and impatient, and sat up.

'Don't touch me,' he choked angrily. 'Don't you know anything?'

'No, I don't know. I haven't got a mother now, you know that. Please, Reuben, I can't stand it when you're angry with me. What have I done?'

Tears welled into her eyes and Reuben couldn't stand that either. He kissed away the tears and held her more gently, stroking her hair and her face. The tempest in his loins subsided and he pulled the shoulder of her frock back into place.

'Now you're all neat and tidy again,' he said, as if he were dressing a child for Sunday church. Sometimes Dolly was like a child to him. An enchanting child in a woman's body. He would not find the strength to resist her forever.

Kira stared at the painting of the girl flying across the sand, bridging time with each caught breath. Was this her grandmother? There was something familiar about the girl's face, almost as if she was looking at herself. A long time ago,

Tamara had told her that her grandmother's name was Dolly. Kira didn't remember exactly. It could have been in a dream.

She left the painter's house and continued walking. Some of the chattel houses had been abandoned to the elements and rotted away. There were quite a few fire-gutted ruins. Wooden homes were a fire hazard.

The concrete houses were newer, mostly built in the plantation style with a central flight of steps up to the front door, raised to avoid the rain.

Kira lost herself trying to remember what her mother had said. But it had been a difficult time and there was nothing she could do to clear the fog. And now she wanted to know, desperately. It was like a pain in her side, she wanted to know so much.

CHAPTER 4

Kira delighted in the wild flowers blooming everywhere; they lightened the moment of gloom. Every nook and cranny was a cascade of blossom: hibiscus, wild orchids, bougainvillea, the delicate frangipani, the flamboyant poinsettia growing wild. It was a riot of colour, such a contrast to the grey London she had left behind. She noticed many trees on the leeward side of the beach on which warning signs had been nailed:

'*These green apples are poisonous.*'

The trees were heavily laden with small crab-like fruit.

'They're manchineel trees,' a small boy had explained, seen her looking. 'Very bad to eat. Make stomach bad.'

'Thank you,' she said. 'I won't eat them.'

Kira asked several times for directions to Fitt's House. The answers were pleasantly vague but she gathered that she was going in the right direction. Walking the leafy lanes, she could almost think herself back in England, except that no English hedgerows were laced with such exotic blooms.

Benjamin Reed must be influential, if not rich, if he was the President of the Sugar Growers' Association. He would have bought his property and land before the prices soared with the tourist boom. Kira imagined a grand colonial house with an imposing entrance and flight of steps; her thoughts were momentarily bitter with memories of damp bedsits.

She wandered along a lane, looking for house names but there were none. Two square gate-posts flanked a pair of rusty ironwork gates and beyond was a garden that was a disordered tangle of trees and shrubs and flowers. A winding central drive led to a house that was built of pink coral, the coral bleached and faded by years of sunshine and rain.

She caught sight of a wide flight of steps that led up to a blue-green veined stone archway, decorated with diamonds of turquoise stones. A jungle of plants and flowers in terracotta pots fought for position on the steps. Two life-size stone wolves – or were they dogs? – guarded the entrance, their expressions benign and not in the least fearsome.

Kira began to laugh. It was like something out of a Disney film. A stone balcony went round three sides of the first floor of the house supported by columns, ornamented with scrolls and Grecian urns, the two front corners dominated by large stone eagles, or perhaps doves. They had hooked beaks and pantaloon legs, but short bodies, plump and domesticated, both eyeless birds staring forever out to sea.

Kira's gaze followed the stone balcony up to a replica balcony, a storey higher, crenellated like a castle, edging a flat roof, the tall windows shuttered against the heat . . . A castle. A pink castle . . . The words came back into her memory. What had her mother said? Grandfather lived in a sugar-plum-fairy castle. This was a castle set in a jungle of flowers and creepers that threatened to grow into a impenetrable thicket and hid the house forever from the world. She wondered if there was a sleeping princess inside, then decided it was more likely to be an ogre.

The lane was overhung with branches and several times Kira had to duck her head. A green breadfruit swung towards her forehead, looking as hard as a cricket ball. She dodged the fruit but her lame leg let her down and she slipped, staggering sideways.

'I'm sorry, young lady. If you'd come along five minutes later, that branch would have been pruned.'

The gardener shook a pair of pruning secateurs at her as if to prove his good intentions. He was standing on a ladder leaning up against the tree. A pair of pale blue eyes peered at her from a brown face topped with cropped grey hair. He wore a tattered shirt that seemed to shout aloud how little his employer paid him.

'Are you all right? Gonna sue? That's what people do these days,' he growled.

'It was a bit unexpected and I slipped,' said Kira. 'Is this breadfruit? Can you eat it?'

'Ain't you ever tasted it? Baked, boiled, fried. Good done any way. The trees were brought over to Barbados a long time ago to feed the slaves. I'll see if I can find you a ripe one.'

'You're very kind, but I'm staying at a hotel and couldn't cook it.'

The old man rested his arms on the top of the wall, wiping gnarled hands on his shirt. 'You on holiday, then, miss?'

'Yes . . . sort of. I was in a road accident and the doctor at the hospital thought I ought to get away.'

'You couldn't have come to a better place. People have been coming to Barbados for their health for years. Even George Washington came, with his half-brother, Lawrence, to get over some lung infection. And there weren't no jumbo jets in 1751. They think he stayed at a house in Bay Street – put up a plaque, they did – but nobody really knows for sure if it's the right place. So how come you got hurt?'

'It was an ordinary street accident in London, me and a motorbike. A sort of collision on a windy day.'

'Don't sound too good. You'd better not walk too far before it gets dark. It gets dark very quickly. Comes down like a blind and there are no street lights out this way. You could get lost.'

'Thank you,' said Kira. 'I don't fancy walking along the sea road in the dark with all the traffic and no pavement. This is a funny house, isn't it? Like something out of a Walt Disney film. And all those weird statues. It looks a bit like a fairy-tale castle.'

'Ain't a funny house, miss,' said the gardener,

a bit ruffled. 'Built for a special person, it was. Long time ago.'

'A castle? You're going to build me a castle? Oh, Ben, you are a darling! I don't believe it. No one has a castle on Barbados. There's only those old forts, out Gun Hill way. You're teasing me. You're always teasing me. It isn't fair.'

'Dolly, I'm not teasing you. It's a real promise. If you marry me, I'll build you the most fantastic house on the island. Something that will be the perfect setting for my princess.'

Dolly's eyes lit up. 'Me, a princess? Now you're joking. I'm the daughter of a poor white painter and I don't know why you're bothering with me, Benjamin Reed. You're a rich sugar planter and could marry any girl on the island. I bet they're lining up from here to Speightstown for your attentions.'

Benjamin found it difficult to string any words together. He was not used to talking with women, especially a wild young girl with flying hair and green eyes that were always laughing at him. He could not feel really comfortable with her. All his life he had worked, not courted.

'Dolly . . . believe me. I love you. I'm mad about you. Can't get you out of my mind. It's like an illness for which there ain't no cure but you marrying me. I'd look after you, take care of you. And you could do what you liked. I shouldn't mind. Paint, swim, ride . . . anything you wanted, all day long.'

'That's not very flattering, Ben Reed, calling me an illness like spot-measles or the plague. Fidget, I think I'll be going, Mr Reed, until you can think up some more pleasing and flattering words for a lady.'

Benjamin Reed groaned aloud and struck his head. 'Dolly, I'll never get it right. Never. I can't say proper words; I can only do things. Doing is my way of showing love. I'm building you a castle, girl. I know just the right place, facing westwards, only a run from the beach.'

'A pink castle?'

'Any colour you like . . .'

'I'm sorry, I didn't mean to make fun of the house. It's very beautiful, but you must admit that the statues are a little strange,' said Kira quickly.

'The statues? Yes, I suppose you holiday folk might think them strange. They were made by a young local sculptor who hadn't ever seen the animals. He did his work from pictures and photographs.'

Kira detected a note of irritation in the old man's voice. Perhaps she had kept him talking long enough, halfway up a tree.

'Thank you for the offer of breadfruit. It was nice talking to you. I hope I haven't kept you from your work.'

'Work's never finished. Fitt's House might seem a rum old place to you, young lady, but it ain't all out of the history books. It's got four solar panels on the flat roof,' he said as he disappeared down the ladder, tangible hostility in the air. 'Hot water from the sun. I'd call that modern technology.'

So this was Fitt's House. Kira felt a surge of excitement that she was within yards of her grandfather's house, the house where her mother had been born and grown up. Perhaps Tamara had even climbed this breadfruit tree as a child, run along this lane, picking flowers, straddled the stone animals in story-play.

'How enterprising of your employer,' Kira called out. She could hear the gardener sweeping up branches and a muffled oath.

'No point in wasting heat from the sun,' he replied from the other side of the wall.

That sounded like Benjamin Reed's philosophy of life. He would be a thrifty man, counting the pennies. Kira could not remember all the poverty of when she was a child but she knew her mother had worked hard in a corset factory, spending hours at a sewing machine till her eyes were red and blotched with tiredness. Sometimes Tamara had brought home pieces of waste material, ivory and pink silk and brocade, to make doll's clothes for Kira. But the scraps frayed and were quickly of no use.

How easily her grandfather could have sent some money. A few pounds would have made no difference to him; he even had food growing free in his garden. A shiver of anger went through Kira as she glanced back at the coral-pink house and its absurd statues. The setting sun was casting wild orange and crimson rays in all directions, making the stone glow with light. Benjamin had certainly chosen the right site for his house. It looked glorious, bathed in the fiery warmth, deep shadows from the trees adding a steely blue to the picture.

Kira turned away abruptly. At the end of the lane she crossed the sea road and cut down to the beach between trees and houses. She did not want to get lost inland. She took off her sandals and the sand was cool on her feet. She hitched up her skirt so that she could paddle on the edge of the lapping water.

There were evening joggers now, kids out of school playing cricket on the sand, people walking dogs, swimming after work. These were the lazy, hazy hours of evening. Everyone smiled and said good evening. Her anger faded. If she stayed too long in Barbados she would have little hostility left in her heart towards her grandfather.

Kira was seeing Giles in every distant runner, his brown body glistening, muscles rippling, long legs moving with ease in easy strides over the sand. But she was in no mood for any man to start taking over her thoughts, even though she could still feel the magnetic power of his eyes. He was a devastating man, someone to die for. Everything about him, his looks, his voice, his touch . . . she shivered at the thought of his touch. His skin would have the tangy salt of the sea in its taste . . .

She stopped herself firmly. This was foolishness. She must put all thoughts of him out of her mind.

Instead she was suddenly drowning in tormented pictures of Bruce and Jenny, and the

lingering hurt came back, cramping her stomach. The baby would be born in the au-
tumn, a tangible sign of his new love and
their commitment to each other, their future.
She meant nothing to Bruce any more, and she
had to accept the hard fact.

A young woman was playing with a baby on
the shore. The baby was brown and chubby,
covered from head to foot in sand, clutching
fistfuls which his mother gently directed away
from his open mouth. She wrapped him in a big
towel and swung him around until he gurgled
with delight. Kira noticed that the baby was
very dark but that the mother's skin was paler.
There were many black youths walking with
white girls, talking, laughing together, hand in
hand, all very natural.

Giles was white-skinned but darkly tanned.
She wondered about his ancestry. His dark hair
was crisply short but every feature was mid-
European. Not that it was any business of hers,
nor did it matter.

Back at Sandy Lane, Kira stood in the shower,
letting the tepid water wash off the salt and sun
oil. The scar on her leg was vivid but she
was hoping a tan would soon camouflage its
ugliness.

Kira was not a vain woman. She thought her chestnut hair and green eyes merely passable. She was quite unable to see the elusive quality that shone in the depths of her eyes or the tawny red that brought a burnished shine to her hair.

The scar was a misfortune but it could have been worse. It did not matter if her leg marred her looks. She belonged to no one but herself. Men were not the centre of her world. The nerve-ends near the scar were still sensitive to any touch. She patted them carefully with a towel.

Her hair dried into a wild tangle on her shoulders and she didn't bother to style it. She didn't know how much she resembled the girl in the painting. She put on a strawberry-coloured cotton dress that would turn heads. It had a blouson top, hip sash and hem appliquéd with cut-out flowers. All very Thirties, slim and svelte.

She spun round in front of the mirror. She looked like a pink flame. 'You'll do. Sandy Lane, here I come,' she said.

Forget about everything, she thought, forget about Bruce and the baby he had made with his new love. She wandered into the bar, fighting back waves of loneliness. It was full of people, laughing and talking. They gave her a cursory look, then went back to their drinks.

'May I join you?'

Giles's deep voice broke into her thoughts. A dizzy sensation flooded through her at the unexpected sight of him, making her skin tingle. She had no time to think of a reason for saying no.

He sat down opposite her, hitching up his slim fawn trousers to allow his long legs to stretch. His matching jacket was unbuttoned, revealing a thin black silk shirt open at the neck. He had a small glass of raw rum in his hand. Not a man for fancy cocktails.

She was thrown by seeing him again so soon, confused by his rugged looks and masculine assurance. It was easier to nod briefly and let him call over a waiter. She tried to stay cool and calm. There was no way he would get the slightest inkling of how she was feeling.

'Planter's Punch for my guest,' he ordered without asking her. 'They make a good one here. It's a mixture of rum, green limes, a dash of Angostura bitters, cracked ice, nutmeg and mint. One of sour, two of sweet, three of strong, four of weak – that's the recipe for any good cocktail, they say . . .'

Kira listened to his voice, knowing that she could listen to it forever. It had a warm and magnetic quality and his eyes never left her face. He signed the chit for the drink without looking at it. She could become addicted to this man and this life, she thought. Perhaps she would become a beachcomber, sell necklaces like Moonshine and live on rum and free breadfruit. Forget about becoming someone, forget about Bruce and his new woman, and the fruit of their hot and writhing flesh . . .

He seemed to have forgotten about their abrupt parting that morning and was choosing to ignore her chilly silence. But the rum was creeping its insidious way into her veins, making her relax into a pleasant warmth.

'The decoration is a little over the top,' he went on, referring to the harvest of sliced mango, paw-paw, glossy red cherries and fancy straw in her long glass.

'But the drink is wonderful,' she couldn't stop herself saying approvingly.

'I like the dress,' he said. 'Very Thirties, and it brings out the red in your hair. Did you know that your hair is an enchanting mixture of colours? A painter's palette gone wild.' He put out a hand as if to take hold of a lock but

Kira jerked back. He changed the direction of his hand and called over the waiter, indicating his empty glass.

Kira was annoyed at her reaction. She should be taking pleasure from being in the company of the handsomest man in the room. She was well aware of the envious glances the other women cast in his direction and the fire of their desire.

'Is Sandy Lane Hotel your second home?' she said, passing over his compliment on her hair and dress.

'It's my third home. I have a beach house on the estate here. Sugar Hill is a greathouse, one of the last plantation houses. It's too big for me to live in even when Lace is there. I like the simplicity of the beach house. It's quite beautiful, so peaceful and undemanding.'

'Does Lace like the house?'

'She likes Sugar Hill enough but does nothing to help keep it together. She has never worked in her life; lazy little madam, if you'll excuse the language. Her life is one long round of parties and dancing and buying clothes.'

'How nice,' Kira murmured, thinking of her long hours at the House of Commons and her small flat in Pimlico, everything so compact that she could prepare a meal in her kitchen without taking more than three paces. 'But what about your mother? She lives at Sugar Hill?'

'No, she's in a nursing home. She's in bed most of the time. It's MS. She needs constant care. There's little that can be done for her.'

'How very sad.'

'Perhaps you'd like to come and visit her, and then see Sugar Hill,' he said over the top of his glass. 'It's worth a visit. Stately home and all that. Very colonial.'

Kira wanted to refuse but if his mother was so ill it would be very impolite and cruel.

'Thank you, but not just yet. I've allowed myself twenty-four hours to get over my jet-lag and now it's back to work.'

'Very commendable. But you could take a lunch break. It gets very hot. We could drive to Sugar Hill in less than twenty minutes.'

'I don't know. I have masses to do.'

He inclined his head as if to acknowledge her tight working schedule and dropped the subject. He was looking at her again with a disturbing look that was playing havoc with her senses. She forced herself to sit still even though she longed to turn away, run to somewhere safe, miles and miles.

'Are you sure we haven't met before?' he asked. 'There's something about your face . . .'

'Quite sure,' said Kira. How could she ever forget if she had met him before? She took a deep drink, which was a mistake, for despite the cracked ice the rum was strong and potent. A knot formed in her throat as if the liquid had burned her. She stirred the ice quickly and swallowed some of the melting coldness to still her starving desire.

'Careful. Rum is apt to go straight to the head,' warned Giles, mistaking her uncertainty. 'I didn't mean to make you feel you were under a microscope. Not only are you a very beautiful woman but you do remind me of someone. And I can't think who it is. You know how elusive memory can be, and I can't pin this one down.'

She looked towards the darkening sea. 'I went walking today. There was this strange house, all pink, built like a castle, with statues and turrets and battlements.' Kira was probing cautiously, hoping Giles could throw some light on the subject.

'That's Fitt's House, Benjamin Reed's home,' said Giles drily. 'Or Reed's Folly, as it's sometimes called around here. He built it for his young bride, to tempt her into marrying him. He had grand ideas of turning her into a princess, they say. But the house didn't bring him any luck.'

'How unfortunate,' said Kira. 'It doesn't sound very sensible.'

'Don't waste your sympathy on Benjamin Reed,' Giles snapped, putting down his drink. 'He's not worth it. It was a kind of madness. He's a twisted, bitter and stubborn old man and he deserves his unpopularity.'

Kira's heart fell in a long swoop, not quite anchored in space. The open-air bar was a moving field of light. Everything Giles was saying only confirmed her own opinion of her grandfather, yet it did not help that other people felt the same way. It seemed disloyal, in a funny way, to listen to them. It made her more determined to confront the man herself and tell him what she thought of him for his treatment of her mother . . . yet somehow she ached with a raw sweetness for the old man, so alone, so bitter. What had happened to his fairy-tale princess?

'Doesn't anyone like him?'

'His old workers dote on him, the loyal ones. He has a few friends. But he cut himself off. It's his own fault.'

'Will you excuse me? I'm feeling quite hungry for once after my day in the fresh air. I think I'll go in to dinner. Thank you for the drink.'

'What an excellent idea. I'm glad you're feeling hungry. I've booked a table at Sam Lord's Castle – you said you wanted to meet a pirate. Do you want to fetch a wrap? I usually drive with the roof down.'

It was a bittersweet moment that pulled her two ways. He had a nerve, yet she was in too fragile a condition to cope with a man so sure of himself. But the idea of dining with him was tempting. Perhaps she could allow herself one slice of the cake.

'I take it that was an invitation, not an order? Or am I mistaken? I've made arrangements to eat here at Sandy Lane.'

'You can eat here any time. A pirate's stronghold is far more exciting, don't you agree? Think of the publicity, Kira. There are always swarms of reporters at the Castle, looking for an item for the morning's front page.'

The planes of his face were thrown into dark shadow as they went outside. The night air was warm and balmy, full of glorious scents from the gardens; the sea murmured in the background as it washed the sand smooth for the coming day.

The lights in the gardens drew the insects and they buzzed around the glowing magnets like a grey net.

'Your research company could do with some publicity, couldn't it? Have dinner with me at Sam Lord's and you'll get your photo in tomorrow's paper.'

Giles took her arm lightly and steered her up the steps and towards the car park. His touch was minimal but the pressure of his fingers on her bare skin was electric. His fingers were hard, as if he worked with his bare hands, as if he not only gave orders from his office but rolled up his sleeves too.

'And what do you get out of this?' said Kira, still mentally kicking herself for the way he was manipulating her. He was wrapping his jacket round her shoulders against any chill.

'I get dinner with a prickly female,' he said with a wicked grin. 'A new experience for me. My car is over here.'

'Charm doesn't help in my business,' flared Kira. He was teasing her. 'I'm serious about my work. It's more than a butterfly image. My consultancy is based on efficiency and hard work.'

He chuckled in the darkness. 'I meant no disrespect, ma'am. You ain't no butterfly, that's for sure. More like a tiger cat, I'd say. I guess you've got claws hidden under that pretty dress.'

'I'm eating with you because I'm hungry, that's all. Don't think it's going to lead anywhere.' It seemed a stupid thing to say but the warmth of the night air was intoxicating. Something strange was happening over which she had no control.

The words took her back into a private, empty world where she was really lonely. She was starved for the touch of a man yet she was saying the words that would send him away. A terrible ache filled her, a fear that Giles *would* get the message and go, leave her. Sudden tears stung behind her eyes and she brushed them away angrily.

'Nothing further from my mind. No, lady, I've booked a table for two and afterwards I will bring you back to the hotel.'

He leaned towards her and his mouth was a breath away from her lips. His hand ran lightly down her arm, disturbing the fine hairs in a feathery touch. She found her lips parting in soft anticipation and her body leaning towards him.

He was standing very close in the evening's balmy darkness, every angle of his face etched in shadow.

'But I'm damned hungry,' he said. 'And not just for food.'

CHAPTER 5

Kira turned her face away. He was not going to get to kiss her and she was not going to make herself cheap. Bruce had taught her that it was dangerous to succumb to male magic even when the silver moonlight was adding to that magic and a sheen hung on the evening air. Giles was too close, towering beside her.

'I do appreciate your hospitality to a complete stranger but I assure you I'm no helpless lady. I've been looking after myself since I was a little girl, and eating alone is the least of my worries,' she said.

'You mean you've been living on your own?' He sounded surprised, his voice also tinged with apprehension, as if he suddenly saw a child at home alone. The Barbados culture was family-orientated. A child would never be left alone.

Kira shook her head, unaware of the red lights reflecting from her hair in an auburn aura. Giles was watching her, suddenly seeing a different person emerging from the cool businesswoman, someone vulnerable and afraid.

'Not exactly. My mother died when I was young. I was sent to a convent and the nuns were good to us but it was still a lonely existence. They're not given to hugs and kisses, more a pat on the head and "hurry along, there's a good girl".'

'Then I insist on taking you out to supper and spoiling you.' There was a new awareness in his voice. 'My car is here. Allow me to play Prince Charming for one evening.'

'Cinderella has to be home early.'

'Of course. Though I'd rather like to see my Merc turn into a mouse.'

'It was a pumpkin,' she corrected.

She should have known he would have a white Mercedes. At a touch of a button, the roof folded back. Kira felt the last of her resistance slide away, as if she was walking into another life and taking that walk as if it were the only course open to her. She was being tempted by a car, and she ran her hand along its smoothness. She had never ridden in an open car before. She did not know that Dolly, her grandmother, had been tempted by a bathroom.

'Nice car,' she said, more abruptly than she meant to, as he opened the passenger door for her. The upholstery was a pale blue with cream trim. The floor was carpeted in the same blue. She sank back into the comfort with a tiny sigh. Bruce had had a rust-ridden Ford Fiesta, a company car. She did not care what happened to the rest of this evening now. She would let it run and run. It was something out of time, a magic she should not allow herself to experience again.

Perhaps fate had decided that she was owed this kind of evening after the dark months of loneliness and pain. It was definitely the Cinderella syndrome. She looked sideways at her Price Charming, his dark profile outlined against the lights hidden in the palm trees. He fitted the role well, though his strong, arrogant nose and firm jutting chin had none of the softness associated with a gallant fairy-tale prince.

She knew nothing about him. He was a stranger and yet she was letting him drive her across a Caribbean island to a place she had never heard of; an island that until yesterday had only been a name in a travel brochure. She must be out of her mind. It would serve her right if they found her tomorrow trussed up in a cane field. It was a dangerous world – yet somehow she trusted Giles. A gut instinct told her that the danger was to her heart, not to her body.

When did trust begin? It had to begin some time. At some point a woman had to recognize when a stranger became a friend and could be trusted. She already had this feeling about Giles Earl. He was only dangerous in the strong feelings he aroused in her, like electricity humming along the wires. His authority had an uncanny power and she was afraid of that power.

A wry smile touched her face in the darkness. She had trusted Bruce and look where that had got her: a nightmare of hurt and anguish that was only now beginning to subside but which could flare up with just as much immediate pain at a thought, an image, a memory. That bouncing baby on the beach . . .

'Another sigh, Kira? Two sighs in one evening is the limit on Barbados. It's a government regulation. Sam Lord's ghost won't take too kindly to a melancholy visitor. He likes to be the centre of attention.'

'A ghost? Really.' She stared out at the passing countryside. It was swaying with strange grey, cobwebby images.

'Not really, but there should be. Enough people died at his command, they say. It's said that he used to hang lanterns in the trees and in the windows of the castle to lure ships on to Cobbler's Reef. The ships would be wrecked on the rocks and Sam Lord's slaves would loot the wrecks and drag the spoils back to the castle through an underground passage.'

Kira shivered, though the night air was not cold. She could almost hear the cries of the drowning sailors. The dark countryside was sliding by in swiftly changing shapes, tall mahogany trees blotting out the ivory moon, mysterious gates leading to secret villas, clusters of painted chattel houses, glimpses of the sea glimmering with phosphorescence and shot with light. Fields of cane rustled in the wind. The sweet smell of flowers and the lush cane drifted on the same wind.

'I don't much like the sound of Sam Lord,' she said. 'Do we have to eat there?'

'It's only a legend.' He leaned across and touched her arm momentarily for reassurance.

'Admiralty records show that he was off the island when many of the wrecks occurred. And no one has ever found the underground passage. Yet there's no doubt he was a ruthless and dishonest man, and he treated his family and wife with terrible cruelty.'

'And now his castle is a popular restaurant?' said Kira with a touch of irony. 'A funny kind of justice for those people.'

'We can't dictate history. Perhaps Sugar Hill will become a holiday camp or a theme park one day. Sam Lord's Castle is a luxury hotel, very elegant, with a lot of his pictures and furniture preserved, like a museum. But if you don't care to eat there, we can go to Cobbler's Reef, the restaurant in a garden which is more informal,' Giles suggested with a touch of sensitivity she had not expected in the man.

'Which one is the nearest?'

'Sam Lord's.'

'OK. The pirate place it is.'

He drove steadily but not fast. The speed limit on Barbados was low compared with Britain. The lanes twisted and turned, very like Devonshire, and even late at night a mid-road game of cricket brought the big car to a halt. The boys pulled up the stumps and stood back to let the car pass.

'Hiya, Mister Giles,' some of the boys called out.

'Come and bowl, sir?' asked another, cheekily.

'Not tonight,' called Giles. 'I have a lady with me.'

'Is that my promised publicity?' Kira asked.

'Half of it.' He was laughing to himself and she liked that. She liked the fact that she had amused him.

They drove through the village and passed the high walls of sugar cane in the fields beyond. The surprise was the flatness. Her eyes roamed over so much space.

Giles knew a way of cutting out the tortuous route through Bridgetown. He struck out on to Highway 7, which was only an ordinary two-lane thoroughfare despite its title.

'The other half is that the news is already round the island that you're dining with me. They love gossip. They probably check when I have my hair cut.'

A few minutes later he turned right into Bel Air Road and she watched the deft way his brown hands handled the car. The discreet commercialism of the area became apparent;

another way of life had taken over, yet egrets flew overhead on their way home to roost. It was geared to tourism, almost a resort in itself with arcades of shops and mock village accommodation in the grounds. There was a uniformed security guard at the gate of Sam Lord's who checked Giles's reservation.

'They're very careful,' Kira commented, returning the guard's big smile.

'They have to be. A lot of very wealthy American tourists stay here. They pay to be looked after, although there's little crime on the island – mainly bags and cameras lifted on the beach – and we want it to stay that way. We have a superb police force based in Bridgetown, highly trained. Have you see the harbour police yet in their sailors' uniforms from Nelson's time? There's a good photo opportunity for you.'

'I'm not a tourist. It's the way people live that interests me. I shall hire a mini-moke to look round the island.'

'Very easy to get lost. The narrow roads twist and turn in a most confusing manner.'

He slid the car into a parking space. It was quietly busy. Taxi drivers hung about waiting for a call from the hotel. Rows of yellow beach-buggies, hired by visitors, cooled down after racing round the island. The security guards did not look quite so friendly in the dark and Kira was glad to have such a tall man at her side. She knew her fears were unfounded; it was just the fear of the unknown.

'It used to be called Long Bay Castle,' said Giles, steering her towards the massive house. 'It's the finest old colonial house in the Caribbean. Its thick walls even survived the terrible hurricane of 1831.'

There was a definite pride in his voice though Kira was aware from the tone and timbre of this words that he did not take the place all that seriously. Yet the commercialism that had robbed the castle of its uniqueness had saved it from falling into a ruin.

'The hurricanes are pretty devastating,' he added. 'I hope we don't get one while you're here.'

It was a white wedding-cake of a building; the 18th-century plantation house had been extended into an elaborate French-style mansion of the period. It stood on a low rocky cliff that looked out on to a coral beach shaded with coconut palms and sea grape trees. It was turreted and crenellated along the top of the flat roof and Kira was reminded of the smaller pink castle that her grandfather had built for his young bride . . .

Dolly pressed herself against Reuben with all the vigour of a young, untamed body. Reuben wrapped his arms round her tightly, then even more tightly, almost crushing the breath from her slender frame. They had not seen each other for two days and the urge was overpowering.

He was tasting the sweet, hot scent of her skin, feeling the softness of her hair against his neck. It drove him mad. Her strong young hands were digging into his back, pulling him closer.

'This is my living and loving,' she murmured, her thoughts in disarray. To be apart from Reuben would be like death itself. Yet she had to tell him.

'Benjamin Reed has asked me to marry him,' she said at last, when the urgency of their hot kisses was lost in exhaustion.

Reuben jerked back. 'No. Dolly, you can't mean it? Damn him! Tell him you can't. You will, won't you? You're going to marry me.'

Dolly smothered a giggle. 'But when? You haven't asked me and Benjamin has. He wants to marry me soon at a big church and he's going to build me a grand new house in St James. He's bought the ground already, right near the sea. It's going to have proper bathrooms with water, and a kitchen.'

'Dolly, do be sensible. Don't even think of it. Benjamin Reed is an old man. Let him marry somebody else, someone nearer his own age. There's plenty of single women who would jump at the offer. Dolly, you and I, we're together, aren't we? I thought for always, forever.' His voice was tinged with bitterness.

Her laughter rang out. 'Of course we're together,' she teased. 'But Benjamin wants to marry me and he's not that old. He's only thirty. That's not middle-aged. This house is going to be all pink,' she added dreamily.

'Listen, you idiot girl.' Reuben put his hands on her bare shoulders and tried to make her look at him. 'You don't marry someone for the sake of a house or bathrooms. You don't prostitute yourself for a pile of pink coral. I hope you told him no. A very definite no, thank you.'

'I didn't do nothing of the sort,' said Dolly shaking his hands free. 'And don't use that nasty word about me or I will think you've been free with those buy-me-now girls down by the market with their swinging hips and painted eyes. Oh, yes, I've seen them making mouths at you.'

'Don't be a damned fool, Dolly. As if I would go with any other girl, any girl at all, when I'm crazy about you. You know that I love you. Wait for me, please. You know marriage is out of the question until I'm twenty-three at least. Twenty-five would be better; that's when I come into my grandmother's money.'

'Money doesn't matter,' said Dolly, snuggling up to him, twisting her foot round his leg and rubbing his bare skin. It was a slow, sensual movement. 'I would live in a shack on the beach with you.'

He groaned with frustration. 'You're going to live at Sugar Hill when I'm the master. Promise that you won't marry Benjamin.'

'Promise,' she whispered, her lips against his mouth, her tongue tracing the warm curve of skin. His nerves tingled as she wove her spell.

They approached the four flights of blue and white marble steps leading on to the open porches. It was like the set of a Thirties movie. Kira half expected a row of dancing girls with Fred Astaire and Ginger Rogers or Gene Kelly.

She could hear the pounding surf of the reef that perpetuated the Sam Lord legend. It was easy to imagine flickering lanterns in the trees and the wind-blown ships crashing into the treacherous reef amid the terrible cries of the drowning sailors. She shivered.

'I told you there were ghosts,' said Giles. 'The island abounds in stories.'

'I don't believe in ghosts,' said Kira firmly. But she did believe in a different kind of haunting. Her ghost was a young woman called Jenny gazing up at Bruce with adoring eyes, telling him that she was pregnant and loving the moment.

She hardly took in the interior of the castle, noticing only that it was beautifully preserved with the original woodwork and ornate plaster ceilings. She saw herself in huge mirrors that also reflected the fine paintings and Regency furniture that might have been treasure-trove from a wreck. Carefully tanned women in long dresses were coming down the elegant staircase under the high-domed ceiling. Glittering chandeliers enhanced their jewels.

'I'm not wearing a long dress,' said Kira.

'People wear what they like. There's probably a special function in one of the rooms. Don't worry, you'll see other guests in Bermuda shorts and sun-tops.'

Giles took her arm possessively and this time Kira did not flinch. The atmosphere of the castle was evocative and bewitching, as if Sam Lord was luring her into his clutches too.

'Upstairs is Sam Lord's bedroom with the original four-poster bed and drapes. Downstairs are the dungeons where he imprisoned members of his family who got in the way, even his poor wife. I think they've been turned into offices now.'

Giles slowed his long stride, alerted by a sudden tenseness in Kira's body. She was surprised that she should feel so deeply about the suffering Sam Lord had caused, as if the elegant decoration covered over real bloodstains and the soft music disguised the whimpers of those imprisoned. A small, inarticulate sound escaped her lips and in a moment his hands were on her shoulders, turning her face towards him.

'This place upsets you, Kira,' he said slowly. 'I'm sorry. I didn't realize there was a soft core to the cool Miss Kira Reed from London. We'll leave immediately and find a fish restaurant in Oistins.'

Kira shook her head, trying to clear the strange feelings, to be in command of herself again. To rid herself of Bruce's cruelty too.

'No . . . there's no need,' she said, taking a deep breath. 'But I think I would prefer the other restaurant in the garden. All these antiques are a little overpowering and it's so hot. I'm not used to your marvellous climate yet.'

'Cobbler's Reef it'll be, then. You'll love it. There'll be a steel band playing and the gardens are gorgeous.'

Giles was right. They were shown to a moon-lit table set with gleaming silver and crystal glasses reflecting a flickering candle-flame from among a wreath of flowers.

Kira began to relax to the soft beat of the music. Here she could forget the decadent white house at the back of the gardens, with its terrible history. She deliberately chose the chair which had a view of the not too distant sea.

'We have wonderful food in Barbados,' said Giles, not handing her the second, unpriced menu. 'But I'll introduce you to our exotic Bajan dishes slowly. Will you let me choose for you tonight?'

Kira nodded. She doubted if she could read any menu in this light. And Giles was implying with his remark that he would see her again. That threw her. It was probably an inborn politeness, though. They were such polite people. He glanced at the menu then put the heavy leather folder aside.

'We'll start with the flying fish and spicy dip. Flying fish is practically our national symbol,' he added. 'Then grilled red snapper and side salads. I hope you don't mind two fish dishes? The chef here cooks fish to perfection. It's his speciality.'

His charm could be devastating. His eyes glittered with a wicked cast of humour that Kira was not used to. They smiled over their glasses of chilled German hock. No subject was taboo. He even made fun of her leg.

'So you've had a busy day, limping the length of St James?'

'The beaches are lovely. I met a man washing his goat in the sea. Then I went inland and bumped – I mean literally; fruit nearly hit me – into an old gardener pruning a breadfruit tree. It was that pink house I told you about earlier – the one you said belonged to Benjamin Reed.' She was probing again.

'Yes – Fitt's House,' said Giles. 'One day I'll tell you some more about its history.'

* * *

'Is this really going to be your house?' Dolly asked with awe. She hesitated in the unmade drive, staring up at the half-built villa. 'Wow!'

'Yes,' said Benjamin. 'I've always dreamed of living somewhere special. Not a traditional greathouse like Sugar Hill or Farley House but something so different that people will stop and stare.'

'They'll certainly stop and stare at this,' said Dolly, stepping carefully over the piles of rubble. 'It looks like a castle, a pink fairy castle.'

'Careful: the stonemason's chippings are sharp. You might cut your feet.'

Dolly looked at Benjamin with interest. People didn't usually care if she hurt herself. She often fell from things. He was older but he had a nice face, pleasant and easygoing with seafaring eyes. Not handsome like Reuben. Nor was Benjamin tall. He was lean and wiry, his thatch of hair bleached by the sun.

The coral stone was a rich shade of pink that would soften with time. The house was already built to the first floor, a sweeping flight of steps leading up to the front door and veranda.

'What are these?' she asked, running her hand over half-finished animal and bird shapes that stood about.

'Statues. They're supposed to be lions and eagles but the stonemason has never seen a lion or an eagle. He's doing the work from pictures.'

Dolly laughed and the sound rang out like music. 'They're funny,' she commented. 'They don't look anything like eagles and lions.'

'Don't tell him they're funny,' said Benjamin, unable to take his eyes from her face.

'Of course not, silly. I would never hurt anyone's feelings deliberately.'

'I know that,' he replied seriously, watching her closely. 'That's why I care for you so much.'

'Don't say that,' said Dolly, suddenly panicking. 'I haven't said anything. I haven't agreed. Look, I've only come to see your house.'

'I know that. I won't push you into anything. I'm just glad that you've come. I wanted you to see what I'm building for you.'

Benjamin reached for her hand but Dolly was already skipping away, her interest taken by something else.

The meal arrived and it was delicious. Giles was right. The chef cooked fish to perfection.

'I'm glad to see that your appetite has returned,' said Giles as Kira picked at the decorative design of sliced fruit and vegetables in the side salad. 'You had a mere sparrow's breakfast this morning. In fact the sparrows ate more than you. I was beginning to think you were one of those women who are always on diets. You're far too thin – all bones.'

'I've always been this slim,' she lied.

It was not true. The weight had fallen off her since Valentine's Day. It was one way to lose weight but not to be recommended. She went quiet. The aching place inside her head hardened into a knot of pain. Her mind was lost in a prison of her own making.

'Thin, I said, not slim.'

Their eyes locked across the table. Kira could not fathom the message in those dark, glinting nuggets of ocean blue. It was more than a casual interest. It was a burning look, as if he was striving to imprint his authority on her. Cinderella never had to cope with that kind of look from Prince Charming as they waltzed around the ballroom floor. Not that Kira could waltz any more. She loved dancing and dancing was out.

Giles was even on her wavelength.

'So how come the limp?' he asked briskly. 'Some irate client trip you up on the way out of a high-powered board meeting?'

'Do you always ask so many personal questions?' Kira was being bewitched by the music.

'No, only when I like someone. Then I want to know all about them. You are a mass of contradictions, one minute angry and the next so sensitive and easily upset. Sometimes you act the efficient businesswoman, then in a flash you're a lonely little girl. Kira, you intrigue me. I want to know what the real Kira Reed is like,' he said evenly. 'And I'd like to understand you.'

'That's an unlikely event,' Kira heard herself saying. 'I doubt if I shall ever see you again after tonight. There'll be no reason.'

His eyes narrowed and his tone became intolerant and patronizing. He was gauging her reaction.

'But what if I offer you a research job connected with my sugar plantation? Would that tempt you to stay around? What do you think? I'd pay well. Somehow I want to find a way to melt the snow that surrounds your heart,' he added whimsically.

'Well, I thought it was you, Giles. So this is where you eat these days. I thought you had given up civilized eating for the casual beach life

– coconuts and things.' A young woman stopped by their table, her pixie face full of mischief. She was wearing a skimpy red satin dress with narrow straps, her dark hair tumbling on her shoulders. She put her arms possessively round Giles's shoulders.

'Don't exaggerate just because you're always in bed when I leave Sugar Hill.' Giles stifled a sigh. 'This is Lace, my sister. Twenty-five going on barely twelve.'

'He's so hunky, isn't he?' Lace went on, helping herself to a strawberry from his plate. 'I wonder how long *you'll* last. No woman lasts long with Giles. He's a workaholic, you see. No female can compete with the plantation or Sugar Hill.'

'Kira may be going to work for me,' said Giles drily.

'Kira?' Lace was already losing interest. 'What an unusual name!'

'It's Russian,' said Kira.

'Oh, you're a foreigner. That's the attraction. Giles likes something different,' said Lace, her hand going to Giles's glass of wine. He stopped her. 'Don't be a meany, Giles. Just a sip.'

'I think you've already had more than a sip. Go back to your friends.'

123

'We're going on dancing,' said Lace to Kira. 'Do you want to come with us?'

'No, thank you,' said Giles, answering for her. 'We're not in the mood for dancing.'

'Then what *are* you in the mood for?' she laughed as she walked away swaying to the music. 'Or would that be telling, big brother?'

CHAPTER 6

'Take no notice of Lace,' said Giles. 'Disconcerting people, especially me, is her main hobby.'

'Perhaps she needs a job to keep her occupied.'

'She'd never arrive on time. She's not like you. You're probably a nine-to-five slave-driver.'

She acted casual. 'It would depend on which slave I was driving,' she said.

Giles had many advantages over her. He was one of the plantocracy: he owned a plantation and a sugar factory and a greathouse. He probably owned another chain of businesses she knew nothing about. He would be the kind of person who would invest his money and time in local enterprises.

She was an emotionally adrift secretary with big ideas that had not yet taken shape, but she knew she was not destined to pound a typewriter or keyboard for the rest of her working life. There had to be more to life than that for Kira. She was never going to be as short of money or worn out as Tamara, her mother.

'So what do you think of doing some research for me?'

'That also depends on the area of research. It has to be realistic. You could be contriving some lightweight problem with no depth to it, simply because you don't think I'm capable of real work.'

Giles gave a short laugh and spiked a slice of mango. 'Surely you give me more credit? There would be nothing in it for me; you've made that clear enough. No, this is a genuine piece of research that I want and I need it done accurately and efficiently. It also has to be completed fast. I've been waiting long enough for the information.'

Kira felt as if she was drowning in gallons of black molasses. Work for Giles? It would be like picking her way through a minefield. 'Well, I don't know . . .' she said, with a cautious attempt at a smile.

A flicker of impatience crossed his face. He would be a formidable person to work for. Kira did not know if she could cope with the day-to-day contact.

He cut in abruptly. 'Make up your mind, woman. We're up to our necks in problems, not the least of which is the falling world consumption of sugar. We have an enormous capital investment in the sugar-refining factories and a large workforce in the fields. Fortunately for Barbados, sugar is not only stirred in tea and sprinkled on cornflakes. The healthy gurus of the Western world have given us the calorific thumbs-down but our sugar still goes into the making of excellent rum. Barbados fine and mellow rum is the best on the market.'

'Alcohol?'

'Don't be a puritan. World-famous.'

'What do you want researched?'

'Grass-roots problems.'

'Not those awful monkeys . . .?'

Her dismayed expression softened the hard line of his mouth.

'Relax. It's not the monkeys,' he grinned. 'Though I'd pay good money to get rid of them.'

'Tame them. Open a zoo.'

'OK. That's your second project.'

'I can't stand the creatures,' she burst out. 'So what is it? Fire-bugs?'

'No, that's for the police department. One of my men was killed earlier this year. He was caught, trapped in the circle of fire that rushed towards him on the wind. There was nothing anyone could do for him. He was dead before we got him to hospital.'

Giles's voice dropped to a harshness that did not disguise his feelings. He obviously found it difficult to control his anger at the incident. It was as if he was miles away from the moon-drenched garden setting of Cobbler's Reef and the racing white waters, reliving the stench of the burning cane.

'I'm so sorry,' said Kira, breaking the silence. She was remembering vividly the misery on Bruce's face. 'People do cruel things to each other for no reason. That was barbaric.'

He dragged his thoughts back and covered her hand with a swift movement. He rubbed his thumb over her skin in contemplation, as if reassuring himself that she, at least, was real.

'But you would never be cruel, would you, Kira? There's a gentleness about you that tells me the cool look is a cover.'

'Gentle yes, with animals and children. But never with men,' she said, withdrawing her hand, though not wanting to. 'They have to earn my approval, and not many of them do.'

'I plan to be the first man on Barbados to win your approval,' said Giles. Kira could not see his expression clearly in the nebulous gloom but she was sure he was laughing at her.

'You're too late,' said Kira with one of her rare smiles. 'A young man called Moonshine on the beach this morning got there first.'

'Ah, yes. Moonshine. I know of him. He's trying to put himself through business college.'

'That's very ambitious and I'm sorry I didn't buy anything.' Kira was stricken with guilt. 'I should have.'

'Don't worry. You're earmarked now. He'll be back till you do. Anyway, when you learn how many dollars I'm going to pay you for this research, your generosity will overflow into his briefcase of necklaces.'

Kira didn't ask ask how much, even though she wanted to know. 'But you haven't told me anything yet about the work.'

'It's transport, basically,' he said, back in control. 'Sounds boring, eh? But it's vital, I assure you. Let me explain. There are lots of small growers, family smallholdings, even one-man cane fields, scattered all over the island.

They need to get their cane to my factory. At the moment there is an inefficient local lorry system and a lot of complaints. The small growers feel they're being swindled.'

'And you need to keep your factory working at capacity,' Kira cut in.

'We need each other. I haven't time to go around and talk to everyone but I want an overall picture before I can come up with some solution. Could you do that? Or perhaps it's not sophisticated enough for a smart London woman?' he added with a touch of sarcasm. 'Noisy lorries are hardly status.'

Kira hid the surge of eagerness and relief. It was exactly the kind of research she *could* do. She was good with people. She could ferret out the real facts of a situation. She'd always been able to find answers for Mr Connor and wondered how the blonde temp was getting on. Giles wasn't asking her to do anything that was beyond her.

'Lorries are OK,' she said casually.

'Your eyes are saying they're more than OK. Never underestimate your eyes, Kira. They mirror your soul. That's settled, then. You'll need a Barbados registration from the police so that you can drive. Get one at the police station at Holetown. It's only up the road from Sandy Lane. I'll lend you a vehicle so that you can get around. Charge me expenses.'

'Hold on, Giles. I haven't said . . .'

'There's a file this thick at the factory, all the complaints that you'll need to go through, and a list of the small growers. I'll give you some kind of written authority, in case anyone is suspicious of your questions. Though I'm sure, with your personality, you'll be able to sweet-talk the most reticent grower.'

'My non-existent charm,' Kira said acidly.

'Your air of vulnerability,' he said smoothly. 'And your limp. They'll be sorry for you, and curious.'

'I'll wear an accident declaration badge.'

'And they'll be too polite to ask how you got it. Not like me; I want to know everything about you. I want to take you to pieces and then put you back together again.'

'That doesn't sound very nice,' Kira murmured, shocked, as if he had actually violated her body.

Giles was saved from replying by the arrival of a waiter with a laden sweets trolley. The selection was mouthwatering but Kira did not have room for even one of their famous ice-creams.

'How about the lime soufflé, light and sharp like you?' said Giles with a straight face. 'Or the coconut flan, rich and sweet like me?'

'Just coffee, please,' she said, ignoring the absurdity.

'Two coffees, please. And two French brandies, the best. I hope you like brandy. It's the finest way to end a meal.'

'Not Barbados rum?'

'Rum is an anytime drink. Elevenses, before lunch, on the beach, before an evening meal, when one is relaxing and socializing. We invent the most fabulous sundowners. I'll get my housekeeper to show you how to make them, then, when you're back in your wet and gloomy London, you will be able to cheer yourself with thoughts of sunny Barbados.'

A surprisingly lazy warmth invaded his voice which sent a silver shiver of recognition down her spine. He was getting too personal. She wondered if there was a woman in his life. No man so attractive and influential could exist on this small island without a woman wanting to share his bed and his life.

So what if he had a string of women? Kira remembered that the moral code of the island accepted sex before marriage. It was important that a woman was not barren. Marriage was important too, and many brides went to their weddings already pregnant.

Kira wondered what Giles's current lover was like . . . some dark beauty with voluptuous curves and masses of tumbling curls. She saw them entwined in bed, all naked legs and more legs, thrashing and straining, the woman's voice husky with orgasmic pleasure. She shuddered, eyes half closed.

'Cold?'

'No . . . just thinking of London,' she lied. 'Yes, it is a cold, grey place.' And it had become colder and greyer without Bruce to lighten her days.

'I think I should take you back to Sandy Lane soon. I don't often have a dinner guest falling asleep on me. Do you think that you could manage to stay awake long enough for a quick glimpse of Cobbler's Reef?'

'Sorry, it's just the balmy air and left-over jet-lag.'

'It can take several days to recover.'

'But yes, I'd love to see the reef. As long as we don't meet a pirate.'

'Haven't seen a genuine one for years,' said Giles, folding some dollar bills without counting them and leaving them on the table.

The garden was full of the sweet and spicy aroma of tropical flowers, hibiscus, bougainvillaea, frangipani, growing like weeds, the grass strewn with the day's fallen petals. They took the path to the sea in silence, their hands occasionally brushing. Each encounter brought a sensation to Kira's body that she had not felt for a long time and thought she would never feel again.

She stepped aside and put a distance between them. His tall figure hesitated in the dusky light, as if unprepared for her defensive action. The distance felt like a empty mile.

Giles noticed the way she moved to one side as if no one must invade her space. It saddened him immeasurably that someone had hurt her so badly that she trusted closeness with no one. It was strange that he should already feel so drawn to her; it had not happened to him for a long time. Those eyes seemed seemed to dominate her smooth, calm face. He wanted to touch her face to see if her skin was really as silken as it looked. He could smell the sweet perfume of her body in the warm air and it stirred his senses. He wanted to drown in that sweetness and hold her in his arms till the cool dawn came.

The path ended with a small viewing area at the cliff edge. A wooden seat invited a rest but instead Kira went as close to the edge as safety allowed, watching the breakers crash and foam over the reef. The sea roared as it pounded the coral. No ship had any chance against the power of the waves and the jagged rocks.

'We still have lots of shipwrecks,' said Giles, reading her thoughts. 'This part of the coast is very dangerous. Fishing boats and small sailing boats get caught in riptides. It's the meeting of currents or abrupt changes of depth in the water.'

'I can feel it,' she said.

'It's the ghosts you can feel.'

The beach below Sam Lord's Castle was bone-white in the darkness, dotted with trees and stacks of striped loungers. It was easy to image those long-ago slaves creeping down in the gloom to hang lanterns of death in the swaying branches.

'I've enough ghosts in my life,' she said without thinking.

Giles towered beside her even though Kira was tall. Everything about him was so splendid, so aggressively masculine and powerful. He was like a strong wine going to her head, taking her into an enchanted garden where she could walk on clouds.

He did not ask her what she meant.

'I'll take you home now,' he said, as if the island was already home for her. He laced his fingers through hers and the touch was electric. She felt her breasts tingling although he was not that near.

She tried to extricate herself from his grasp but it was already too late. He was moving closer and his other arm went round her shoulders, his hand tracing her back though the thin material. She felt her breasts crushed against his hard chest and the sensation was bliss.

He kissed the furthest curve of her neck and the few inches of shoulder that were bare, with light, feathery touches. The kisses felt like a butterfly supping nectar from her skin. His nose brushed the lobe of her ear, and his hand came up to tangle itself in the softness of her hair. She stood still with wonder.

Now she could feel his breath quickening on the skin of her cheek. She moaned, not able to take any more, yet quite unable to stop him. She turned her face aside and he took it as an invitation to stroke the back of her neck, to slide his hand across her shoulders, to rasp his nails lightly on the delicate skin between the blades.

'Kira . . . Kira,' he murmured.

She felt her body curving with desire, leaning into him, taking a wanton pleasure from the ardent and skilful touches. This was not her way; love had to come first. Yet she could not tell if the pounding in her ears was from her heart or from the reef.

When his mouth reached hers, Kira was beyond resisting. She let him part her moist lips and deepen the kiss, his tongue invading her mouth. Her body began to weaken as the kiss moved from tenderness to growing passion. Her eyes were closed but she knew that his were blazing.

Suddenly he pushed her aside, as if the lapse had been her fault. For a moment, Kira was hurt, then the turmoil quietened in her breast and she knew he was right to stop. The closeness had all become as darkly turbulent and danger- ous as the waves that lashed the reef.

'Home,' he said, briefly.

When they reached the car park, Giles took off his jacket and slipped it round Kira's shoulders as he had before. It was still warm from the heat of his body. The heat touched her bare arms and it travelled along her skin like fire.

'You may feel chilly on the drive home,' he said, tidily lifting her hair over the collar. Her hair was soft and the wind curled a tendril round his finger. Giles had never touched anything so soft. It made his heart contract with longing. He did not know how he had managed to break the spell in the garden. He wanted to know why she was so thin and troubled, longed to comfort her.

'Can't have you getting cold,' he added, on one of the warmest nights Kira had known for years.

He reached out and folded his arms round her loosely, breathing in her sweet scent. He could not stop himself. Kira froze, her arms pinned to her side. It was a long, suspended embrace, intended to be casual but with both of them acutely aware of the shape of their bodies and the fact that those bodies were touching. She lost herself in the clean, masculine smell of him, the healthy fragrance of good soap, the tangy scent of aftershave . . . he had no right to smell so good.

Wonderingly, Kira stayed still in his embrace, letting him hold her. Her mind was spinning.

Why did he seem to need her? For months she had thought only of herself and her pain, her betrayal, her injuries. But now this man, this man of stature and strength, was wearing some suit of sorrow that she could not understand. She was sure it was not another woman. It was something else.

Giles stepped back and Kira would have fallen if he had not steadied her. She braced her balance but her injured leg let her down and the pain was sharp.

'Are you all right?' They stared into each other's eyes, wondering at what they saw. Kira knew that something was happening to her icy heart but she fought against its stirrings. She did not want to be hurt again.

'I'd never hurt you,' he said, doing it once more, reading her thoughts. 'Not intentionally.'

'I'll never let you,' she said, the pain putting an unnecessary coldness in her voice.

'I'm glad we've sorted that out.'

He drove her back to St James, through the balmy night, past the ghostly sugar cane fields and whispering palms, stopping outside the hotel entrance. He did not get out, but sat staring ahead impassively, his hands on the wheel. A bell boy came and opened the door.

'I'll get one of my employees to bring you a car. Get that visitor's licence at Holetown and I'll see you in my office tomorrow after lunch. I'll send you directions for getting there.'

'I'll call you first,' said Kira, fighting back. 'I may have other things to do tomorrow.'

'Cancel them. Two sharp, in my office,' he repeated firmly. 'Goodnight, Kira.'

'Goodnight, Giles,' she said, forgetting to thank him. She began the words but it was already too late.

She collected her key, only half hearing his powerful car speed away. She had come to Barbados for peace and quiet and to make some contact with her grandfather. To right some wrongs. Instead she was being caught in a web spun by a man she knew she should be keeping away from. She slid open the doors to the balcony and stepped out for a last look at the glimmering sea. Her spirit was singing a brand new song. But the cold voice of common sense at the back of her mind told her to beware.

Kira dreamed of Giles. He came unbidden into her sleep and took her body without force. It was a dream of glorious passion and unutterable sweetness. Rapture beyond all her imaginings hung in the air like spun gold, lancing their pleasure with joy and happiness.

She awoke, drenched in sweat, her legs aching, still feeling the pressure of his warm weight. She stretched languorously beneath the smooth cotton sheet as if indeed her body had been satisfied. Then she curled on to her side, her hand on the empty pillow, hungering for his presence.

Her physical longing for Bruce had long since gone. Once she had wanted him, in those early heady days, but she'd dreamed of being a virginal bride. What a mistake! But waiting had seemed right at the time. Perhaps that was why Bruce had fallen so easily into Jenny's arms.

How could she continue to want a man whose body had so recently been pleasuring another woman? The reality had quickly dampened her desire for lovemaking, cooling the physical passion, and now her pride would not allow her body to want him still. Desire had faded, leaving Kira an empty husk: no longer was she the warm and loving woman she had once been.

Kira turned over in bed, her hand now cupping her cheek, reliving her dream, wondering if Giles was going to bring her body to life again. It was strange that she should even contemplate such a happening, when in reality she strove to keep him at a distance. She wanted time and space and distance in which to heal and make herself whole again.

Bruce had demolished her spirit that awful evening. She could not remember his exact words now, didn't even try. The pain was enough. A living nightmare arriving unexpectedly out of a haze of love-blindness.

For once, Kira did not cry at the memory, and that was something new. Dry-eyed, she looked back dispassionately, remembering how he could not bring himself to meet her eyes, how he'd found excuses. Time was helping ease the anguish – or was it Barbados, weaving its magic spell?

She drifted back to sleep, half-smiling, unaware that she was letting Giles into her thoughts again.

They had not met for a week. Reuben had kept away but he dreamed of Dolly every night, longing to invade her body, wanting to quench the fire that burned in his loins. He was going mad with wanting her. It was crazy.

'Don't you love me?' said Dolly, leaning up on one elbow, stroking his hair with gentle fingers. 'I want more kisses . . . here and here . . .' She touched the hollow of her throat and a small place on the curve of her shoulder, twisting her body towards him. 'Love me, love me . . .'

'I can't,' he groaned, rolling on to his side. 'You know what it does to me. It's driving me mad.'

'What does it do to you? Tell me. Is it here?'

Reuben jerked away and sat up. 'For God's sake, woman. Don't do that again. You're a little devil,' he choked angrily, recoiling from her. 'Don't you know anything?'

'No . . .' Dolly was bewildered by his reaction. Tears smarted in her eyes. 'André tells me nothing. And if you don't tell me, how shall I know? I've no mother, no friend to ask. Don't be angry with me. How shall I ever know if you don't tell me about life, my sweetheart, my darling Reuben.'

Reuben could not stand the sight of her tears. He kissed them away gently, stroking her face and hair as if she were a kitten. He loved her so much, and even more when she acted like a child. But one day she would be a woman and then she would share his life.

'Firstly, you do not take your clothes off,' Reuben said, rearranging her dress. 'You do not drape your legs over a man. And you do not touch him . . . here.'

He planned to marry her, one day. He was barely twenty so it had to be a long way off. First he had to learn the business, save some money, build a family home. Sugar Hill would not be his for a long time. But one day he would own the great white plantation house and he wanted Dolly to share it with him.

'I'll tell you everything if you promise to behave, Dolly. And no going off and dazzling the other boys with your bare legs and bare shoulders.' Reuben relaxed back on to the sand and folded his arms behind his head. A dappled palm fluttered shadows across his face.

'You can talk. That smug girl Elise is always eyeing you. She'd go out with you any time you asked. And flaunting her money and posh clothes, just because her father's going to build a smart hotel and a golf course.'

'Waste of good sugar land,' Reuben muttered. 'It shouldn't be allowed. Someone ought to stop this rot.'

'Get yourself elected, then,' said Dolly, wondering if she dared unbutton his shirt and touch the dark hair on his chest. She loved the coarse curls that lay like a raven's sheen on his skin. When they went swimming, she often pretended she was out of her depth so that Reuben would hold her against him and the water would wash over their cosely treading limbs. 'Be a representative at Congress. You'd could be our youngest representative ever,' she giggled.

Dolly let herself bathe in the reflected political glory for a daydream moment. She saw herself attending balls and dinners with Reuben in a variety of dresses, though where she got them from wasn't clear in the dream.

'I've too much to do, thank you. There's no time for politics. Why don't *you* get yourself elected? Become the first woman in Congress?'

'Now you've laughing at me. How would I know what to do or say? No one has ever taught me anything. I can only cook and clean paintbrushes. I can barely read.'

'It's your own fault for not paying more attention in class, always skipping school to go swimming or sell your father's pictures in Bridgetown market on cruise days.'

'But I had to. The big cruise ships only anchor off Bridgetown for a few hours. The passengers come ashore to shop-buy. American dollars, you know. We would starve if we didn't sell to the tourists.'

She straightened the rest of her frock and stood up, shaking off the sand, her face composed and motherly now. 'I must get my father's tea,' she said.

'I'll walk with you to the end of the lane. My bike is in the bushes.'

'Don't wait too long to marry me,' said Dolly, suddenly very matter-of-fact. 'I don't want to be an old maid, a spinster, all crumbly and dried up.'

CHAPTER 7

Facing Benjamin Reed for the first time was going to be difficult. Kira did not relish meeting him, nor was she certain how she would react. Her anger at his treatment of her mother was begining to lose its impetus under the relaxing spell of Barbados. It all seemed such a long time ago – and perhaps the old man had had reason for his behaviour.

She was lazing in bed, enjoying not having to rush to work with crowds of commuters. She poured herself a pineapple juice from the refrigerator and turned on the radio.

The 'Voice of Barbados' was a mixture of music request programmes, phone-ins and quiz games. There was regular local news and world news, parochial items about local people and choirs, and then, following solemn music, announcements of deaths on the island and details of funerals. It seemed that, no matter how lowly or unknown, everyone got a mention on the radio when they died.

Lists of mourners were read out and Kira was surprised at how the families had split up and went to every part of the world – America, Britain, Australia. It was sad listening to funeral details so she turned the tuning knob and found another station – just in time to hear her own name.

'More out-and-about Barbados news. Seen dining at Sam Lord's last night, Miss Kira Reed, a London-based research consultant, with Giles Earl of the Sugar Hill Plantation. Miss Reed is newly arrived on the island and staying at Sandy Lane, St James.' The warm, throaty voice added a footnote. 'It is rumoured that Miss Reed is here to do some research for the sugar industry.'

'So I made the radio,' Kira smiled to herself. 'But how did they know about the sugar research?'

The dewy morning was so fresh and beautiful, she could not lie abed for long. Slipping into her one-piece swimsuit, she went through the gardens and on to the newly swept sand. She dived into the crystal blue water and swam strongly out to a moored sailing dingy in the bay. She felt the weakened muscles of her damaged leg obeying her commands.

Later she would collect the business cards from the printers in Bridgetown and a driving licence from the police station. She had her UK licence with her so it would be a mere formality, plus paying the registration cost.

Giles had not mentioned money. She wondered how much he was going to pay her for her work. She hoped it was going to be a fair return.

And some time that morning she would find Fitt's House again and meet Benjamin Reed. She had come here to see her grandfather and see him she would, without disclosing her identity at first if possible. He had made it clear long ago that he wanted nothing to do with his grandchild, and that suited Kira too.

She sliced through the water. She wanted no man in her life . . . not a grandfather, not Bruce and certainly not Giles Earl. Even Percival Connor had not treated her fairly. Well she could stand on her own two feet now – even if one of them tended to let her down occasionally!

She ploughed back towards the shore, anger and frustration lending a fierceness to her strokes which sent sprays of water flying through the air.

She waded into the shallows, her feelings calming down. A splashing from behind told her that someone else was up early. Why was she not surprised when she turned around? Water was streaming off his long, tanned body as Giles emerged from the waves, his skin glistening and muscular. He wore black trunks fitting low over his hips, his legs moving with strength through the powerful waves.

'I thought for a moment you were being chased by a shark. Then I remembered that we have no sharks inshore. What was it? A crab?'

'Several crabs,' said Kira, waiting for him to reach her. 'I have several crabs permanently nipping at my toes.'

'Ah, that accounts for the occasional hunted look.'

'What are you doing here?' she asked, ignoring the remark.

'I live here. I told you, I have a beach villa,' he added, waving towards a thick screen of casuarina and sea-grape trees on the white shore. Kira could see nothing through their foilage. 'My house is over there. It's called Copens.'

'Copens? What does it mean?'

'Samuel Copen. He drew what he called a "prospect" of Bridgetown in 1695. Probably the first ever draughtsman's map. It was an impressive Dutch-style seaport then, with red-tiled roofs, brick chimneys, wharves and quays, and its bay was full of three-masted ships. A prosperous port. I have a framed copy of Samuel Copen's prospect.'

Kira was impressed. 'Did Bridgetown stay prosperous?'

'No way! We're an island of hurricanes. In 1780, the whole town was reduced to rubble by a hurricane. The cathedral was destroyed, the harbour filled with sand and stones and wood; many people died. They hit us and they kill. There is no discrimination.'

Kira stood in the shallows, hugging her arms across her chest. A swimsuit circa 1905 would have suited her growing modesty at that moment. This skimpy, high-legged sheath of Lycra left little to the imagination. Why had she put it on again? Because she had not expected to meet Giles.

'When was the last bad one?'

'We had an abnormal hurricane in 1955. They called her Hurricane Janet. The forecasters thought it would pass north of Barbados but the wind shifted north through east to south. The worst ever was on 10 August in 1831. It lasted eight hours and there was little of the town left standing by the time it moved on.'

'When's the hurricane season?' Kira asked apprehensively, scanning the sky for horned black clouds.

'You're safe,' said Giles, shaking water from his hair. 'August through October are the hurricane months. You'll be back in foggy old London before then. Where did you get your Russian name?'

'My father,' said Kira without thinking. 'My father was Russian.'

She bit on her last words and gave him a swift, startled look. But Giles was only paying polite attention. The island gossips had long forgotten that Benjamin Reed's daughter had married a Russian dancer.

'You were right about the publicity,' said Kira quickly. 'There was a mention on the radio this morning. Not exactly one hundred per cent accurate, but . . .'

Giles chuckled. 'I signed the visitor's book at Sam Lord's. I know the radio reporters keep an eye on it for anyone new.'

'You signed for me?'

'Why not? Admit it, now. It was fun to hear the item on the radio this morning. A surprise for you. Didn't it give you even a small thrill, or are you so used to publicity and the media?'

Mr Connor had hated the media. He always got uptight about journalists' questions and insisted he was unfairly reported. 'No, it was the first time for me.'

'Any other firsts last night?' he asked lightly. His eyes lingered on her a second too long for composure. He wished he knew what was troubling her. She looked so uncomfortable in her deliciously cut-away swimsuit. He wanted to taste again that full, sad mouth. He wanted to make it smile, to make her eyes glow, for the tension to melt from that stiff, straight back.

Giles planted his hands on his hips. It was the only way he could stop them touching her. This was a kind of madness, he groaned inwardly. How long had he known her? Only two or three days, yet there was already something elusive between them – a something that was exciting and full of promise.

'I'm sure I don't know what you mean,' she said, striding on to the soft, dry sand. She tried to dismiss the image of the tall, dripping man following her, the expanse of broad chest glistening with dark wet hair. He was too earthy, too primitive, too disturbing.

'Come and have breakfast with me,' he called out. 'At my place, on the patio.'

'No, thank you.'

'I won't ask you any awkward questions or chase you round a grapefruit.'

'I don't intend to give you the chance.'

She heard him chuckle as he veered across the sand to the left of Sandy Lane, towards a thicket of glossy leaves.

'By the way,' he turned and added, 'If you ever meet Benjamin Reed, don't mention Hurricane Janet. I'm warning you, he gets upset.'

Kira stopped in her tracks. How did he knew she was going to see Benjamin Reed? Her heart thudded, then good sense took over. He was president of the Sugar Growers' Association so a meeting would be on the cards. Perhaps Giles himself would pencil in such a meeting.

'Why?'

'Because he does.'

Giles pushed aside the tangled branches and she caught a glimpse of a one-storey building, mostly white stone and a flash of floor to ceiling window glass. A white table and cushioned chairs stood on a patio. Then the branches closed behind him and she lost her view and her chance of sharing breakfast with him in a beach paradise.

She was consumed with envy. She thought of the cheerless grey mornings in London, her small but compact kitchen, wet and steaming raincoats in the Underground, the crush of backpackers; waiting for crowded buses that arrived in conveys, always having to stand.

This life was a million miles away from reality. Like Giles . . . not real. He, too, was part of the island culture, a different world from hers, and the sooner she dismissed him from her thoughts, the better.

After breakfast, Kira changed into a parrot-red sun-dress and took a square scarf to drape over her bare shoulders. She did not want to break any local bye-laws by wearing the wrong gear in their capital. She waited outside Sandy Lane and boarded the first rickety bus to arrive, much to the amazement of the taxi drivers touting for custom amongst the hotel guests.

The bus was highly mechanized, despite being an ancient vehicle. Kira had to drop her money down a plastic shute under the eagle eye of the woman conductor in a military-style uniform. She was handed a ticket. Kira moved along the crowded bus and took a seat next to a buxom matron whose lap was piled high with empty shopping baskets. The other passengers looked at Kira with interest, their faces friendly. She smiled back.

It was a scare-a-minute drive into Bridgetown. The driver took corners on two wheels, emergency-braked for stray hens and dogs, made numerous unscheduled stops for people whose homes were on the route, stopped mid-road to exchange ribald comments with a mate driving a bus out of Bridgetown.

Kira even enjoyed the confrontation between the stern conductress and a long-haired, bleary-eyed beach wino who climbed unsteadily aboard and then refused to pay his fare.

'We ain't starting until you paid your fare,' she said.

'We all paid our fare, man,' said the indignant matron beside Kira, the abundant flowers on her brimmed hat bobbing. 'We all gotta get to Bridgetown. You making us late.'

'You drink all your money. That's your business,' bristled another old man, his face wrinkled and veined like a map.

There was no sympathy from the busload of passengers held up in the soaring temperatures.

The leatherette seats were hot and sticky. Kira felt like paying the wino's fare so that they could get moving, but decided not to interfere. The conductress was on top form, quoting rules and regulations.

Eventually the wino climbed down and tottered off to find some shade, trailing rags and a gnarled walking stick. They opened the windows wider to clear the air of alcoholic fumes.

Kira stepped off the bus at the bus station into a swirling throng of people and cars and bikes and buses. The hot air was pulsing with the smell of sweetmeats and spices from pavement stallholders; crushed-ice vendors mingled with the fruit sellers and the whole atmosphere was pungent with motor exhaust fumes. Kira was glad she didn't have asthma!

She wandered about, drinking in the sights like any another tourist. She delighted in the Harbour Police Force in their Nelson-era sailor uniforms; the schooners in the Careenage harbour and the preserved warehouses; the great ocean-going ships anchored out in the bay; the sugar bulk stores and loading towers, cargo ships and the gleaming white cruise-liners calling at Bridgetown for a couple of hours of intensive shopping.

Six international banks were neighbours to old wooden houses with overhanging balconies. Many of the side streets were in poor shape and awaiting demolition, though Kira thought these quaint old ramshackle buildings gave Bridgetown much of its unique character. Swan Street, Mahogany Lane, Sobers Lane . . . with their deep gullies to take torrential rain, the unmended narrow pavements were a hazard of pot-holes and broken stones. Rows of shabby pink and brown shacks sold a few vegetables or peddled some repair service or another.

The air-conditioned police headquarters in Coleridge Lane was full of smartly uniformed officers, spruce and welcoming.

'Good morning, ma'am. How can I help you?' said the officer behind the counter.

'I'd like a visitor's driving permit, please.'

In no time Kira had a local driving permit and a registered licence.

'Take care, ma'am. It's getting really hot now.'

Heat blistered the pavements. She had not felt the heat so much yesterday, as she was wandering in and out of the sea. Today, though, she was feeling quite sick by the time she found the printer's shop in a dusty back street.

'Come in, Mizz Reed,' said a wiry Barbadian, pulling up a chair. 'Can I get you a Coke or a coffee?'

Kira accepted an iced can of Coke, savouring the cool wet feel of the can before the icy drink.

The printer had a fairly old printing machine, but a very modern electric typewriter and photocopying machine. He had made a good job of her business cards: the gold print on brown card looked smart. The price was a bit steep but Kira realized she was a sitting target. Still, the Coke had saved her sanity.

That had been worth its weight in any currency.

Kira bought a thin buttercup cotton slip of a nightdress with shoestring straps at Woolworth's. She had to smile at the outrageous colours and the huge sizes of many of the bras and knickers in stock. There were also masses of household goods, bright and cheap, with a strong American influence.

She knew she was flagging. The tourist office in Harbour Road gave her a map and a sheaf of leaflets on places to visit.

'Where do you suggest I have lunch? I'd like to try some real Bajan dishes.'

'The Brown Sugar at Aquatic Gap is very good. You must also go to some of the wonderful old houses that have become eating places in order to survive.'

'Like Sam Lord's?'

'No, Sam's is very commercialized. There are real country houses where you are made to feel like a family guest. Brown Sugar is near the Hilton Hotel. Any taxi driver will take you.'

Kira fell into a taxi. She was feeling dizzy and dehydrated. Her breakfast had been only fruit. She was glad when the taxi stopped outside an old single-storeyed house with white-latticed windows and a riot of plants climbing the walls. An all-round veranda was full of pots of ferns and small palms, and Kira was relieved to sit in the shade with a cold drink while they found her a table.

'I'm afraid you may have to wait a while. We're very busy. Everyone makes reservations.'

'I don't mind,' said Kira, thankful for the shade. She slipped off her sandals under the chair.

Local girls in ankle-length flowered skirts and turbans waited on the tables. A long trestle offered a hot and cold buffet of local dishes and the spicy smell was tantalizing.

'Madam . . . a gentleman has offered to share his table with you. Is that acceptable?'

Was Giles following her? She peered into the garden, knowing she would be able to spot his classy presence and height. 'What sort of gentleman?'

'An elderly gentleman.' The waitress tried to conceal a grin. 'One of the island's most respected citizens.'

'That's all right, then,' Kira said demurely, putting on her sandals.

Slanting sunshine came through the raffia shades as the waitress led her to a table in the garden. The restaurant was full of wealthy Barbadians, dark, handsome and mostly bearded, and visitors in smart summer clothes. Kira recognized a couple from Sandy Lane. A tall, exotic Caribbean woman with a pronounced American accent and assured manner was laughing with them. Kira wondered if the new Miss Reed would ever gain that kind of assurance.

She turned a smile towards her host, half expecting a large, dark Barbadian. But the respected citizen had tanned skin, was thin and wiry, going bald, and casually dressed in creased white slacks and a short-sleeved white tennis shirt. His scrawny arms were covered in scratches and she knew where she had seen him before.

'Have you tried breadfruit yet?' he asked.

'No.'

'Then this is your chance. It's over there on the buffet table, cooked a dozen different ways. Let me show you round and explain the dishes.'

'I saw you yesterday, didn't I? You were gardening, up a ladder and pruning a tree. What are you doing here?'

His faded blue eyes twinkled in his browned face. 'Having lunch. Same as you. Even gardeners have to eat.'

'Sorry, I didn't mean to sound patronizing. I was just surprised to find you here.'

'No offence. I'm delighted to have a young lady's company. It's a pleasure frequently denied to men of my age. Did you find your way back to your hotel all right?'

'I took the road down to the beach and then headed north along the shore.'

'Let me get you another drink,' he said, waving one of the girls. 'You look as if you could do with it. It's always hotter in town than one expects.'

'Is this your day off?' Kira asked.

He chuckled. 'No, I never get a day off. Too much to do. I had some time off during the Fifties.' The good humour faded from his face and was momentarily displaced by a cloud. 'But I'm in town today on some business. Even gardeners sometimes have financial transactions to complete.'

Kira tried to apologize again.

'But I try to avoid coming into town too often. These days it's much too hot for me. When I was a young man, I could work and ride all day in the sun, from dawn to dusk. But not now. I have to take it easy when it's hot.'

'You look very fit,' said Kira quickly.

'Fit enough,' he said with a quirky grin. 'But I'm getting old and I don't like it. What's the matter with your foot? Surely not that little stumble yesterday? I noticed you were still limping when you came over.'

Kira found herself telling him about the accident, the time in hospital and the sudden free time afterwards.

'What selfish behaviour from a man in authority,' he said. 'Can't you take him to court or something? It wasn't your fault, after all.'

'I suppose I could, but I can't be bothered,' said Kira. I'd like to keep my options open.'

'Wise girl. But I'm sure an attractive and intelligent young woman like you could walk into any job she liked. Why don't you look around and maybe find something quite different?'

'I may well do that.'

The girl arrived with two long iced lime drinks. The man seemed to know her and thanked her by name. She flashed her dark eyes at him and Kira smiled to herself. Perhaps he *was* a respected citizen after all.

'Let's eat,' he said. 'I get tired of my own cooking, which is pretty basic.'

Kira allowed herself to be guided along the buffet table, taking the old man's advice on the dishes to try. There was simple steamed and fried flying fish; baked swordfish with spice sauces and dips; suckling pig, chicken, turkey and a big black pot of meat pieces called jug-jug.

'It's been cooking for months,' he said. 'Traditional food.'

She put one small unrecognizable piece of blackened meat on her plate just to show willing, but found it too hot and peppery to eat.

There was cornmeal, breadfruit, yams, sweet potatoes, rice, white eddoes, kidney and lima beans, pigeon peas, blackeyes, runcival peas, beet tops, spinach, swiss chard, avocado pears, chris-tophenes, egg-plant, okra, pumpkins, squashes, cucumber, tomatoes and sweet peppers.

'I've never seen such a choice,' said Kira.

'Have a little taste of everything.'

He was an easy table companion, never pry-ing, and it was a relief to talk naturally after the confused conversations and charged atmosphere that surrounded Giles and herself. When it was time for Kira to go, the man insisted on taking care of her bill.

'No, please, it's too much,' she protested. 'I mean, this is just an accidental meeting. I'm not your guest or anything.'

'A charming accident. And I've had the pleasure of a lovely woman's company, rare these days, my dear. Allow me the privilege of paying for your meal. I appreciate your concern but it won't break me.'

'My treat next time,' said Kira, meaning it.

'What a delightful idea,' he said, rising with old-world courtesy. 'I shall take you up on that.'

Kira thanked him again and hurried out of Brown Sugar, aware that she was late for her appointment with Giles. It was going to be a prickly meeting from the word go and she was not looking forward to it.

'Your bill, Mr Reed,' the sassy waitress said. But Kira was already out of hearing, heading for the ladies' room to tidy up.

'What a beautiful young woman,' said Benjamin Reed. 'But a little sad, wouldn't you agree? I quite forgot to ask her name.'

'You'll see her again. Barbados is a small island.'

'She said she headed north from the beach,' he mused.

'Then she's staying at a hotel in St James.'

'I'm too old for sleuthing.'

'Nonsense, Mr Reed. It would only take a few phone calls,' the girl grinned. Her smile broadened when she saw the tip he had left.

The heat was bouncing off the pavements as Kira left the shady garden of the Brown Sugar. She had been told to go to another bus station where she could catch a service that would drop her near the Reed and Earl Sugar Processors. Kira fell into a seat, thankful to sit down. The heat was draining all her engery.

The southern part of the island was much flatter and less picturesque than the West Coast. The road went through flat plains and treeless fields where only the pale sugar grew in plantation after plantation. There was wave after wave of pale green and golden cane. It was a slow, bumpy ride and Kira finally stopped looking at her watch. The driver yelled out 'Reed and Earl' and jolted Kira awake.

The bus left her on the road by the side of a tree. A lorry slewed off the road and thundered up a lane, dust flying from under its wheels. It was full of cut sugar cane, the sweet smell following in its tracks. In the distance Kira could see the shimmering silver outline of a collection of buildings and chimney stacks, corrugated iron rooftops, rusty and silver in the shooting rays of sunshine. She was almost there.

She trudged along the dusty lane, a blister forming under the strap of her sandal which rubbed her skin, sweat running down her neck. Giles would have a stack of caustic remarks to make on her lateness.

She could already smell the heady sweetness of sugar in the air. Her head was beginning to ache with the sun and the pungent odour and she was regretting her generous lunch.

Even out here on the flat plain there were riots of flowers, more dusty and stunted and wind-blown than on the west coast. She remembered Giles's comments about the wild monkeys and looked around nervously. Nothing stirred except the breeze through the waving cane.

The buildings loomed larger, busy and noisy, and she could see lorries unloading piles of cut cane in the yard; a huge conveyor belt took the crop up and into the factory.

A man was striding towards her out of the heat-haze, wearing a wide-brimmed hat, khaki shirt open at the neck, long boots, dusty jeans.

'You're nearly an hour late,' he said.

'I know,' she croaked, her mouth too dry to allow her to speak.

'Why didn't you drive down?'

'In what?'

'I sent a moke to Sandy for you this morning. Why didn't you use it? Heavens, surely you haven't walked . . .?'

'I came on the bus from Bridgetown,' she said defiantly. 'I've been in Bridgetown all morning as I had some errands to do, including getting a licence. I plan to tour the island.'

'And you're not wearing a hat, you idiot woman. Do you want to get sunstroke? Come into my office and have a cold drink.'

Giles had spotted her from his office window on the first floor, a lone figure trudging wearily along the road. She had been limping badly, far more than he had noticed before. A long day on her feet had not improved the condition of her leg.

He wanted to lift her up in his arms and carry her into the shade of the veranda which ran round the upper floor of the administration block. But he fought against the desire. She would protest, fight like the little tiger she was, and he had no wish to provide his workmen with a juicy item of gossip.

'Thank you,' she said, following him. She hardly made it up the iron stairs to the first floor. His air-conditioned office was an oasis of cool. She sank into a cane chair, her throbbing leg outstretched, and restrained herself from rubbing the aching muscles. He poured a glass of orange juice from a silver Thermos jug and added chunks of ice.

'Drink this.'

She did as she was told. Giles gave her a few moments to recover. She looked dusty and dishevelled, her burnished hair coming loose from its clip and sticking to her forehead. Her shoulders looked a patchy red despite the draped scarf.

He looked at her gravely, taking off his hat and tossing it aside, unware of the demarcation line flattening his hair. Kira was already regretting coming and was changing her mind. It had been a foolish idea to think she could work with Giles Earl. She would finish her drink and catch the next bus back to Bridgetown. She could endure a dozen bumpy rides in order to be miles away from the disturbing sight of this bold, aggressive man.

'Thank you for the drink,' she said, draining the glass. 'I've come to tell you that I can't do the research work for you after all. You'll have to find someone else.'

'Can't or won't?'

His words were clipped, blunt. He looked as if he was about to break the ruler he was tapping in his hands. His eyes narrowed, sweeping over her.

'I don't believe you,' he added. 'What's made you change your mind? And you'd better come up with something good.'

CHAPTER 8

She was trapped. There was no way she could tell him that it was his unnerving presence she could not stand, that her total fascination with him needed stamping on. Nor was she prepared to say as an excuse that the project was too difficult for her, when she knew she was quite capable of the work.

'I doubt if I shall have time after all,' she said, trying to appear off-hand. 'I've discovered a million more interesting things to do.'

'I don't believe you. You mean like swimming and sunbathing and taking rides on buses? You've burnt your shoulders this morning.'

She ignored his last comment although the skin was beginning to tingle. 'Something like that,' she flipped.

'Put some cream on your shoulders or they'll be sore,' he said. He began to draw patterns on an old-fashioned green leather-bound blotter. Everything on the big mahogany desk was well-used and old. 'I've arranged for you to attend tomorrow's monthly meeting of the Sugar Growers' Association. You would meet all the big plantation owners and listen in on our current problems. The members have agreed to your sitting in as an observer. It would be useful background for your project.'

Kira swallowed the bait. This was going to be difficult to refuse. It would be a perfect way to meet her grandfather, judge him as a man, gauge his reaction to the prospect of an unknown granddaughter appearing on his doorstep. It was not fair of Giles to make the situation even more complicated.

She shrugged as if undecided. Why had the first man she'd met on Barbados had to be Giles Earl? And why did he have to be connected with Benjamin Reed? Although she gathered from his coolness that they only talked on business occasions.

Giles got up from his desk and was standing against the window watching the workers below. His tall form looked powerful and resilient against the brilliant blue of the sky. He had no right to look so neatly sewn into the fabric of his life. Kira caught a glimpse of happiness for herself but knew it was just out of reach. She could imagine herself calling his name to the wind just so that she could hear it spoken aloud.

Kira could hardly contain the relentless yearning she felt for those strong arms to hold her again. Yet when he *had* touched her, that strange and dangerous moment at Cobbler's Reef, she had been alarmed; all the bells had been ringing.

'You might as well see around the factory while you're here,' he said flatly. It was more of an order than an invitation.

'Since you put it so charmingly, I can hardly refuse,' said Kira. She rose, but stopped at a framed photograph hanging on the wall behind her. It was of a handsome tousle-headed young man, trowel in hand, obviously laying a foundation stone. His expression, caught forever by the photographer, was as chilling as looking at a coffin and Kira felt a minute breeze of fear across her skin.

'Who's this?' she asked.

'That's Reuben Earl,' he said. 'My father. He was laying the foundation stone of the new plant. He was the one with all the ideas for expansion. Benjamin Reed wanted to stay in the Stone Age. But he's glad enough now when the dividends roll in twice-yearly from his shares.'

'You will be there, won't you, Reuben?' Dolly pleaded in his ear as they lay entwined on the deserted, sun-flecked beach. 'I can't go to this dinner party unless you're there. Benjamin said it would be all the best people, so he must mean you. Then you'll see my new dress.'

'Yes, I am going, but I'll be too busy talking to Benjamin about the plans for the new factory to take any notice of a new dress,' Reuben teased. 'Man's talk. You can chat about dresses with the minister's girls.'

'Not those horrid, stuck-up girls,' she said, pushing him back on the sand. 'All pious and pink dresses. I shall make you pay for that remark. You must kiss me a hundred times.'

'You can't even count that far.'

'I'm betting I can,' said Dolly, smothering his reply with her young body and crawling arms. She pinned him down, her hips pushing his legs apart in a parody of the male role. She bit the lobe of his ears, the tip of his nose, the dent in his chin, tugging his hair, behaving like the wild, untamed creature she was till the first passion was spent and she fastened her mouth on his, her tongue duelling with his, and the world around them disappeared into a sun-baked haze.

'Dolly, Dolly,' Reuben groaned, reeling from the sheer physcial assault. 'For heaven's sake, stop. It's more than any man can stand.'

'You're at my mercy,' she growled, but then they heard the voices of some fishermen approaching and they struggled to untangle themselves, assume expressions of innocence.

'Afternoon, Mizz Dolly,' one of the fishermen waved, grinning.

'Afternoon, Mister Reuben,' said another, teeth flashing.

Dolly flung herself back and lay inert. 'Now the whole of Bridgetown will know.'

'The whole of Bridgetown already knows,' said Reuben caustically. 'This is merely confirmation for the gossips. The only people who don't know are your father and Benjamin Reed, it seems. Get up, girl, and I'll walk you home. I don't want people making fun of you.'

'I won't let people make fun of us,' said Dolly, beginning to cry. 'If everyone knows, then they know I love you and that one day I'm going to marry you.'

175

'Calm down. You know I can't marry you for years. I've told you a dozen times. Don't you ever listen? I've got to learn the business first before I take a wife. Now there's this new factory to get built and a new partnership to cement. We're going to be the number one world exporters of sugar from Barbados.'

'Number one exporters of silly dreams and stupid ideas,' retorted Dolly, exasperated. 'Oh, such big ideas you men have. And I'll be a shrivelled-up spinster by the time it happens.'

Kira followed Giles out of his office, along the iron veranda and down the steps into the yard. The thick, sweet smell of sugar filled the air. The yard was piled with coarse-cut canes being unloaded from the lorries. In one area, the loads were being weighed in and checked for trash.

'You'll need a hard hat,' he said, taking a yellow one from a shelf stacked with hats in tipsy piles. Kira put it on carefully, tucking her hair behind her ears.

The heat and noise and dust inside the factory was unbelievable. Giles raised his voice, explaining how the feeder tables cut the cane into small pieces with knives. He pointed out the two great cane engines, roller mills and four presses crushing the stalks and the constant swish-swash of water washing so that the juice got cleaner and purer.

'This way, Kira. Be careful.'

They climbed up narrow ironwork steps to the numerous upper galleries so that they could look down on to the great furnaces. A blast of white-hot air seared Kira's face as she peered down into the glowing furnace holes. It was like looking into a flaming pit of hell fire itself. Kira drew back. But her fear left her as she became absorbed in the mechanics of producing a spoonful of sugar.

'We burn the dried husks as fuel,' Giles shouted above the noise. 'Nothing is wasted here. The island isn't blessed with an abundance of coal or trees or offshore oil.'

He took her arm and showed her where the juice was clarified and evaporated to produce syrup. 'The centrifugal force then separates the syrup into raw sugar and molasses.'

'Text-book talk,' she complained.

'How else are you going to learn?'

They walked along an almost surrealistic avenue where huge vats of frothy sugar were bubbling and splashing. Inside the vats the liquid was becoming thicker and moving around more lethargically. Kira peered through each glass viewing-window on to tons and tons of molten sugar. Technicians in white coats moved about with clipboards, checking dials and instruments.

Her fear of heights vanished in her fascination for the different processes in the factory. Giles explained everything clearly and with thought for her ignorance of the subject. He often took her arm, and guided her along some narrow walkway, as if their fights and conflicts had never happened.

The strong, lingering smell of sugar was everywhere. A headache suddenly ran like a crack across her eyes, her vision became confused with pipes and cables, guards, vats, drums, bags of lime, parked bicycles, men tending and watching machines. Everyone and everything was saturated with the overpowering heat and smell inside the high, corrugated-roofed building.

'We work twenty-four-hour shifts in top season,' Giles said, turning to help her down the steep iron steps. And she had thought he was a playboy, jogging, breakfasting on the beach at leisure, dining at Sam Lord's. She took each step carefully, not wanting to catch her heel in the open grid. 'It's a race against time.'

'This is sugar from your own plantation?'

'Yes, it has to be harvested at exactly the right time. Then we take cane in from the small growers. We work as a co-operative in order to help them get their crop processed.'

'The theory is good,' she said almost inaudibly, moistening her lips.

'It's not working well. That's why I need this research. We get a lot of complaints. Non-arrival of crops, short weight, disappearing deliveries, lack of quality control in mixed consignments.'

Kira staggered out into the fresh air, wrenched off the hard hat and shook out her hair. Her scalp was wet with sweat.

'Are you all right?'

'So hot . . . and the noise! I don't know how you stand it.'

'I'm used to it, but I forgot about your delicate ears. Stand in the shade for a few minutes. There's a breeze under these trees.'

The air was still sweet but the heat from the furnaces was contained by the corrugated building. Now it was the late afternoon sunshine which warmed her face, and a whiff of ozone from the nearby sea breezed across her skin.

'Please think again about taking on this research,' said Giles, fanning her face with a spray of palm leaves. It was such a touching and funny action. 'You'd be exactly right – an impartial and neutral observer.'

Kira wondered if Giles would still think she was impartial when he discovered she was Benjamin Reed's granddaughter. She doubted it.

'I'll admit I'm interested, and the sugar process is fascinating. I can see how Barbados depends on its sugar industry. But I honestly don't think I have the time to get all the information, let alone collate it and produce a comprehensive report.'

'I'll get you a computer.'

Kira laughed, feeling better in the fresh air. 'That doesn't solve the time problem. A report doesn't just write itself on a computer. The information has to be fed in. But I love the fields of sugar cane,' she added, her voice trailing away. 'Waving like an ocean of green water.'

'You're so right, Kira. The fields do look like green waves when the wind is blowing through the cane.'

He peered at the shadows so finely etched beneath her green eyes, and the vulnerability visible in their depths. Whatever had happened to her to make all that hurt so transparent?

His eyes were wandering over her with a tender caress that made Kira's heart miss a beat. She jerked her gaze away. She knew that when Giles looked at her like that, her brain would not function properly. He was manipulating her as she had vowed no man ever would again.

His face was sweaty, dusty, the crisp dark curls plastered to his forehead by the rim of his hard hat. There were patches of darkening sweat on the shoulders of his shirt, grease stains on his jeans.

He pulled her towards him, nothing gentle or tender in his eyes now. He bent his head, his lips moving lightly over hers as if coaxing submission. Kira held her breath then let it escape in a shuddering sigh. His hand slipped down her long, straight back, curving her body against his hard chest. There was nothing Kira could do. Her senses were reeling in the balmy dusk. The sensual case of his touch was melting her body and she longed for the moment when his mouth would take hers in the kiss he was silently promising.

'I can't stop kissing you,' he said huskily. 'You have the most beautiful mouth, so soft . . .'

'No, please don't . . .' But her protest was unconvincing.

'Don't kiss you, or don't stop?' he teased, threading his fingers through her hair.

She struggled weakly. 'Your workmen are watching. Let me go.'

'It's their tea-break. Shall I ever get to know you, Kira? You've caught me in your spell. You're using the island magic. I can feel it. You're the witch of the water, singing at the edge of the sea, leading me astray.'

He pulled her further out of sight against a stack of cut cane, taking the rows of sharp edges against his own back. The aroma of the cane was heady, but not as heady as the firm leanness of his body moulding her against his hips.

His mouth came down warm and demanding on her lips and the growing fire parted them, seeking the softness inside. In the swirling darkness, a sensation grew that pushed all thoughts of caution from her mind. She could only think of his body covering her own. His hands were resting on her rounded hips, moving up to her waist, moulding the flesh, tracing the curves. She hardly knew where he ended and she began. She had no will to stop him.

Shock waves ran through her body as he tasted her mouth with a fierce longing that matched her own. She leaned against the hardness of his thigh, moving, giving herself up to the slow, exquisite assault on her senses.

Her heart was hammering as he held her at arm's length. She could not believe that he was pushing her away after such kisses. He was smiling, slow and mysterious, his real thoughts hidden.

'I think we should go back to my office before I make love to you, right out here in the yard,' he said. 'Now that *would* shock my workforce! I've some lists to give you, then I'll drive you back to Sandy Lane.'

'But I haven't said . . .' Kira began.

'Yes, you have. You've said yes with every word, every gesture, every look in your eyes. We're going to be partners.'

'Partners? Are we going to be partners?' she asked tremulously. 'What do you mean?'

He tipped her chin up and gazed into the glowing depths of her green eyes, amazed by the brightness of the gold flecks. They were the most beautiful eyes he had ever seen. He wanted to live with those eyes forever.

'Give it time, Kira,' he said huskily. 'Give me time.'

Reuben could not take his eyes off Dolly during the long, slowly served meal. Course after course arrived at the table and Reuben did his best although his appetite had fled. Conversation with the minister's eldest daughter and the doctor's wife was hard work when Dolly was sitting opposite, flirting demurely with every man in the room except him.

He could not believe it was the same harum-scarum Dolly looking so grown-up, toying with her food and slipping the wine. He imagined her hosting dinner parties at Sugar Hill, bewitching all his friends and their wives.

Dolly looked enchanting. She had tamed her hair into a twist on the top of her head, but tendrils had escaped, framing her face and neck. Her mother's pearls were perfect for the simple dress of ivory silk which Dolly had finally chosen after days of window shopping. At the last minute she had tucked a gardenia into her hair and the perfume clung around her.

But under the table, she had eased her feet out of her mother's brocade shoes. They were too tight. And there had been no money for new shoes.

'My husband tells me that this new factory will have all the modern safety requirements,' said the doctor's wife. 'No more workers falling into vats or being crushed under cranes.'

Reuben shot back to the present, nearly spilling his wine. 'Of course. Absolutely. Every new regulation observed to the letter.'

'I do hope there will be an official opening,' the woman continued. 'Such an event will deserve everyone of importance being there. Members of the Senate, of course.'

'And you and your husband will be among our special guests,' Reuben murmured politely, tensing. Cool bare toes were touching his ankle, sliding slowly up his trouser leg. He glared across the table but Dolly had assumed an expression of total innocence, head tilted, pretending to be listening to her neighbour.

The caress was touching his nerve-ends and desire flooded his body, destroying all his concentration. The doctor's wife prattled on but he did not hear a word.

Dolly was driving him crazy. Reuben exhaled through his nostrils, trying to control his thudding heart and sweating body. He slid his hand under the tablecloth, as if to retrieve an errant napkin on his lap. Instead he grabbed Dolly's ankle and held it in a fast grip. He looked at the sudden shock in her eyes and tugged a fraction of an inch.

Her alarm increased. If Reuben pulled on her ankle, she would be off her chair and under the table in a humiliating heap. She pleaded with him silently but his expression did not alter. He loved her, he loved her desperately but he could stand no more of her games.

With his other hand he pinched one of her toes, quite tightly. He saw the pain spark a tear. He did not mean to hurt her but he was angry.

'Having trouble?' enquired the doctor's wife.

'You could say . . .' he said, eyes granite-hard. 'Damned napkin. Lost it.'

'I'll get you another one.'

Dolly looked as if she was about to faint. She was gripping the sides of her chair, bracing herself for the moment when Reuben pulled her off balance. She knew he would do it. She had never seen his face look so hard and so unforgiving. It frightened her.

'I wonder if I could have a glass of water?' she murmured, all choked up, hardly daring to turn her head.

Suddenly Reuben rippled his thumbnail down the sole of her foot and Dolly squealed out loud. He let go of her foot.

'Ticklish, Miss Le Plante?' he said with a glimmer of amusement.

Dolly was pink with embarrassment. Everyone round the table laughed. Benjamin did not understand what the laughter was about but, since his guests seemed to be having a good time, he did not mind. And Dolly looked pale and lovely, every inch a perfect lady.

Giles drove Kira back to Sandy Lane later in the afternoon after he had seen to some disputed loads which had arrived in his yard unannounced. The lorry drivers were unknown to him and he was reluctant to take delivery of the cane.

It was easy for Kira to see that the men respected his authority and that his decision was a fair one. The loads would remain stacked in the yard until some identification could be produced.

They did not talk much on the return drive across country, though Giles did point out sights of interest . . . particularly the Lion Monument on Gun Hill. The great white beast stood out prominently from the hill, roaring its silent defiance into the air.

'Little did that young English officer, all that way back in 1869, know that his idle, off-duty stone chipping would become a tourist attraction a century later.'

'Do you know his name?'

'Oh, yes. It was Henry Wilkinson. He was stationed with the Imperial Forces.'

'You love this island, don't you?'

'Of course. It's my home,' said Giles, as if that was enough.

Giles also pointed out the quiet, tree-shaded road leading to the Villa Nova. The house itself was hidden by royal palms and huge bearded fig trees.

'It was Sir Anthony Eden's retreat from the world and from illness,' he said. 'I'll take you there one day. It's a beautiful house and the views are magnificent. And I'll take you to Bathsheba to the see the wild East Coast, then Harrison's Cave at Welchman Hall Gully.'

'Harrison Ford?'

'Harrison who?'

'If I'm to take on your research, then I won't have time for the tourist track,' said Kira resolutely.

'You can't come to Barbados and ignore its beauty and history. You're allowed some time off. You might as well be working in some dreary industrial town. Did you know that the first King Charles was at his wit's end to decide whose grant to this land was valid? He might have saved his head if he had come to live here himself.'

'It must have taken months at sea to get here. What a horrendous voyage.'

'The sailors survived and Barbados became another Little England.'

Kira wondered if one of those sailors had founded Giles's family, or perhaps an aristocratic English gentleman, one of the deported political rivals, come to make his fortune growing tobacco and cotton. Sugar had not become a crop until a long time later.

She did not ask about his family roots. A Barbadian beauty might have captured the heart of a male Earl some time in the past. Giles's skin had a deep, healthy tan but his dark hair had a crisp thickness that might once have been tight curls in a distant ancestor. Then she remembered the photograph of Reuben Earl, and that his hair had been a blond thatch.

He dropped her at the end of the driveway to Sandy Lane. Golfers were coming off the course, pleased with the day's game, ready for a swim and a drink.

'I have to leave you here, I want to reach Speightstown before everything shuts down. You *could* come with me.'

'No, thank you,' said Kira, getting out of the car. 'Thank you for the guided tour of your factory and the cold drink. It was all most interesting.'

'And the kiss? Are you going to thank me for that? Was it interesting too?' His face was brooding, his voice neutral.

'I didn't realize I was supposed to thank you for kissing me,' said Kira. 'It's not normally expected, is it? Or does a kiss come under the heading of hospitality?'

'Part of the tourist promotion scene. Always make the visitor feel at home.'

Giles sped off with a burst of acceleration, scattering home-going cyclists from the fields with uncharacteristic carelessness. Kira did not understand what had upset him. He was usually a controlled driver of the powerful car and he showed courtesy to all road-users; even hens and dogs asleep in the middle of the road got the courteous treatment.

Perhaps she had failed him in some way. If he had been expecting a quick holiday affair, then he was going to be disappointed.

She wandered on to the shimmering white sand, decorated with long shadows now, and waded into the sea to wash away the stickiness and heat of the day. The skirt of her sundress wrapped itself round her legs but she did not care. People wore anything in the sea. Her dress could be mistaken for a sarong. She lay on her back in the lapping waves, gazing up at the cloudless sky, her eyes half closed against the setting sun, the cool water easing her burning shoulders . . .

The sea was turning to liquid silver from the rays of the sun. On the shore, the noisy birds were roosting in the casuarina trees, the branches alive with birds fluttering and socializing, telling the world about their busy day. Birdsong had taken over from the rustling wind and the birds had become a part of the living trees.

Kira dined alone in the restaurant, not eating much, then strolled for a while in the darkened gardens of the hotel, enjoying the music from the steel band and watching the dancers on the patio. She envied the couples dancing closely, obviously in love, some cheek to cheek. It must a wonderful place for a honeymoon.

Honeymoon . . . she had dreamed of a honeymoon with Bruce somewhere warm and romantic. Bruce and his new woman would be married by now. He would want their baby to be born within a legal marriage. Kira waited for the usual quiver of rage and surge of anguish but it did not come. She had used up her strength in overpowering jealousy and hatred but where were they tonight? For the first time she faced the thought of the baby without emotion.

That night she slept well. She did not fall asleep with tortured thoughts of Bruce. Instead she curled against the pillow and remembered another kiss, a bold, demanding kiss from a muscle-hard man, hot and sweaty from a day's work.

The meeting of the Sugar Growers' Association was being held at Fitt's House at nine o'clock in the morning before the day grew too hot. Meeting Benjamin Reed for the first time was going to be a difficult encounter. Kira was not sure of how she would react. And she was nervous. She was breakfasting on her balcony and her hand shook as she stirred her tea.

She dressed with extra care, deciding on a plain white cotton suit with a pale blue silk shirt. She fastened the belt from the suit round her slender waist, slipped on high-heeled sandals and sunglasses, put the new business cards in her bag.

'Research Consultant – here I come!' she said with bravado to the mirror. But something was wrong. It was her hair in its usual tidy, upswept style. She took out the grips and let it fall on to her shoulders. Not so efficient, but much more glamorous. Mr Connor would have disapproved if she had arrived at the Commons looking so outrageously flamboyant.

She drove the mini-moke to Fitt's House, following Giles's directions. The open-sided yellow moke was a noisy vehicle with a gear-change that sounded like a battering ram in reverse. But at least the through-breeze made it a cool journey.

She drove slowly along the driveway, taking in afresh the strange architecture of the house, the unreal stone statues dominating the veranda and balcony. The trees were laden with blossom, strewing flowers and fruit over the untidy lawns and their unkempt edges. A new and younger gardener might be able to cope better than the present one.

Other cars were already parked in the semicircular forecourt in front of the sweeping steps that led to the front door. Giles's white Mercedes was there. There was a round basket on the back seat, full of a variety of different melons and sweetcorn. It seemed that he had been early to the market.

She brushed aside overhanging branches, flowers shedding petals onto her shoulders. Her tidy mind longed to take a broom and sweep up the debris of petals and leaves and scattering of sand that littered the veranda on either side of the front door.

She went up the steps cautiously, remembering her high heels. The scent from the pots of rioting flowers and hanging ferns was not enough to quell her apprehension now that she was actually here and, at last, about to meet her grandfather. She conjured up a picture of her mother, bent over a sewing machine, sewing far into the night. She was here to avenge her mother and her mother's death. The thought was enough to drain some of the tan from her cheeks.

An elderly Barbadian woman showed her into a big, cool room running the whole width of the back of the house. Her immediate impression was of furniture. So much furniture filled the room. Wall-to-wall heavy antique furniture, Victorian, Colonial, Edwardian. The dark polished wood of the long central table seemed to take light from the windows into its veneer. Every other surface had a vase, statue or ornament of silver on it. It was like going into a sales room at Christie's before the auction of treasures from a stately home.

Giles unfolded himself from his stance of leaning against the marble fireplace and came over to her. He was in a pale grey suit with a shoestring tie laced loosely under the collar of a darker grey shirt. His highly polished boots reflected the gold from the old watch-chain slung across his waistcoat.

He took her hand and pressed it lightly to his lips, his dark eyes smiling.

'Barbados agrees with you,' he said in a low voice. 'You're looking relaxed and the tan is coming along nicely, slow and even.'

'Thank you, Dr Giles,' she said mockingly. 'I appreciate your concern. When am I going to meet Benjamin Reed, the chairman?'

'In a moment. Here comes everyone. Once they meet you, they'll want to make you a permanent feature of the Association.' He bent towards her and Kira jerked backwards but he was only brushing a petal from her shoulder.

A group of men came over, all smiling, shaking hands with Kira as Giles was making the introductions. Their names did not register. She was listening for her grandfather's name, searching the weathered faces.

'And may I introduce Benjamin Reed, chairman of the Sugar Growers' Asociation, my father's partner and now my own partner?' Giles's voice gave nothing away. It was deferential but devoid of any warmth. Kira tensed. She felt something stir inside her that had been dormant for many years, a reaching out for family. She turned to face her grandfather, the man who had contributed to her mother's death.

She had masked her face to begin a polite greeting but instead she did not know what to say. The words trailed into the air.

'Mr Reed,' she began again. The old man took her hand in his and the skin was thin and papery. 'So is this the gardener's day off?'

He chuckled. 'The poor soul's a bit past it, you know. And I don't trust him up those ladders. He spends more time talking to young women over the wall than getting on with his work. I'll have to get someone younger.'

'It seems a pity for such a pretty garden to be neglected.'

Benjamin Reed took her arm and led her towards a sideboard containing a selection of iced drinks. 'I can't tell you how pleased I am to see you here. I've thought a lot about you and hoped we would meet again. I thought after our last encounter that we had a lot in common.'

'We have,' said Kira simply. 'We have.'

CHAPTER 9

Benjamin Reed straightened his back. He felt fate had been kind to lead this enchanting young woman into his life once again.

'Miss *Reed*,' he said, taking in the burnished hair and the plain white suit and blue shirt. 'So we share more than the same surname. We share an interest in breadfruit and Bajan cooking. I trust you have recovered from your morning's shopping in Bridgetown.'

The unexpected kindliness chipped straight through Kira's defences. Her face lit up and she smiled. Both men immediately noticed the tiny dimple at the corner of her mouth.

Benjamin put on his wire-rimmed glasses and, in focus, he saw that her hazel eyes were pools of sadness and the faintly glossy lips were vulnerable with hurt and an appealing sensual softness. He was also immediately alerted to Giles's apparently indifferent interest in Miss Reed.

'Yes,' said Kira. 'And thank you again for the lovely lunch at the Brown Sugar and for taking the trouble to describe all the dishes to me.'

'It was a pleasure. It's been a long time since I had the company of a beautiful young woman for lunch.'

'So you two have already met,' said Giles, not particularly liking what he heard. 'I didn't know.'

'We met over, or under, my inept pruning of a breadfruit tree and Miss Reed's expert dodging. And yesterday I was able to offer Miss Reed a seat at my table. The Brown Sugar was packed, as usual.'

'But we hadn't got as far as exchanging names,' Kira said.

'Miss Reed thought I was the gardener,' Benjamin said. 'Not a surprising mistake, since I was halfway up a tree.'

'Or halfway down a tree,' Kira added.

Benjamin grinned and a look of same-wavelength amusement flashed between them. 'Shall we start the meeting, gentlemen? Time is money and we have a very full agenda. Miss Reed, perhaps you would care to sit at my side, and then I can explain any unclear points to you? Gentlemen, I should like to introduce Miss Kira Reed from London, who has agreed to undertake some independent research for Giles Earl on the transport problems of small growers.'

Giles pulled out a chair for Kira, then sat down on the other side of her. 'You say time is money, Ben, yet you're letting your plantation deteriorate for lack of investing funds in new machinery and crop care. When did you last ride round your cane fields? They're going to rack and ruin for want of attention and money spent on them.'

'When I want it, I'll ask for your advice about my plantation,' said Benjamin Reed curtly, shuffling a pile of papers. 'This is not the time or place.'

'And the factory would go the same way if I didn't fight you for every dollar. The slave days are over, Ben. We must adopt new technology if we're going to survive in the market.'

Kira stared at her lap. She could feel the antagonism flaring between the two men and it was not rivalry over a lunch at the Brown Sugar. This was deep-seated hatred and more than simply about a disagreement over the running of a sugar factory. Something must have happened in the past to allow such strong feelings to take root.

'Gentlemen, please,' a man said, clearing his throat. 'We're wasting time.'

'What does it matter anyway about my fields?' murmured Benjamin, suddenly weary. 'Who's going to care about the Reed Plantation when I'm gone?'

His bitterness and despair came plainly through his words. Kira paled, her fingers gripping the heavy carving on the arms of her chair.

'You should have taken my father's advice,' Giles could not resist saying.

'And look where it got him,' said Benjamin sharply. 'A nice view from St John's Church, eight hundred feet above the Atlantic. Only Reuben can't appreciate the view from where he is.'

There was a shocked gasp from the group of men around the table. Giles's knuckles were clenched white. Kira saw a muscle twitch at the corner of his mouth as if he could barely contain his anger. Kira searched for something to say to cool the situation. She racked her brain for a safe subject.

'Do you have no family, Mr Reed?' she asked quickly. 'I thought this was an island of big families.'

She knew she was deliberately opening a wound but she wanted to know what Benjamin would say about her mother, Tamara. She wanted a clue about how he felt, all these years later.

He stiffened. 'No family, Miss Reed. I never had any children.'

Her contempt grew. He was denying the existence of his daughter. Kira wanted to stand up and shout at him, 'But I'm here! I exist! I'm your daughter's daughter.'

But she controlled her anger, focusing her gaze on the window and the cluttered garden outside. It was a jungle of flowers and shrubs, full of noisy birds and lizards sunning themselves on the hot stones. More animal statues glared between the fragrant blossoms. One had a frangipani bloom rakishly placed over an ear, morning glory climbing up sturdy stone limbs.

Kira's heart sank. This was not going to work. She was not going to be able to confront Benjamin Reed with her accusations. She had planned for years just what she would say to her grandfather, to confront him with his despicable treatment of her mother. Now she saw that she could not do it. She actually liked the old man and, despite his public denial of any family, he was not the monstrous person she had been imagining since childhood. She reminded herself of the unanswered letters, the pleas for help, the long hours her mother had worked just in order to keep a shabby home together. Why had Benjamin refused to help them? She could not understand it.

'I'm sorry,' said Kira. The choice was still hers. She could announce her identity here and now and shame him in front of his friends and colleagues, reveal him for the cruel and heartless father he had been. It would atone in a small way for her mother's suffering.

But it would mean the end of everything good that was just beginning. She liked Barbados, felt happy on the island, wanted to do the research to prove to herself that she could. She even dared to like Giles Earl, was excited by the danger he represented.

Or she could say nothing. There was something about Benjamin Reed that made her want to befriend the old man and find out why he had acted so badly. Kira agonized over her decision. She was being seduced by the sunshine and a crazy garden full of grotesque stone animals.

'Don't look so upset,' said Giles. 'Ben and I always fight like this. It wouldn't be normal if we didn't.'

'Let's start the meeting,' said Benjamin gruffly. 'Minutes of the last meeting, Mr Howard, please.'

'If I can read my notes,' said a wizened man with thick pebble glasses. 'I'm sorry I didn't get round to circulating copies.'

Kira made her own discreet notes in a small notebook. It was so easy for her. She had been taking minutes for years, could almost do them on auto-pilot . . .

It was a fascinating meeting. Sugar was no longer simply sparkling white grains to her, to be avoided at all costs. It was the island's life blood. There was apparently a shortfall in this year's quota. No one factor had contributed to the decline, said Giles.

'What about all the cane fires?'

'The late start of the crop.'

'And the heavy rains. We can't control the weather but we can do something about the fires.'

'Twenty-seven per cent of our crop is damaged by fire,' Benjamin told Kira in an aside.

Kira was appalled. When Giles had mentioned monkeys and fires, she had thought of them as being irritations, not a major problem.

'We need patrols, fire patrols.'

'And who would pay for them?'

'We'd have to . . . the owners,' said Benjamin. 'More money down the drain. Patrols, bah! We're not an automobile association. You might as well try to ban smoking or the import of matches.'

'I caught an arsonist last month,' said Giles. 'He came at me with a petrol can.' He touched the back of his head tentatively. 'Still feels tender.'

'Heavier penalties in the courts,' said Mr Howard, who had apparently forgotten he was supposed to be minuting the meeting. 'It's the only way.'

When they came to the item on the plight of small growers, Kira listened even more intently. Her notes grew. She refused to look at Giles even though his deep, occasionally harsh voice held her spellbound. She could listen to him forever. She willed herself not to look at him, not to betray by the flicker of a single eyelash that he had any kind of hold over her.

'There's been a disastrously sharp drop in the production of sugar from small growers,' said Giles. 'Their gross output is thirty-two per cent down. That's bad news for all of us, especially those of us with big factories to keep running and a large workforce to pay.'

'Bad news for the small grower too,' Benjamin muttered.

'No one is denying that, but without our factories, he'd never get his cane processed. It's a very sharp drop — one out of every three tons normally produced by the small man just gone.'

'Gone with the wind,' said Benjamin, who had clearly lost interest. 'Good book. Have you read it, my dear?'

Kira could see that Giles was becoming irritated. Her grandfather was obviously not a man for meetings. He was clearly itching to get away.

'Not enough is being done to give them realistic help,' Giles went on resolutely. 'The main problem is transport. The centralization of factories didn't help them. How are they supposed to get their cane to the factories? Many live miles from any grinding facilities.'

'And now the sugar mills have gone . . .'

'That's why we need this research,' Giles started again with immense patience. Kira could almost feel him exercising control over his breathing, the tension in his fingers clutching a pen.

Benjamin leaned towards Kira. 'This island used to be dotted with sugar mills. Mostly all gone now. There used to be one here, in the garden behind the house. It got blown down in a hurricane.'

'How awful.'

'Would you like to see the remains?'

'Yes, I would. Thank you.'

'Would you mind, Mr Chairman? The meeting hasn't finished,' Giles snapped. Kira felt like a schoolgirl caught talking in class.

'Only talking to the chairman, sir,' she said meekly. There was a maddening glint in Giles's eyes which baffled her. Did he disapprove of her even talking politely to Benjamin?

'The cost of lorry transport is sky-high,' Giles went on. 'Even if a cane crop does arrive safely, the grower's profit is already eroded, if not wiped out by the transportation cost. Deliveries go astray; weight is disputed, quality control is difficult to enforce. Miss Reed, perhaps you will make a full report on the situation? You can clearly cover it far more thoroughly than we can ever hope to do.'

An excited Kira could suddenly see her work spreading in all directions. 'I'll interview all the small growers, detail their individual difficulties. The overall picture may help you come up with something,' she said, tired of not saying anything, of keeping quiet.

'Good idea,' said Mr Howard, nodding. 'I approve.'

A chorus of approval came from round the table. Kira was pleased with the way Giles had presented the situation and introduced her to the Association. She had only been on the island a couple of days but already she felt involved. Some of Giles's nationalistic pride was brushing off on her. Benjamin's blood ran in her veins and he obviously loved the island more than anything or anyone.

The meeting closed. The men came over to talk to her, adding suggestions for things she should look out for. Kira explained that Giles was employing her but it was plain he was going to share the results with the Association.

'Isn't that so?' she asked as he brought her a cup of coffee.

'If there *are* any results,' he said flippantly. His sternness had totally gone. What an unpredictable man! 'You'll probably be off swimming half the time.'

'Be patient and you'll see.'

'I'm not a patient man, Kira. You should know that by now. There's only one thing I'll wait for . . . with infinite patience. Even when you disguise your femininity in a severe business suit, you're still all woman.'

Kira was thrown. How dared he say anything so embarrassing, in front of all these people? He was so sure of his own masculinity, he thought every woman must be clamouring for his attention.

'I assure you that your patience will be stretched to its limits as far as I'm concerned,' she said. 'I've looked at those lists you gave me yesterday, and the map. Some of the smallholdings must be so small, it seems they're not even marked.'

'And some farmers are not even on the list. They probably send their crop in with a neighbour's.'

'Recipe for chaos,' she agreed.

Giles was looking at her over the rim of his cup.

She had lost weight since her accident and the exquisite bone structure of her face fascinated him. She did not seem to know how becoming she looked with a faint flush staining her cheeks or how it quickened his pulse. Beautiful women had pursued him all his life but there was something about this ice maiden that set her apart. He had a feeling she was a mixture of fire and ice, a lethal combination for any man to cope with. He felt suddenly alarmed, almost threatened, and set his cup down with a rattle in the saucer. 'When are you going to start work?'

Kira was baffled by his change of mood. 'This afternoon. I have my route planned.'

'Why not now?'

'Because now I'm going to enjoy a tour of Mr Reed's garden and see the ruined mill.'

'Don't let Benjamin influence you,' Giles said abruptly. 'He'll try to get you to do things his way. He's a devious old man.'

'I don't think that's true,' said Kira, rising to the defence of her grandfather. 'You move too fast for him. Older people need time to get used to changes.'

'He's got you on his side already.' His dark brows met as he scowled. 'Don't you have a mind of your own? I thought you were a woman of independence. I didn't expect you to be

211

swayed by a lunch with an old-fashioned charmer.'

Kira collected her bag and notes. Her feelings about her grandfather were confused enough without Giles adding complications. Her manner was aloof, her back rigid.

'I'll contact you when the report is ready,' she said, as if it might be some weeks. She swept across the room, her high heels tapping on the polished floor, hoping her leg would not let her down.

'Don't forget to take a hat and don't drive into the late evening. There's no street lighting out in the countryside. It's easy to get lost when you're off the beaten track.'

'Get lost on an island this size? I'd just keep driving till I'd found the sea!'

The heat on the veranda outside took Kira by surprise. The big room had been cool, the wide-bladed ceiling fans coping as efficiently as modern air-conditioning, and she had forgotten the rising temperature.

'There's no need to worry about me,' she added, unbuttoning her jacket for coolness.

'I had no intention of worrying about you, Kira. I'm more concerned about my moke. Don't drive it into a ditch.'

Benjamin was tugging off his tie and his grizzled hair was standing up as if he had recently run his hand through it. He took Kira's arm in a proprietorial manner and drew her down the steps.

'Let's tour Fitt's House from the other side of the wall. The sugar mill is only a ruin but you can still see the old furnaces. We'll forget all about stuffy business worries. The problems will still be there tomorrow.'

'The Barbadian malaise. That's your trouble, Benjamin. It's always tomorrow as far as you're concerned. It it was left to you, Reed and Earl would be as ruined as your old sugar mill!'

Benjamin swung round to face Giles, his mouth contorted with distaste. Something had obviously touched him on the raw.

'Hard hats, guard rails, research consultants . . .' he raged. 'We never needed all these new-fangled contraptions in my day. The factory ran all right till you started meddling with everything. I've been in sugar all my life, since I was a boy. There isn't anything I don't know and there isn't anything new. Fires, monkeys, plagues of rats, dogs . . . cane diseases. I was coping with them before you or your father were big enough to hold a cricket bat. So don't talk to me as if I'm old and written off. And if I'm old and crabby before my time, blame your father, Reuben Earl, and what he did to me.'

It was a long, hot night. A melancholy horn blared out to sea. Creepers whispered in chorus against the long glass window panes.

Dolly had never been in such a grand house before. Even the size of the rooms was intimidating, made her feel like a child again, on the fringe of the grown-ups at a tea party. She stared at the ceiling.

She lay in the big bed, her heart pounding. She had brought her best nightie, white lawn trimmed with broderie anglaise. She had made it herself and it had lain in a drawer, unworn for over a year.

Shadows played across the ceiling and Barbadian folklore flew into her mind. Was it Papa Bois, guardian of the forest and small animals, or was it La Diablesse, the devil woman? Dolly had been to see a wise woman who lived in a shack on the edge of the water and the wise woman had given her a potion.

'Sip this at every new moon,' she had whispered, sparse white hair flowing like light. 'And you will marry the man of your choice.'

Will-o'-the-wisp shapes, grey and mysterious, moved across the curtains, fluttering as the trade breeze caught their flimsy folds and sent them spinning into orbit. Dolly closed her eyes against the shapes and the thoughts that went with them.

Reuben was coming. He said he had to see to his horse. That horse, Storm, was his pride and joy. His parents were staying with old friends at the other end of the island. They were not expected home till the next afternoon.

There was a jug of iced lime juice by the bed and Dolly drank nervously. Her mouth was as dry as an old boot. Reuben would expect her to taste as sweet as a flower. There was just time to wash again in the empty, echoing bathroom across the wide landing.

She slipped her bare feet out of the bed and hurried across the polished floorboards, but the door opened before she could reach it.

'Dolly, where are you going? Are to trying to escape? Have you taken fright like a little bird?' said Reuben, half laughing.

'Reuben . . . I didn't expect you back so soon. I was just . . . is Storm all right?'

He was stripping off his shirt, ripping buttons, and his muscles gleamed in the half light.

'How long did you think it would take me to stable a horse? A couple of hours? How could I waste a moment when I knew the most gorgeous and lovely girl in the whole world was waiting for me?'

'Oh, Reuben . . . I don't know if we should. This house is so big and your room is so strange . . .'

Reuben stopped abruptly. 'But Dolly . . . I thought we agreed. Five years is a terrible long time. We can't wait that long when we love each other so much.'

Dolly held out both hands to him. Now that Reuben was here, her fear was disappearing. She was not afraid of him; it was only the great house that intimidated her.

'Much too long,' she whispered. 'I can't wait that long. I want you so much.'

'But we will get married,' he promised hastily. 'Of course we will get married.'

They were reading each other's thoughts as clearly as if the words were spoken aloud, feeling the shape of the words and listening to hidden meanings.

'We will, won't we?' Dolly clung to him desperately. 'Tell me that we will marry some day.'

'Baby, baby . . . trust me,' he soothed.

He was unbuttoning his riding breeches and stood before her, his young and proud manhood a new sight for her. For a moment she was terrified by his boldness, his size, that she might be responsible for this reaction. How could it get inside her? She would burst. She would be ripped apart. Her body dissolved in fear.

'Don't be afraid,' he said, taking her in his arms, so that she felt him hard against her thigh. 'I will be careful, gentle. Keep holding on to me. We've wasted all these years. I won't hurt you. Sweetheart, darling, darling . . . trust me, love me . . .'

His mouth was kissing away her fears and he lifted her and carried her back to the cool smoothness of the bed. She didn't struggle but wound her arms round his neck, longing for their beach feelings to return. It was all so simple on the beach, under the dripping palms, bathed in the warmth of the sun, the lapping of the waves soothing her fears and making a lullaby for her love feelings. She loved Reuben so much that sometimes it was as if she would die in that love, unable to breathe such intensified air for one minute more.

One day Reuben would be master of this greathouse. Would he have time for her then? She was only the half-wild daughter of a poor island painter. Or would he find the well-brought-up daughter of some other planter more to his liking?

He was slipping the straps of her nightdress off her shoulders, mouthing the silken skin, letting his lips stray lower to the curve of her breasts. She gasped as he touched the softly rising nipples. He was tantalizing her, teasing and touching and tonguing. Her nipples rose to pebble hardness.

He eased his body atop hers, firing her body with the glory of his weight. He was crushing her beneath him, moving her with long, drugging kisses. She spread her arms to her side, surrendering to his slow and rich exploration of her ivory skin.

An exquisite sensation shot through her body. It was something she had never known before. She threw back her arms in delight, shivering at the same time, her limbs weak with longing. Perhaps it was going to be all right after all.

Giles's mouth settled into a hard, firm line. Kira held her breath. The hostility between the two men could be cut with a knife. Giles's eyes were like pieces of granite. He came down the steps, all man, all dominant, swiping his wide-brimmed hat against his thighs like a whip.

'You and my father damned near ruined both the plantations and the factory with your near-suicidal rivalry. If it hadn't been for me, you'd be living in a beach shack by now and Fitt's House would be just another restaurant for well-heeled tourists. When are you going to wake up to the fact that sugar is big business and even personal conflicts don't mean you can run it like a cottage industry?'

'Personal conflicts,' the old man snarled. 'Blast you. Dolly was mine.'

'Reed and Earl would have been bankrupt in another five years if Reuben hadn't come to your rescue.'

'How dare you talk like this? You think you know everything but you know nothing. You have some dangerous ideas, Giles. Bad blood always come out when you least expect it. Thank God I didn't have any children.'

Kira gasped. Both men looked at her, suddenly aware of her, alarmed by the dismay on her face. She slipped away across the grass, her heart thudding. No children, no Tamara, no Kira. Had she been mistaken? Perhaps Benjamin wasn't her grandfather after all. Perhaps it was some other Reed . . . surely not? He seemed so right. She tried to calm her breathing but there was no calming the emotional bruising that hurt her to the bone.

She had been right to keep men right out of her life. For a while she had been lulled into thinking that there might be room for her grandfather, even Giles. But she had been wrong. Giles was dangerous. Bejamin was bitter to the point of madness. And her own treacherous weakness had found in Giles a man who stirred her emotions.

Perhaps it was she who was harbouring insanely wild ideas. And that had to be stopped.

The Anglican church in the centre of Bridgetown was packed to the doors. The Barbadian women almost outshone the planters' wives with their finery. They wore their best Sunday dresses and colourful straw hats, decorated with flowers and fruit and feathers. White gloves and high-heeled pumps completed their outfits.

What the local women lacked in modish style, they made up for in sheer joy in the occasion.

The planters' wives sat in the front pews, the subdued colours of their clothing in direct contrast to the riot of fruit and flowers and multicoloured veiling nodding on the hats of the women in the back rows. The men sat, sweating and beaming in their best suits.

The music from the organ occasionally rose over the subdued chatter and greetings of friends. Everyone was smiling. This was going to be a great day. Bridgetown loved a big wedding.

The groom waited, solemn and smart, in his place, at the far end of the aisle.

The bride stood nervously in the porch. She was late and clung to her father's arm. She made a beautiful bride. A dressmaker in Broad Street had dreamed up an ivory tulle dress with layers of skirt and she looked like thistledown, floating down the great church on a brush of the wind.

Half of Barbados was there, from cane workers to plantation owners. All had been invited.

Dolly was shaking, her fingers gripping her father's arm, her skin pale and clammy. She had been sick in the outhouse that morning, holding on to the basin while nausea heaved through her stomach.

She could hardly recognize anyone through the gauze of the veil. The sea of faces came up at her like a floating sea washing into the Cave of Flowers. She hardly recognized anyone, least of all the man she was going to marry. God help me, she prayed, already dying inside.

CHAPTER 10

Kira had been driving inland and northwards for about an hour during the hottest part of the day. The sun was beating down relentlessly like rays of fire. She had a litre bottle of mineral water beside her and some fruit saved from her breakfast.

She had checked out of Sandy Lane and paid her account, hardly flinching at the total. It had been money well spent. The luxury beach hotel had proved a relaxing experience, a paradise among the waving palms, but Kira could not afford it any longer. If she was to be moving around the island, she would find somewhere to stay each night. There must be plenty of guest houses and small hotels dotted round the coast.

The first of her interviews was a smallholding in the north of Maycock's Bay beyond Hangman's Bay. She drove past an old whaling centre. She saw an old ruined fort and evidence of the Barbados Defence Force. The landscape was changing to magnificent cliff scenery with wild and rugged hills.

Kira stopped the moke on a high point and gazed at the natural beauty of the area. It was criss-crossed with rough tracks that she would have to traverse to get to the scattered small-holdings. All right in the dry season, but it must be treacherous in the rain.

Courtney Blackwell Johnson was as big as his name, a middle-aged Barbadian who farmed a few acres of sugar on the lower hills, but he could not get the cane directly to the factories for grinding.

'I take the cane to a depot point in my van where's it's picked up by a lorry for transportin' south to Reed and Earl's,' he told Kira. 'But if I make any money from m'sugar then I count myself lucky.'

'It doesn't seem right that all your profit is swallowed up by the transport cost,' said Kira.

'No, ma'am. I'm thinking of turning over to vegetables. I can feed my family on vegetables and sell a few over. But I don't like the idea. I'm a sugar man like my father. But we always had mills. St Lucy had six or seven mills, all within a mule's ride.'

'Whose lorry takes your cane?' Kira asked.

Courtney scratched his head. 'Don't rightly know, miss. Some fella we call Hopalong.'

'How can I contact this Hopalong?'

'I dunno. He just comes along.'

'That's not very satisfactory.'

'That's the way it's always been.'

'Well, thank you,' said Kira. 'I'll put it in my report.'

'Thank you, ma'am. Nice seeing you.'

As she drove away, Kira was saddened by the economic problems that Courtney faced so stoically. She admired the simple man working the land as his father had. The inland roads deteriorated until she was driving along rutted tracks of stone, pitted with pot-holes. She was shaken from side to side in the driving seat, wrenching at the wheel in an effort to avoid the worst of the craters.

She thought about the two men at Fitt's House that morning, the angry words that had flared between them. She could have taken sides, defending both of them. Both men had been tugging at her feelings. How could they argue so fiercely? What had happened all those years ago? It had been a strange day. She had discovered a grandfather she really liked and somehow wanted to keep in her life and another man she dared not have or encourage. Yet she had to deny a family bond in order to keep Benjamin as a friend.

This work is going to be good, she thought, and it's real. I needed to do something entirely different, get away from the same old constituency problems and the tug-of-war political scene. She kept her eyes skinned for the next sign of habitation. The wild and rugged landscape could not have been more of a contrast to the elegant and touristy St James Coast.

'And I needed to leave London and start doing something that wouldn't remind me of Bruce and Jenny and the baby,' she said aloud, convincing herself. It was a relief to say the words, the names, and face the reality of the situation.

In the distance, tucked against a hill, she saw the usual style wooden chattel house with steep roof and doll's house windows. A woman was nursing a baby to her dark and swollen breast, a picture of happiness. It didn't help. Kira felt a stab of envy at the cameo of maternal joy.

She stopped the moke in the yard and hung on to the wheel, fingers clenched. Skinny chickens scattered in all directions, wings flapping. A floppy puppy scratched lazily in the sunshine and went back to sleep. It was a hazy, lazy, peaceful picture.

'Hello,' said Kira, swinging her long legs out of the moke. Her cotton skirt clung to her thighs. Her skin was sticky. 'I'm Kira Reed. Giles Earl has asked me to come and talk to your husband about transport problems. Is he around?'

The young woman's face broke into smiles. Kira had discovered her passport into any home on the island. She had only to mention Giles's name and she was welcome anywhere.

'From Mr Giles? Why, ma'am, that would be a pleasure. Just you sit here in the shade and I'll go find Kingsley. He's out in the fields.'

The young woman hoisted the baby on to her hip and with another wide smile set off down a path towards the lush sugar cane. It was some distance but she did not hurry, her walk a rhythmic sway from side to side. Her dusty brown feet splayed out, the bright cotton of her dress flattened against her body.

Kira sat in the shade of a gnarled old tree,

letting the sugar-scented breeze lull her into a doze. In her mind's eye she saw the magnificence of Giles' height and his unyielding muscles. She remembered the way his hands had rested on her full rounded hips, and the lazy confidence in his voice as he teased her. Giles, she breathed, her eyes closed, let me feel the wall of your body again . . . soon . . . now. I can't endure this tantalizing delay . . . She hugged herself, aching with longing . . . the image of his strong face before her robbing her of all thought.

She jolted herself into consciousness, shaking her hair out of her eyes.

'I'm an idiot, a fool,' she told the shaggy puppy that was watching her curiously. He grinned hugely in agreement, panting.

She knew what it was. The hangover from her grief over Bruce was making her long for comfort and love, for physical contact with someone who thought she was desirable. It was as simple as that. Giles obviously thought she was attractive, so perhaps – why not let him have his brief summer affair? Perhaps he had a 'tourist' belt on which to notch up his conquests! Kira knew it was a wanton idea but did not care.

Kingsley arrived along the path, a bulky young man with flashing teeth. But his grin soon faded as he poured out his troubles to Kira. His wife brought drinks of fresh pineapple juice and Kira accepted, knowing that to refuse would offend their hospitality. They were poor, they had hardly anything, yet they were so happy. Kingsley could not stop touching his young wife, stroking her bare arm, tickling the baby, letting his hand rest easily on her knee.

'Something's got to be done,' he said. 'Before we all go bankrupt. I'd hate to have to sell this bit of land but we gotta eat.'

'What would you do?'

'Get a job in a hotel, I suppose. I'm strong. I could be a porter or a gardener.'

'That doesn't seem right. You'd have to move south, too.'

Kira wanted to give them something. But what did she have to give them? She could only put their problems in her report and hope that Giles could find the answer. She went silent with determination, his name and the promise of his help almost on the tip of her tongue.

She had some English money in her purse and took out a brightly minted pound coin, pressing it into the baby's brown hand.

'A lucky coin from England,' she said, not believing it was truly lucky but not knowing what else to say.

Kingsley and his wife thanked her and waved her off their land. As she drove away, with promises to return that she knew she would not keep, Kira felt a new sadness. What was happening to her? Was Barbados weaving its promised spell or was her true blood beginning to assert itself? She had to remind herself that she was here for a month or two, no longer. Giles's fee and her savings would last that long if she was careful.

She had been planning to be back at the Commons in mid-October in time for the State Opening, to see what else there was available, which other MP she could work for. Her flat in Pimlico was gathering dust. And yet . . . and yet . . . with a jolt, Kira realized she had nothing else to make her go back to England. Only her flat. She did not really want to work in Parliament again.

It began to rain with an abruptness that was hard to believe. The clouds opened. Rain poured off palm leaves in sheets, splashing into the road, washing away the dust in rivulets, drumming on road bins. She drove for several miles in the downpour, her speed reduced to a crawl. She was nearing the east coast and tried to peer through the overworked windscreen wipers for somewhere to stop and stay, or at least take shelter. She had forgotten the advice that the eastern coast was wild and barren. Not for nothing was it called the Highlands.

Suddenly she glimpsed the sea ahead and rammed on the brakes. Great rollers thundered in from the Atlantic, breaking over outcrops of rock with powerful plumes of white spray. The long curving beach was deserted, the manchineel trees swaying under the onslaught of rain, their leaves washed to a dark green gloss. There was not a hotel or any habitation in sight.

'I think I'm lost,' she said.

She managed to turn the moke in a clearing with much grinding of gears. Gusts of rain were blowing in both sides of the open vehicle on to her bare arms and face. Soon she was drenched. The wind was whipping her skirt up and off her knees, bunching it round her hips. She clutched at the sodden material in her lap like a bundle of wet washing.

Through the rain she caught sight of a line of workers hurrying from the fields using their straw hats and banana leaves for some protection. But their faded clothes were soaked. They balanced bundles of cane on their heads, too precious to drop and run. She called to them but they could not hear and disappeared into the mist.

Now she could hardly see through the torrential rain, the road ahead a swirling mass of mist and water. She had never seen rain like it. Dreary swathes washed in from a low blank sky. English rain was merely April showers compared to this deluge.

'Hey, you there, sunny Barbados,' she called out loud. 'Where have you gone?'

A tall stone building loomed sideways out of the mist, its strange beehive shape at first unrecognizable. Then Kira caught sight of four broken blades and realized that it must be one of the ruined sugar mills. Its pitted stone surface was overgrown with weeds, but it looked solid enough for temporary shelter. She wrenched the moke off the road and drove erratically along the hidden track towards the shape of the mill.

The yard was littered with rusty machinery, brown water running off the iron components. There were no houses about. The disused mill was completely isolated.

Kira made sure the handbrake was on firmly, then, collecting her handbag, she braved the onslaught and ran through the rain to the ruin, praying there would be an easy way inside. The heavy mahogany door yielded at the first push and Kira staggered inside.

At first she could not see, not only because of the gloom but because her lashes were stuck with water. She wiped her face with her hand and looked around. Her heart fell. She had picked a ruin all right. It was empty except for some derelict machinery and a stack of old canes, dry and withered. She sank down on to her knees on the dusty floor and cradled her head in her arms. Her body was stiff with the tenseness of driving but at least she would be out of the rain here and off the treacherous track. If she waited until the rain stopped, perhaps she would be able to move on eventually? Surely it couldn't rain like this for long?

She thought of her case in the back of the moke but no way was she going outside again, not even for dry clothes. She had had the foresight to lock her notes away in her briefcase. She had no idea where she was. These roads were certainly not on Giles's map.

She peeled off her wet skirt and looked for somewhere to hang it up. A couple of nails in a beam were a convenient height and the drips were soon failing on to the dust, creating tiny craters. Her skirt hung like a wet ghost in the gloom; the only sound, apart from the lashing rain, was the dismal dripping on to the floor. Perhaps she ought to sing or something.

Outside, the palm fronds rustled wildly, pounded by the rain, tossing wildly, this way and that in the boisterous wind.

Kira wrapped her arms across herself, standing back from the doorway, watching the relentless deluge. The sun was going down but there was no glorious sunset tonight. The heavily laden clouds scurried across the sky like winged creatures from Greek mythology. Kira shivered in her damp undies and silk shirt as the temperature dropped.

Dolly shivered in the big Edwardian wrought-iron bed. She had on the same pristine white nightie, resolving that she would wear it all night and never, never take it off. She was cold despite the heat lingering from the day.

It had been an exciting day in a strange way, with everyone watching her. Her father had beamed like a beacon; he saw all his financial problems being solved. The present the groom had made him had been generous and the cheque crackled in his pocket.

But Dolly did not remember much of what had happened. Time passed slowly in a white haze of voices and words and music and food and wine. There were so many people she did not know. She'd drunk greedily of the wine, accepting every refill, hoping to dull the ache in the pit of her stomach with an overcoat of alcohol. Someone took the glass away.

'You don't want to drink too much wine, Mizz Dolly,' the housekeeper said kindly, seeing the pallor of the girl's skin and the fear lurking in her eyes. 'You gonna be all right. He's a good man.'

'Yes, a good man,' Dolly repeated.

She drew her knees up in the alien bed and hugged them. She wanted to go home. Her childhood bed was a rusty single one with sagging mattress, but right now she wanted to be there more than anywhere else, curled into a tight ball. She felt like a wilting petal in the heat, all the life draining out of her body.

A door opened. Someone was moving quietly about the room, knowing their way around.

There was a rustle of clothes. She squeezed her eyes shut, obliterating the shape of the man, but shadows danced against her lids.

'You can't . . . you can't, please . . .' she cried out, clutching at the sheet. She was shaking with fear.

What on earth was she doing here, marooned in a ruined mill with only mice and bats and goodness knew what else for company? Kira's shiver deepened with thoughts of the thin-legged creepy-crawlies that might exist in the old stonework.

A familiar sound disturbed the steady pattering of the rain. It was an engine, somewhere in the distance, climbing the hilly track in low gear.

Kira hesitated. Should she run out and try to get a lift from the driver to some sort of habitation? She thought with longing of hot water and a bath and a cup of tea. She really did not fancy spending the whole night in the old mill.

It was not easy to weigh up the advantages of a night in a hotel against the risk of cadging a lift from a stranger. There was less crime on Barbados than in England but Kira was still apprehensive. A sudden gust of wind blew rain in through the open doorway and Kira backed away, cowering from the blast of chilled air.

'Kira? Kira, are you here?'

Her name was buffeted far away on the wind, like an eerie echo in the distance. The engine cut out. She held her breath. That voice, deep and gravelly, could only belong to one person. A surge of panic and relief swept through her at the same time. Surely he would help, whatever he thought or believed of her? His chivalry was unshakeable.

'Giles?' she said, realizing he would not hear over the rain.

'Kira! Where are you?' he shouted, the words swept away on gusts of wind.

Now it was panic that hammered into her head. She wanted to see him again and yet she was terrified of her reaction to him. It was too late to run away, nor did she want him to go. He was dangerous, attractive, aggressively masculine, too exactly what she wanted. But she was frightened. No matter what she told herself or how she tried to prevent her response to him, this special man could melt all her resistance.

'Hey, woman? Where are you? I know you're here somewhere. That's my yellow moke you've parked in a ditch.'

Kira's anger flared. She peered briefly into the rain-misted dusk, bristling with indignation.

'I did not park in a ditch,' she yelled back. 'The moke is in the yard and I took a lot of care. There's not a scratch on it.'

Giles appeared through the rain, trenchcoat flapping against his legs, the collar turned up, hair plastered against his head. The rain dripped off his face, running down his neck.

'I knew that would bring you out of hiding,' he said with satisfaction. 'Need any help?'

'No, thank you,' she said stubbornly. 'I'm managing perfectly well on my own.'

'Managing perfectly well on your own, are you?' he drawled, taking in her bedraggled appearance. 'A half-drowned rat would beat you on looks.'

'Thank you. That makes me feel a whole lot better.'

His eyes travelled down her long bare legs and the damp silk shirt clinging to the line of her lacy panties. A blush of embarrassment warmed her face. She tried to cover up, wrapping her arms across her breasts, but the movement only lifted the hem of her shirt higher.

Giles's breath sharpened as he came into the mill, his tall figure blocking out the last of the fading light. He was looking at her with an appreciation that should have warmed her heart, but which only served to alarm her.

It was an electric moment. Kira stood very still, unable to move, hardly daring to breathe. She could not take her eyes from his face. Squally blasts of rain-laced wind whipped across her skin. The chill was icy along her spine. She was afraid of her longing for him. She was also very cold.

'Why did you check out of Sandy Lane without telling me?' he asked with more restraint than he had intended.

Her departure had annoyed him. He had been surprised to find that she had checked out and it had taken him hours to track her route across the island that afternoon as she criss-crossed St Lucy then took the road towards the East Coast. He'd realized she was asking for trouble when he lost track of her in the rain. He knew these roads in the north like the palm of his hand. She didn't, mad woman! He little thought that she would find the track that led to the old mill.

'Do I have to ask your permission to leave a hotel? I can go when I want to!'

That smudge of yellow appearing between the windscreen wipers was the sight he had been searching for desperately in the last hour. He'd been sure she was lost, the tropical rain blurring all landmarks.

'Why didn't you leave a message? This isn't an island for wandering around on the off-chance of picking up a room. You need to book in advance. And you should have left your next address with the hotel in case you broke down. There's no auto pick-up service waiting to tow you home.'

'I'd have found somewhere,' she argued. 'It was the sudden rain that threw me. It just fell in sheets. I couldn't see where I was and that map of yours is out of date. It's got roads that don't exist and others that aren't on it.'

'So, a place changes. I'm beginning to think this whole idea is a big mistake,' said Giles, face set coldly. 'I can't keep coming out to rescue you. I'll get the facts myself. Go back to the beach, Kira, and get yourself a nice body tan. Buy a few necklaces.'

Kira swung round, facing him angrily, the colour burning in her cheeks.

'Don't patronize me, please. I haven't broken down and I'm not lost. I've done a good day's work. If it hadn't been for the rain I'd be sipping a Mount Gay Flapper cocktail in a bar at River Bay right now.'

'The nearest hotel is at Bathsheba and that's small and miles away and you need to book in advance. We'll scrub the whole idea.'

She was fast losing her control. Kira hoped he could not see her conflicting emotions or guess at her confusion.

'That's ridiculous,' she said coolly. 'I'm not a baby. No one could get lost on an island this size so there's no need to fuss. As soon as the rain stops, I'll be on my way and my first report will be in your office by tomorrow evening.'

It was a brave boast. She had no idea if she would be able to deliver a decent report so soon and she didn't care. Anything to wipe that look off his face. Her eyes sought the hollow of his throat, burnt brown by the sun and harbouring a drop of rain like a quivering pearl.

He was out of her reach, even now. He stood like a statue, leaning an arm on the wall, blocking her view of the doorway. She could smell the tangy warmth of his aftershave and the cool freshness of the rain on his dark hair. She imagined burying her face in his wet skin and the thought almost destroyed what was left of her composure.

The moment lingered in the air, intangible and glittering with magic. He was looking into her eyes, delving into her soul. Kira held her breath. Could this be her life changing at last? Was fate going to be kind and deal her something wonderful: a man like Giles, strong, demanding, taking all from her but giving her love, a caring person, everything she had ever wanted.

'I don't think you are going anywhere,' he said firmly.

His voice was still clipped with sternness but, at the same time, with one finger he was lifting a tendril of damp hair from her neck. It was a gesture so gentle and tender that Kira knew she was falling in love with him. She was weakening, stunned by the knowledge, not wanting to run into the arms of pain again but quite unable to stop her headlong forward flight.

He moved closer and the broad expanse of his chest was only inches away from her nose. She turned her head away, feeling more tremors as his hand moved into her tangled hair and down her back. What was she doing here, allowing his man to evoke feelings she wanted buried and forgotten? A small moan came from her lips, escaping on a surprised sigh.

'As soon as the rain stops, I'm going,' she repeated. 'I am. I'm definitely going.'

He shook his head, his eyes glinting with a maddening approval of what he saw. He was looking at the long length of her naked legs. Kira knew the scar was less vivid under her slight tan but it still distressed her for the wound to be on view.

'Don't look at me,' she said.

'How can I stop looking at you? You're so lovely. The road is being washed away and we're stuck here for the night, unless you fancy a long walk. Got your walking boots?'

He was laughing at her. The thought of being marooned with this devastating man was more than she could bear. But she was struggling with herself almost hopelessly until her sense of humour came to the rescue. This crazy feeling could not be real. She tossed back her hair and went over to her hanging skirt, pretending to feel if the fabric had dried. She was giving up on love, letting it go.

'Welcome to the Barbados Hilton,' she said, more cheerfully than she felt. 'Will this room suit you, sir? It's our premier suite. No jacuzzi, but note the magnificent view of the Atlantic if the mist lifts. The mice are reasonably tame and the bats promise not to have a party. Room service is a little unreliable but there's plenty

243

of fresh water as long as you don't mind getting it outside.'

'I've slept in worse places,' said Giles. He inspected the collection of old machinery and debris in a detached way. He'd seen a dozen old mills in this condition. They were solidly built and most of the stonework was sound. 'And I never travel anywhere without my own room service.'

He drew out a flat silver flask from an inner pocket of his trench coat.

'The best Bajan rum,' he said, holding it up to the fading light. 'Will you join me, Kira? Don't look so afraid. I promise not to get you drunk and seduce you. The lady must always be willing.'

'How very reassuring,' said Kira, giving herself time to adjust. 'And this is not exactly my idea of a romantic rendezvous for two. I prefer candle-light and roses.'

'Champagne and a steel band for me.' He grinned, but his eyes darkened as they locked on to hers. 'But Kira, you're soaked through and getting cold. Even in this climate you can catch a chill.'

His face was full of concern. He came and touched her shoulders and she shivered. The silk shirt was clammy with damp and cold. 'Get out of those wet clothes right away.'

'Into what?' said Kira, her teeth chattering. 'There's probably a nice line in sacks somewhere if I could find one.'

Giles shrugged out of his trenchcoat. He was wearing denim jeans and a waistcoat over a black cotton shirt. He peeled off the waistcoat and pulled the shirt out of the waistband of his jeans, unbuttoning the cuffs and front. He tossed the shirt over to her.

'Get into that,' he said. 'And no false modesty, woman. You can't stay in those wet clothes.'

Kira clutched the shirt. It was still warm from his body. She averted her eyes from the matted expanse of dark curls on his bare chest. He was thrusting his arms back in the trenchcoat with jerky movements as if he was angry. And Giles was angry, angry with himself for being so moved by the sight of her fragile vulnerability.

'Don't worry,' he said. 'I'm going now.'

He disappeared through the doorway and was swallowed immediately by the torrential rain. Kira almost ran after him. Was he really leaving? Surely not? She remembered when she used to cry over Barry Manilow singing 'But We Still Have Time' and the same tears came into her eyes. She *wanted* time with Giles. Her fingers were trembling as she unbuttoned her shirt and bra and stepped out of her lacy pants. Her body gleamed like silk in the half light.

For a moment she stood naked, then she pulled on Giles's shirt, glad of its warmth and the fact that it was oversized enough to wrap around herself. It came halfway down her thighs and way past her wrists. She rolled up the sleeves, glad of the extra folds. He'd left behind the denim waistcoat and she put that on too, feeling almost decent with the two garments covering her body.

She went to the doorway but there was no sign of him. She stared into the darkening rain. Had he left her? The palm trees spattered a fan of rain into her face and she drew back, suddenly knowing where Giles had gone. She listened to the wind-lashed waves, crashing on the shore, somewhere not too far distant.

He was waiting out the storm in the Land Rover. The sturdy vehicle was infinitely more comfortable than an old ruin. No wonder he had been amused. She could have the bats and mice. He was probably already stretched out on the back seat, half asleep, waiting for the rain to stop.

No wonder he had said, 'Don't worry. I'm going.' She had been abandoned again.

Kira slumped against the rough stone wall. History was repeating itself in a familiar but different way. Men thought she was strong and resilient and treated her so. She always insisted she could stand on her own two feet and therefore men let her do just that. If they dropped her, with a jolt, it was her own fault.

But she longed for a man with strength, someone who recognized that she needed taking care of. A man who would fight for his woman, who would think of her as a fragile flower, who would cherish her and care for her . . . it was an old dream.

Kira had never felt so isolated. She let the tears come again, unchecked, falling on to the shirt. She wept for Bruce, for the baby, for her mother, Benjamin and her own loneliness. Perhaps this trip was a mistake. She should be in the calm quiet of her flat in Pimlico, working as a temp in an office somewhere or coping with the relentless pressure of the Commons. She wiped her eyes on a sleeve.

'Hey, that's no way to treat my shirt.'

'Giles . . . I thought you'd gone! Where did you go?'

Giles was standing in the doorway, laden with gear, his bulk and height blocking out the remaining light. With a cry, Kira flung herself at him and he had to drop his packages. He tucked her inside his raincoat, murmuring small, only half-heard words of astonishment and consideration.

'There . . . there . . . did you think I had left you? Dear girl, you don't have a very high opinion of me, do you? Oh, Kira, I would never leave you like that . . .'

Kira lay against the warmth of his chest, inside his coat, his arms closing round her, caressing her tenderly with his hands. She was drowning in the miracle of his return. She did not care what he thought of her sudden capitulation. He had come back and that was all that mattered.

CHAPTER 11

'Do I have to stay outside in the rain?' he asked. 'I will, if that's more acceptable to you.'

Kira shook her head, half smiling at the offer. 'Don't be daft. Come in.'

He guided her back inside the mill, his hand firmly on her arm, his thigh brushing her side.

'My shirt looks better on you than it does on me,' he teased. 'It could become high fashion at Sandy Lane. But only to be worn by women with long beautiful legs.'

Kira extracted herself from his grip, hiding the lurking hunger in her eyes. She dabbed at her face with a corner of the shirt, turning away for modesty's sake.

'I thought you'd gone, that you'd left me to endure a night here on my own in this creepy place. I was sure you had sneaked off to the warmth and comfort of your Land Rover.'

'You have no confidence in me,' Giles chided. 'I had gone back to the Jeep, yes, but not to stay. I went to fetch the candle-light and roses ordered by m'lady. The boot of my vehicle is as mysterious as the contents of a woman's handbag. Now, there must be a furnace somewhere so we can light a fire without burning the place down. We must get you dry and warm.'

'A fire would be lovely, but with what?'

He kicked at the bundles of dry cane. 'Remember? It burns a treat.' A shadow seemed to cross his face so quickly that Kira thought she had imagined it. Fire. She had seen that look once before, when he was showing her the furnaces at the factory.

He heaved aside rusty bits of machinery and rubbish, searching for the blackened bricks of an old furnace. Kira watched his deft movements as he cleared a space inside the hollow, put his lighter to a pile of torn paper then fed broken cane to the uncertain blue flames. They caught greedily at the dry cane, enveloped them in creeping red sparks, the flickering tongues growing into a blaze that threw out light and warmth into the crumbling ruin of the mill. The rough lines softened into rounds and curves, shadows swallowing the cobwebs and dirt.

Kira held her hands to the flames. Her chilled body leaned into the heat. 'That's lovely,' she said. 'Thank you.'

Giles was busy unwrapping a bulky polythene-covered package, heaving the weight as if it was nothing. Kira realized how strong he was. He ripped away the last of the industrial tape and shook out the contents. Kira caught her breath in surprise at the rainbow of bright colours that glowed in the firelight as masses of material fell in glorious folds on to the floor.

'It's the new sail for my catamaran,' he explained. 'I bought it this morning. I didn't realize how soon it would be useful. Help me unfold it.'

'Are we going sailing?' said Kira.

'Patience, patience.'

They stretched the polythene packing sheet on the floor first, then arranged the huge sail on top, folding it into several thicknesses. Kira crouched on to her knees, smoothing out the rainbow-striped nylon. A catamaran sail. She had seen the gaudy-sailed craft racing across the bay from Sandy Lane, billowing in the strong wind. It looked so exciting and exhilarating. She might have known Giles would have a boat.

'Will this do for a table?'

'The best in the house.'

He fixed up a length of nylon rope. 'Also from my boat. A washing line for you to hang your clothes. They'll dry in no time then.'

Every movement was deft and economic. He had some ripe melons and a knife. Kira remembered seeing a basket of melons and sweetcorn in the back of his car. 'They're from my plantation,' he said. 'A little appetizer. You'll have to take a rain-check on the full meal.' He raised an eyebrow to acknowledge the low-key joke. Kira smiled again, accepting his offerings with pleasure.

'And this is the nearest I could get to a rose,' he added, his voice suddenly low and intimate. He handed her a sprig of frangipani, still dripping with rain, its fragile tissue-thin petals stuck together like butterfly wings.

There was a drenching silence. Giles was weaving a spell around her as Kira had feared he would, looking at her as though no expression or gesture was going to escape him. This kindness, this imagination and sensitivity to her feelings . . . all so wonderful in a man who was almost a stranger. And in such a big man, yet a man who moved as lightly and sensuously as a panther. She knew his kiss was only a breath away and she both longed for and feared the moment of their lips meeting.

'What about the champagne and the steel band?' She lightened the mood, reminding him of *his* preferences.

He unscrewed the flask and poured a thimbleful of the golden liquid into the top. He handed it to Kira. She put the rim slowly to her lips, knowing the fiery liquid would ignite more than she could handle.

'The champagne will have to wait,' he said, his eyes devouring the silky glimpses of her thigh. 'And the rain is making enough racket for a steel band. But one day, I promise you, we will dance under the stars to the rhythm of a steel band and you will know the pure joy of Barbadian dancing. You will wear a silk sarong, your feet will be bare and your hair loose as it is now, and you'll wear flowers behind your ears. Without any doubt, you will be the most beautiful woman on the island. We should have met ten years ago,' he added with a wry grin. 'Before things changed.'

'What do you mean?'

'Before my mother became ill. I give her all my spare time, and that isn't much. I haven't time for romancing.'

The heat from the fire was reaching her in waves, the air dry and crumbling, gritty with dust.

He cut the melon into thin slices, lay them on a glistening palm leaf. 'Eat,' he said, and they shared the sweet flesh, juice running down their fingers.

They sipped the strong rum in turns, sitting in the wedge of light, letting the alcohol relax their caution as it raced through their veins. They didn't notice that the rain was beginning to ease. They were both so engrossed with each other, imprinting memories, both knowing that the magical night could not last, that reality and the morrow lay ahead. Kira had never felt so happy, knowing this was how she wanted to be with a man, curiously moved that anyone could make her feel so good again.

Neither knew who reached out for whom. It was a blind response, but too late to deny.

In a moment of unbelievable ecstasy his mouth hovered over hers, barely touching, his breath fanning her skin. Then he drew her into his arms, his body becoming a haven and shelter. With a small sob she let old pains fade and vanish as his kiss deepened and he took possession of her mouth as if he had been a lifetime searching for her.

She returned his driving passion with a ravening hunger that matched his, clinging to him, raking his skin with her nails, senses swimming, shivers flying across her silken flesh as his hands sought the softness of her body.

He crushed her against him possessively, lost in the alluring honey of her mouth, his body enveloping her so close she could barely breathe. One kiss slipped sweetly into another, without beginning or end, mouth, lips, cheeks, face, hair, eyes. She threaded her fingers through the soft hair at the nape of his neck, moving, turning, clinging. She could not get close enough, fitting her body against him like pieces of a jigsaw.

'Kira . . . Kira . . .' he murmured against her hair, burying his face in the slope of her neck, finding the tantalizing hollow of her throat. She threw back her head, and was cradled in the curve of his arm, her legs pinned very low, very intimately by his own strong limbs.

He caught at her hand and brought each finger, slowly and exquisitely, into his mouth. She watched, transfixed by the tenderness of his caress, hardly believing that this was reality . . . that she would not suddenly wake up, cramped and stiff from the long flight.

He pushed up the shirt and reached for the soft inside of her thigh and she gasped as he began stroking the sensitive skin with long touches. She stretched the length of her body beside him, not caring that the front of the shirt was being unbuttoned with the same deft movements. He slipped the material apart and drew a sharp breath at the perfection of her body in the glimmering firelight. He put his hand on the flatness of her satiny stomach and groaned.

'You're beautiful . . .' he said, kissing her tilted face, again and again. 'So very beautiful.'

She pulled him down on to her, rejoicing in the weight of his body, cleaving to him, her long bare legs entwined with his, rolling on the multicoloured sail, hardly aware of the hard floor beneath them. Kira forgot the livid scar which had haunted her for weeks. Giles did not seem to notice it, though his fingers were careful not to inflame the sensitive area. He gave no thought to the blemish, took her injury as part of the whole woman.

His hand curved around the fullness of her honey-tanned breast and the nerve-ends contracted with the pleasure of his touch, his thumb stroking the swelling skin. His lips took the brown-rose nipple into his mouth, his tongue tasting the sweetness, arousing her feelings to fever pitch. A tide of passion threatened to drown her; any control she had left was soon lost. All thoughts of reason, sanity and morals had gone and they could only rejoice in the ultimate joy of loving and being loved.

'Don't be afraid,' he murmured. 'I won't hurt you. I've waited years for this moment . . .'

He lowered himself on top of her, finding the moist and aching softness, pinning her down with his powerful hips. She was imprisoned by his steely grip, unable to move, his passion hardened now into inescapable desire, which roused a storm of longing within her.

A flash of panic surged through the throbbing deep in the pit of her stomach. Her body was crying out for release, for relief, for the waves of pleasure to reach the heights of joy. She wanted to feel satiated and fulfilled as never before. But something else was happening, some gremlin from the recesses of her mind, and she began to struggle.

The edges of her mind were fraying with panic and she twisted her head away from his probing mouth, her arms struggling free to push him flat against his chest.

'Giles . . . Giles.' Her voice was raw and uneven. She was trembling, her face tear-streaked, her legs twisting away from under him.

He stopped abruptly, shattered, his breath rasping. 'Don't be frightened . . .' he said again, despairing. 'Kira, please . . .'

'I'm sorry . . . it's not right . . .'

He moved off her awkwardly like a man devoid of any will. 'Perhaps you're not quite ready for the grown-up world,' he said. 'Go to sleep, baby. I won't touch you again.'

Kira lay apart from Giles, a quivering mass of frustration and bruised flesh. She didn't understand what had happened. The flame had flashed out of control and she had panicked, unable to let her body reach the fulfilment she longed for, afraid of that unknown magical realm of womanhood.

She faced the reality of disappointment, humiliation and despair. She had spoilt one of the most wonderful moments in her life. Giles would never come to her now. He had his pride. And there was no need, with so many ripe beauties on the island; he would never look her way again.

'Forgive me,' she whispered, worn thin by an inner emptiness. 'I was afraid.'

He was stretched out, one arm flung behind him, eyes closed, lashes like twin fans against his dark cheeks. She fell asleep eventually, fitfully, feeling sick, her face nuzzled into the strong curve of his neck, her hair drying on his skin.

She dreamed of him loving her again and this time there was no fear and pyramids of stars burst in the heavens. But in her dream his face changed into that of an eyeless stone lion, and she awoke, shuddering and gasping, only to find that he had gone from beside her.

He had walked away.

The embers of the fire still glowed and he had wrapped a fold of the sail over her bare shoulders. But she awoke as cold as ice and sat up abruptly. Her heart once again was frozen. And now there would never be anyone to thaw it out. She had made damned sure of that.

'You fool,' she howled. 'You stupid fool.'

Reuben's face was permanently set in grim lines. The hurt and bitterness had deepened the nose-to-mouth groove overnight. He rarely laughed. A twenty-year-old who did not laugh. His humour had dried up like a vital bodily fluid. There was only work now that Dolly had married Benjamin Reed.

He'd heard that she was already pregnant and the thought disgusted him, stirred memories of their rapture together at Sugar Hill the night before the wedding. He was racked with jealousy and hatred. Surely Dolly would say something to him if she had the slightest suspicion that the child might be his? But she had not even spoken to him since that sunny morning when half of Bridgetown turned out for the wedding of the year.

Reuben did not go to the wedding. He had flown to Jamaica the same morning to tour their new sugar plants, talking to managers, gathering ideas. Right up to the last moment, he still did not believe Dolly would go through with it, thought that it was all part of one of her silly daydreams. And surely not after their glorious time-after-time lovemaking? How could she? But when he returned home and opened a newspaper . . . it was all there. The black and white photographs, the description of the bride's dress, a list of guests; even the name of the baker in Bridgetown who had made the three-tiered wedding cake.

The pain had been physical. Reuben had staggered outside into the garden, sick to his very soul.

The new Reed and Earl sugar factory was being built at speed. Reuben was pouring all his energy and frustration into it, taciturn and short-tempered with everyone. New machinery stood in the yard, crated and waiting to be unpacked and installed, most of it imported from the United Kingdom or the States.

Reuben was intensely proud of the new plant taking shape before his eyes. The progressive systems being installed were the latest in sugar production. He worked from dawn to dusk, barely taking time to eat or sleep. Work helped him through the tormented months when thoughts of Dolly dominated every waking moment. The nights were a different torment, knowing she was in another man's arms and that Benjamin was taking an intimate pleasure in her soft body.

Often Reuben rode half the night, riding his horse through the plantation or down on to the cool empty beaches, its hooves making no sound on the soft sand. The waves soothed his anguish with their relentless wash till the unwilling light of dawn drove him back to Sugar Hill and his responsibilities.

Reuben checked the new furnaces once again. They were an economic innovation and would cut their fuel bills by half. Even Benjamin, who hated waste, had reluctantly agreed to their installation. Not that the two men were talking. They communicated by memo.

'Evening, Mr Earl. You're here late,' called up one of the workmen from below. 'It's not a twenty-four-hour shift yet.'

'It would be if Reed had his way,' Reuben snapped. He could barely say the man's name.

'He's too soft-taken with his new bride-woman to even show his face in the factory these days. We don't see him for a whole week now.' The workman chuckled, wiped his face on a red kerchief, then turned the cackle into a cough. 'Beggin' y'pardon, sir. No offence meant . . .'

'None taken,' said Reuben heavily. Everyone knew. He had been the subject of much well-meant sympathy since the wedding but the conclusion had been that he would find a more suitable partner when he was ready to marry. It didn't help. He only wanted Dolly, his own passionate Dolly: the beach girl, half wild, half tamed, pressing the memory of their love in the pages of his mind. Benjamin had his hands full with his child bride. They said she ran barefoot around his new house.

Reuben breathed deeply into his gut, letting the oxygen intake steady his hands. He knew he was not properly co-ordinated these days. He had never made mistakes before, but now he was making mistakes. Nothing important, but enough to make him extra careful over the most mundane of actions; switching off, cutting a control, adjusting a dial. A foolish accident would be unforgivable, when so much was at stake. His reputation, his pride. And he had to keep working, working, working . . . It was his only salvation.

Kira could not believe that she had rejected Giles with such finality. What had she been doing? Women all over the world, since time began, faced first-ever lovemaking with a new partner with courage tinged with apprehension . . . and with hope in their hearts. What would it be like? Would it be a disappointment? Why had she been so timid and cowardly? Because she did not want to be hurt again?

Common sense told her that it might have been the rum which had released her inner demons.

She breathed deeply, dragging air into her lungs, trying to steady her shaking hands. Just what on earth was she doing here, alone in this ruined mill when all she wanted was Giles's arms around her, holding her close, crushing her body, bringing the wreckage of her spirit back to life? She looked down at her bare legs, remembering how they had wrapped themselves wantonly round his body and then denied their true purpose by struggling.

She was a fool. Her soul was not being fed and she was letting it shrivel. She was starving for love, isolating herself, fading away as a person, yet when this so special man wanted her, she could not let go. She had to let go of these chains. He lifted her spirits just by being there. But he would not want her again. He was too proud a man even to glance her way another day.

And he had every right to be angry. She had given him all the wrong signals. What a fool!

There was no way she could stand another emotional see-saw, and loving Giles would shatter her. Loving Giles? *Did* she love him? After only a few days? Surely not . . . her mind was playing tricks. It was only an infatuation, a fancy, a crush . . . or pure lust.

But Kira *was* sure that she wanted her life on an even keel, and this man caused earth-tremors that rocked her to the core.

The rain was beginning to stop. It dripped from palm leaves in slow, uneven beats. Kira rubbed her stiff limbs. Her bad leg was beginning to hurt. There were dry clothes in her bags in the mini-moke and she went outside to get them.

She did not want to shed tears for Giles, but they were there, waiting to be shed. For a moment she held them back. But they were too strong. She folded her arms over her head and leaned against the rough wall.

CHAPTER 12

Benjamin Reed came to Kira's rescue. She was struggling into her crumpled clothes, determined to get back to normal, when she heard an engine straining to climb over the rough, rocky ground.

The morning was beautiful but she could barely appreciate it. Sun sparkled through the rainwashed sky and there was not a cloud to be seen anywhere. The vista of rolling hills was endless, bright with pure colour, the vibrant emptiness echoing a chord in her heart.

Giles's Land Rover had gone but she could see the ridged tracks where he had driven over muddy earth. The moke was steaming in the hot sunshine, vapour rising from its sodden fabric roof.

She watched an ancient Rover coming up towards the ruined mill. The driver was expert

267

at swinging the vehicle round to miss the worst of the rocks and potholes. Beside him in the passenger seat sat another man whom Kira instantly recognized as her grandfather. He saluted with a battered straw hat.

'How are yer, girl? Are you all right?' he bellowed out of the window.

She nodded, finding a shaky smile. She knew she must look a sight, her eyes gritty and swollen. She could not repair the damage.

'I'm fine,' she called back. She went to meet the car, hobbling a little. The restless night on a hard floor hadn't helped and several times cramp had pinched her lame leg in its crab-like clutches.

'We were worried about you,' Benjamin said, noting the shadowed eyes. He recognized the signs of crying. Dolly had cried a lot before the baby was born. He had been at his wit's end to comfort her but she had quietened down when Tamara had arrived. He had never understood his young wife, never knew why she was so unhappy. He had never seen the light. He didn't want to make the same mistakes with this young woman.

'I guessed you'd be up here, somewhere near the Morgan Lewis Mill. What a night to be stranded, my girl! You look in need of a hot bath and a good breakfast inside you. Come along now. Get your things.'

'But what about . . .' Kira had been about to ask about Giles's catamaran sail but stopped; he could fetch his own sail '. . . about the moke?'

'Josh here will drive it back. You come to Fitt's House with me and don't go wandering off again like that without telling anyone where you are. Giles nearly had a fit yesterday, he was so angry.'

It was small consolation. It did not lift the hurt she was feeling, the aching despair.

She pushed away thoughts of Giles's demanding mouth and hard, muscled body against her softness. She missed him already. But it was no good torturing herself with such memories. With a flash of insight, she wondered if perhaps her peace of mind could lie with this elderly man who was looking at her now with concern and affection. Affection . . . but why? He hardly knew her.

'Thank you,' she said. 'A hot bath would be wonderful. Thank you for coming to look for me. I might have got stuck on the track if the rain has washed bits away.'

'No, you'd have managed. Sheer desperation can work miracles,' he chuckled. He helped her into the Rover, and noticed the limp. 'You're limping again.'

'I got cold last night.'

'That leg of yours needs looking at.'

'It's all right, really.'

'I didn't have too much trouble finding you,' he went on. 'You left a trail of goodwill everywhere yesterday. The growers are all talking about the young lady from England who was really interested in their problems. News travels fast on this island. Everyone talks and chatters on the phone. Giles would like to put a time limit on talking. Tea-break, talk-break. He likes making rules.'

The mahogany and casuarina trees were steaming and dripping, their heavy leaves glossy and freshly green. Kira spotted a lot of rain damage. Small wooden outhouses had been flooded, hen coops flattened. She could see the sense of building the houses on blocks of concrete or wood. The young green sugar cane was rain-lashed and lay flattened on the fields.

Benjamin slowed down as they drove past St Andrew's Church and Turner's Hall

Wood, passing Mount Hillaby, the highest point on the island.

'Turner's Hall Wood is the last of the primeval forest on the island,' he said. 'Some palm trees are thirty metres high. The stringing vines make canopies overhead, real pretty. There's locust trees, red cedar, Spanish oak and cabbage palm . . . such strange-looking trees. You should see the magnificent jack-in-the-box with its heart-shaped leaves and masses of fruit. I'll take you there one day. Would you like that?'

'I'd like that.'

Driving on Highway 2 was quicker despite the flooded stretches. Then they were turning into the drive of Fitt's House and her first glimpse of the pink castle gave Kira a fleeting feeling that she was coming home. Shadows moved and for an uncanny moment she thought someone else was there.

Benjamin took Kira straight upstairs and showed her a big, old-fashioned bathroom with an Edwardian bath standing on curved feet with a marble surround for accessories. He piled towels into her arms and gruffly told her to get on with it, clearly embarrassed.

Now that she was alone, desolation swept over her again and she sat on the edge of the bath, the spurting water from both taps drowning her jerky sobs, her eyes becoming blurred lenses of tears. She peeled off her clothes, dropping them anywhere, and sank into the hot water, trying to control herself. This wasn't doing her any good.

Bruce and Jenny were lost in the past and it was Giles who filled her thoughts now. Someone had brought in her suitcase and put it outside the bathroom door. She put on the first things she found . . . a pair of jeans and a T-shirt. It was too much trouble to put on any make-up. She didn't care what she looked like.

But when she saw her reflection in the steamy mirror, she realized she could not go downstairs looking such a wreck. She splashed cold water over the blotched skin and practised a wan smile.

Benjamin had breakfast ready for her in the large, cool kitchen at the back of the house. The kitchen was left over from several decades back. There was a brown earthenware sink big enough to bath a goat, a stove run off gas cylinders and battered cooking pots that must have been forty or fifty years old.

A huge antique refrigerator hummed and rattled in a corner of the room. Despite the mass of genuine antiques in the house, Benjamin had obviously never spent a penny on the kitchen. It was long overdue a refit.

He was dishing up fried bacon and breadfruit and scrambled eggs on cracked and lined blue porcelain plates. He had an enamel pot of coffee bubbling on the stove. Josh had brought in fresh hot bread from the small bakery down the road.

'I hope you don't mind eating in the kitchen,' said Benjamin, fussing around, straightening everything. 'I've got out of the habit of using the dining room. Too big and too much trouble for one.'

Kira pulled out a wooden chair and sat down. 'This is fine,' she said.

'Sharing breakfast with a pretty young woman, now that really is something,' he chuckled. 'I thought that kind of thing was all over for me.'

I shall have to tell him soon, thought Kira quickly. He can't make passes at his granddaughter! But when would she tell him?

'Don't you have a housekeeper or someone to look after you?' she asked. 'I thought I saw a woman here when I came for the meeting.'

'That's Jessy. She still works for me but only comes in a few days a week. She came to work for us when my wife Dolly was alive.' It was a matter-of-fact statement. 'But I don't need her no more, Kira. I like to cook and cater for myself and I don't want any woman regular about the place, bossing me around. I've been my own master for too long.'

His face steeled itself but the expression was gone in a second. It was the first time he had mentioned Dolly to her. Kira did not probe. He forked the fried breadfruit on the plates and looked up, waiting for her reaction.

'What do you think of it? The fried breadfruit? There isn't anything in the world to beat the taste. God, bless Him, knew what he was doing when he made the breadfruit tree.'

Kira had to admit that the taste and texture was unique and she liked it. But she had even less appetite than usual. She forced down the food slowly, and accepted more of the good coffee.

It was only eight o'clock. Benjamin must have been out soon after six a.m. She was touched by his concern, and worried by his early start, especially when she was no more than a stranger.

She caught a glimpse of her stricken face in a mirror as she helped clear the table. Crying never helped a woman's appearance. It wasn't fair.

She was sitting out in the garden later, compiling her notes for Giles, using work to take her mind off him, when Benjamin joined her and made a staggering suggestion.

'If you're continuing this crack-brained research that Giles wants, then you ought to make watertight arrangements when you travel,' he began. 'We can't send out search parties every day.'

'I'm sorry I was such a nuisance. I certainly don't want another uncomfortable night in a ruin!'

'I've a much better idea. Why don't you stay here at Fitt's House? I've plenty of room and I've been rattling around this old place for far too long. There are five empty bedrooms, back and front. You can take your pick. I'll get Jessy to clean up for you, make it nice and ladylike. You could come and go as you please, just so long as you leave a note saying which parish you're working in. What do you say, Kira? Could you put up with the company of an old man?'

He was leaning forward, trying to hide the anxiety in his faded eyes. He desperately wanted her to stay and he didn't know why. He had nothing to offer her. She was lovely in every way, sitting in the dappled shade of his bread-fruit tree, her eyes haunted with pain. Dear God, he'd like to know who put that hurt there. But now he just wanted to sit and look at her, to have a little of her time before there was no time for anything.

Kira felt a constriction in her throat. She was moved to compassion for her grandfather. He was lonely and he liked her. And he was offering her a chance to get to know him better and to live in this eccentrically enchanting old house. After so much rejection, she was ready to lap up his care and concern, to let him help heal the hurt. Waves of giddy rejection pounded through her brain. Giles. The beating of her heart was crippled. She was so scared and vulnerable. She was missing Giles and her heart seemed sublimely indifferent to how long she had known him.

She smiled at Benjamin, one of those radiant smiles showing the dimple in the corner of her mouth, and he read in it his answer. He knew she was not going to turn him down. He could hardly believe his luck.

Why had her family become so distant? Was there still time to get over, move on from the terrible things that had happened in the past? Kira hoped so.

'How kind, Mr Reed. Yes, I would love to stay with you if I won't be too much trouble. I love your old house and it would be a real pleasure to live here. You'll hardly notice I'm here.'

'That's great, that's wonderful.' He got up with the vigour and energy of a thirty-year-old. He hovered as if he wanted to rearrange the shade on her face so that it would not burn the fragile skin. 'And call me Ben. Mr Reed is so stuffy.'

'I'll always leave you my route for the day, I promise.'

'And go when it's cool. Stop for a rest at midday and return about four. Remember, it gets dark very quickly.' He was agitated, concerned, did not know what to say or do to protect her enough.

'I will. I will.' She nodded.

The moke had been cleaned and refuelled. It stood in the drive, waiting for her. Kira chose her room. She took the big room at the front of the house, which obviously wasn't occupied.

She could see the sea from the tall windows that reached from floor to ceiling. She loved the sea, and was delighted that here she could climb out on to the balcony that ran round the first

277

floor. The room was barely furnished with worn rugs on polished floorboards, an old brass bedstead and a simple, locally made mahogany chest of drawers.

But it was all that she wanted.

Jessy arrived with a cup of coffee, her dark face beaming. 'This is gonna be good news,' she said, putting down the coffee at Kira's side. 'It's about time Mr Benjamin had some civilized female company.'

Kira smiled. 'I hope I won't make more work for you. I know I left the bathroom in a mess.'

'Don't you worry, missy. No more mess than Miss Dolly used to make.'

'You knew . . . Dolly?' Kira concealed her surprise.

'Why, yes'm. I came with her to Fitt's House when she were a bride, a tiny flibbertigibbet of a thing. Always rushing about and bringing in flowers and animals and anything small and hurt, in and out of the sea. Then the little baby came and she carried that baby around all day, like she were a doll-toy.'

Kira wondered how much this elderly woman knew. She would have to question her carefully. It was obvious that her loyalty to the family was unshakeable.

'Was Dolly a good mother?'

'Oh, yes. She were a good mother to that baby. 'Cept sometimes when she had to go off to the sea and run in the water. You can't swim with a baby in your arms.'

'Who looked after the baby then?'

'Anybody. She would put the baby in y'r lap and just run off, like she had to be free. Never knew when she'd be coming back. Sometimes it were hours.'

'How very strange.' Kira wanted to ask how Dolly had died, what had happened to her, but she dared not.

'She weren't properly grown up or brought up. No mother, you see. Just a child herself. Not ready to be a wife and mother. Poor Mr Benjamin, he done put up with a lot.'

Jessy clamped her mouth shut as if she had said too much to a visitor. She waddled away, her ample hips swaying in a brightly patterned frock. She couldn't tell Kira the truth: that she had been the first person to see Dolly's baby, to hold the baby, all slimy and bloodied from the birth and covered in sand . . .

Dolly guessed the baby was due soon. Jessy had tried to explain about the months of pregnancy but Dolly cared little about dates and didn't even try to listen. She only knew that the baby was growing fast and she was as fat as a balloon and her body was beginning to ache with the weight. She worried she was going to burst.

Nothing stopped her from swimming. She swam every day, a loose shift clinging to her voluptuous figure. Benjamin had tried to stop her but nothing he said had any effect. She went her own way.

She had not seen Reuben for months now, keeping out of his way, not wanting him to see her huge and ugly. Her legs had swollen in the heat. He was angry with her and she did not blame him. And she still loved him even though she was married to another man.

She knew now why she had married Benjamin, though on the day itself she had been dazed and confused. She had done it to show Reuben that someone wanted her as a wife, someone cared, someone influential on the island. That she counted enough as a person to become Mrs Benjamin Reed.

It had been a heady moment, accepting Ben's proposal; she'd felt like a lady. She was special now, not just a wild beach girl.

Somehow, in her naïveté, she had thought she would be able to get out of the marriage some time and then marry Reuben when he was good and ready. She had not reckoned on a baby. A baby made a difference.

Nowadays she did not run down to the beach with her fat stomach protruding in front of her. It was a slower progress. She swam more lazily, floating on her back, letting the warm water support her. The sun dazzled her and she closed her eyes, content to be almost asleep in the water bed.

The waves washed her ashore and she lay in the shallows letting the wavelets lift and move her at will. She could stay there forever, not thinking, not worrying, not wondering about what was going to happen . . .

She knew nothing about birthing. Women on the island became pregnant, then suddenly one morning appeared carrying a baby slung across them in a colourful shawl. It usually happened overnight and seemed quite easy.

She had lain in the water a long time and the sun was beginning to go down. The tips of her fingers were wrinkled. She was very thirsty. Fitt's House, although only minutes away, seemed like miles to walk. It was a long way and she wondered if she could make it.

She struggled up on to her knees and without warning was gripped by a violent pain in her groin. She grasped, mind dislocated from her body, staring at her belly in disbelief and protest. Minutes later, another pain rocked her. She floundered in the water, trying to get to her feet, sweat and fear mingling with the salt water. She didn't like it.

'Help me, help me,' she cried out, but there was no one to hear. 'I'm sick . . .'

She crawled up the beach, gathering sand in the folds of her wet shift, stopping each time her body was convulsed. But now the pains were coming faster and she hardly had time to move between them. She reached the fringe of sweeping palms, using the swaying lower branches to haul herself to her feet.

The shoreline swam before her eyes. She could not focus in the fast-fading light. She was gritting her teeth now, crushed under the searing pain that was ripping her body apart. Surely she was dying? The dark hooked presence of death seemed to appear at her elbow.

'Help me, dear God,' she moaned, drymouthed, parched, her tongue swollen.

She spiralled into a swirling red abyss where her mind lost all sense of time and place. Something made her cling to the palm tree, the only strong living thing in a blurred landscape.

There was no time between the pains now; they merged into a red rag of racking torment, crucifying her tender flesh in its grip. It was a long tunnel of pain. Her mind soon spun out of control. Suddenly it changed into an enormous urge to push, to expel . . . she began to pant, little shallow breaths that cleared some of the fog in her head.

Her body was drenched in sweat and there was a warm wetness dripping between her legs.

She stared, horrified, thinking her stomach was falling out. She fought against the urge to push, hanging on to her insides, but she was already too weak to muster any strength. Gravity helped the baby. Dolly screamed, vaginal flesh and skin tearing apart in hot, jagged strips.

Tamara came into the world, upside down on the sand, howling, red-faced and bloodied.

Kira sat very still, half listening. Dolly and Tamara were suddenly very much alive, running round the garden together like children. She heard leaves rustling and imagined it was their arms and legs brushing the branches. She heard high, distant young voices but it was other children playing on the beach.

She felt so close to both women, Dolly and Tamara, women of her own genes. They came to her, beckoning, smiling. It was a strange feeling, not frightening.

But it was time to get back to work. She changed into a sleeveless blue dress and decided to visit the smaller holdings nearer to hand. She did not feel up to a lot of driving.

They left at the same time. Benjamin was going into Bridgetown to a meeting at the bank and to do some shopping. By four o'clock Kira had interviewed so many farmers that their names were beginning to get mixed up in her mind. Her detailed notes were becoming wild scribbles.

Her head was buzzing with information, much of it concerning the two men paramount in her thoughts: Giles and Benjamin. They were both good employers. Benjamin, stubborn and old-fashioned, letting his plantation slip, while Giles was fighting to bring the business up to date and modernize every aspect of sugar production.

'Mr Giles, he really looks after his own,' a grizzled old farmer told her, his face lined like a wrinkled walnut. 'It were him who took my Maiz to hospital when she was taken bad and paid for her funeral. I'm never forgetting that. I don't mind if I get short-weighted on my cane; I'm never forgetting his kindness.'

'But Mr Giles doesn't want you to be short-weighted,' said Kira. 'He's going to put a stop to this and every other injustice if he can. Something is going wrong somewhere along the line.'

'Yes, ma'am. You tell him. Mr Giles'll put it right. He looks after his own.'

He looks after his own . . . Kira warmed herself in the thought. She knew he would. She liked being a small cog in their set-up; it made her feel good. She wanted to help these people, solve their problems, be trusted by them.

Fitt's House was bathed in a crimson sunset as she turned into the drive, its pink walls reflecting the setting rays as its builder had planned. It was a fairy-tale château, the stone animals under some spell, waiting to be brought to life. Perhaps if she kissed them she would find the prince of her dreams.

The front door was on the latch. Ben did not lock up.

Kira went up the old staircase, her leg hardly hurting at all. There was just time for a quick swim before it got dark. It was Dolly's blood in her veins and her passion for the sea driving her onwards.

She threw open the door to her room and then stopped in the doorway. Had she come to the wrong room? She checked that it was the room opposite to Ben's on the central landing.

It had been transformed. The bare, functional bedroom she had chosen that morning was now fit for a princess. The brass bedstead had a flounced and flower-sprigged cover; matching curtains billowed at the windows. Soft white fur rugs scattered the polished boards; an elegant French antique writing bureau had been moved upstairs for her to work at; pieces of rare crystal and porcelain stood on the deep windowsills. An old Victorian button-back armchair in dusky pink velvet and a matching footstool was angled by the long window. A small hand-carved rose walnut coffee table was at the side of the chair. On it was a posy of flowers, a dish of fruit and a silver knife.

Ben had been shopping.

No one had ever treated her like this before. Kira was so moved that she could not think. She went round the room, touching everything, feeling the different textures, the newness. There was even a new divan mattress on the old bed. Ben had thought of everything.

'Do you like it? Are the things all right?' Ben had not been able to resist coming to see her reaction. His eyes were fixed on her face.

'It's just wonderful,' said Kira, impulsively putting her hand on his arm. 'Everything's just perfect. How can I ever thank you?'

'I want you to be comfortable while you're staying at Fitt's House. I'd forgotten how much fun shopping can be.'

'I don't understand why you're so kind to me,' said Kira. 'I'm a stranger you only met yesterday. You hardly know me.'

'We met under the breadfruit tree, remember? And I know when I like someone. As you get older you realize there isn't time to wait around seeing if you're right. If you get a gut feeling, then you have to act on it right away.'

'Am I a gut feeling?'

'An indelicate way of putting it, but yes.'

'I'm going to love this room,' said Kira.

'Now I ain't going to get in your way. I guess you're longing for a swim. My wife, Dolly, used to love swimming. Giles is coming over later, to talk about the month's figures. You're welcome to join us then.'

Kira did not know if she could face Giles yet but it would have to be some time. It might as well be this evening.

'Thank you. Yes, I'll join you after my swim.'

Kira swam out to a motorboat anchored off a small jetty which local residents used. It was a glass-bottomed boat for taking tourists to look at the coral reefs.

She lay on her back, floating in the bobbing waves, letting the last of the sun's rays dapple her skin, trying not to think of Giles, or of seeing him again. The sea was so warm and buoyant, it required no effort to stay afloat, provided she made the occasional paddling movement with her hands.

She closed her eyes, thinking how far away London was. Bruce and Jenny hardly seemed to exist. Barbados was so vibrant and colourful; the rest of the world paraded as a drab place. This was an emerald paradise.

The sun slid behind the horizon, shooting out its rays, and the sea darkened. Time to return to Fitt's House.

Kira had drifted further than she thought, but she was a good swimmer and struck out for shore. There was a sandbank beneath her feet and unexpectedly she felt it moving quite fast and her feet were flung up. She floundered for a moment that seemed an eternity, then righted herself and begin to swim steadily.

But she was making no headway. The shore was suddenly further away. There seemed to be quite a strong current at this point which she had not encountered in the sheltered bay opposite the Sandy Lane Hotel. This was a long, straight stretch of beach.

Kira realized that she was not making any headway – in fact she was being swept further out and along the coast. She did not like the feeling. She felt a small twinge of fear.

CHAPTER 13

Kira tried not to panic. Already the familiar rooftops and receding treeline that hid Fitt's House were some distance away.

She trod water, calling and waving her hands, but her voice was lost in the roar of the waves. She knew that if she kept her head she would be safe. It was exhaustion and panic which killed swimmers in warm water.

The sea was indigo-dark now and lights were coming on in the small houses fronting the shore. She called again, hoping that someone might be taking an evening stroll, or jogging along the beach. She tried swimming against the current but it was very strong, running parallel to the shore, and she just could not make any headway through its racing flow.

Foaming white waves were breaking on the rocks ahead. The reef was approaching fast. A piercing stab of cramp caught her lame leg and she cried out in pain, clutching the muscle. In the confusion, as she thrashed around, she did not hear the vigorous splashing of someone swimming.

A cropped dark head bobbed from under the water and then a gleaming sinewy arm came under her armpits and she felt herself being pulled against a chest. It was a strong man, young and confident. Kira screwed up her face in pain and relief.

'Keep still, lady. Don't be afraid. It's only Moonshine. You gonna be all right now.'

Kira bit her lip against the cramp and allowed Moonshine to pull her along. He was not swimming but letting the current take them along, drifting parallel to the shore, making a few deep strokes now and then to correct their direction and keep the same distance. She tried to relax, trusting him, not wanting to hinder his progress. How strange . . . Moonshine, the handsome and persuasive youth selling beads on the beach.

'You were caught in a rip-current, lady,' he said hoarsely, looking round the surface of the sea for signs of turbulence. He seemed to know what he was doing. 'You have to swim along with it, not against it. You gonna drown if you go against it. You swim along with it and sooner or later, it gonna take you back to the beach.'

It was true. The beach seemed to be getting nearer. A great surge of relief swept through her. Their feet suddenly touched sand and rocks and they began to scramble ashore, uncaring of the sharp edges scraping skin, stabbing toes. Moonshine kept her from falling with a firm grip on her waist.

'Oh, Moonshine, Moonshine, thank you. What would I have done without you?' she gasped. 'I was being swept out to sea and I didn't know what to do. No one could hear me. It was so frightening.'

'These rip-currents just pop up. You don't know where; they change from day to day. I saw you go swimming and thought, there's that pretty English lady who's going around with Mr Giles. You didn't come back and I thought, she dun go get caught in a rip-current. Then I saw you being swept towards the reef.'

His muscular legs stood astride on the sand, chest heaving, water dripping down his ragged jeans. His dark, velvety eyes gleamed in the growing darkness but Kira was not afraid.

'How lucky for me that you came along,' she said, her rapid breathing slowing down. 'I couldn't have swum back from Bridgetown.'

He peered down at her face. 'You all right now? We go pick up your towel, then I take you back to Mr Reed's house.'

Kira felt almost light-headed with relief. She laughed. 'To Fitt's House? Is there anything which happens that you don't know about?'

He grinned in the darkness. 'Moonshine know everything.'

Her heart volunteered an extra beat. 'Then you can put it on the island's grapevine that I'm not going around with Mr Giles. I'm working for him. Quite different. It's a business arrangement.'

'If you ain't going around with Mr Giles then he's certainly acting as if you are. He's charging along the beach now faster than that zippy white car of his.' Moonshine peered ahead into the darkness, grinning.

The air was moist and briny, saturated with moonlight. Kira saw a tall man, striding along the beach, kicking up sand, looking for her as he had that first time on St Lucia. Her heart almost stopped, then quickened at the sight of him. Wild and lonely music played in her ears.

There was going to be no problem after all, seeing him again. Her eyes were riveted on the man coming into sight, the gaunt lines of his face etched in the light glittering off the sea. She stumbled on the clogging sand and he ran forward, catching her in his arms before she fell.

'Kira, Kira . . . what the hell's been going on? Are you all right? Benjamin said you'd gone for a swim.'

'I got caught by a rip-current. Moonshine saved me.' Her head was spinning as she felt his arms go round her.

'Damn it, woman. Don't you know not to swim in the dark alone? I should have told you about rip-currents.'

'I been telling the lady,' said Moonshine. 'You don't get drowned by them if you know what to do.'

'She didn't know what to do.'

Giles swung her up into his arms and began to carry her back to Fitt's House. Moonshine was left behind on the sand, standing in dripping blue jeans, his case of beads flung all over the sand where he had thrown them in his haste to dive into the sea to rescue her.

'Moonshine,' Giles called back to the youth. 'Come and see me tomorrow. I'll settle up for any damage to your goods. And thanks . . . thanks for saving my lady.'

Giles's voice was gruff. Moonshine waved back. He'd have some tale to tell in the bars tonight and that was reward enough. 'Don't worry, be happy,' he called back with the standard Caribbean farewell.

'Thank you, Moonshine,' said Kira.

She lay her head against Giles's shirt-front, ruining it with her wet hair. He didn't care. He gripped her tightly as if she were the slipperiest mermaid from the sea.

'Don't start telling me off,' she said.

'I won't. You didn't know about the currents.'

'No, I didn't know,' she murmured.

He was carrying her as if she weighed no more than thistledown and Kira never wanted the sensation to end. He could carry her to the end of the island. She didn't care how many women he had had or loved; she only knew that the thought of losing him now was unbearable.

He set her slowly down on to her feet, wrapping her towel round her shivering body as if she were a baby, drying her arms and legs. He was not angry. All the anger of the night before had gone, vanished in a wave of warmth and awareness.

'It would be a change to see you dry,' he said, with a slow, ironic reference. He held the edges of the towel close, pulling her against him, his fingers brushing the soft skin below her throat. 'Do you think you could manage it one day?'

'Are you going to dry all of me?' she asked, moving closer to him.

'Kira, don't . . . what are you doing? I could go out of my mind. You're driving me crazy.'

Kira looked up, seeing the angle of his darkened jaw from below. The planes of his face were hawk-like and dominant, the lowered lashes hiding the expression in his dark eyes. She remembered their closeness last night in the ruined sugar mill and hungered for more.

The air was heavy with scented blossom and the stars were struggling against the inky darkness. The moon shone through the clouds like a pirate's silver coin broken in half.

Her swimsuit was wet, clammy and cold but she could not stop herself. She stood on tiptoe, quickly twining her arms around his neck and pulling his head down to hers. She brushed her lips across his mouth and heard his sharp intake of breath.

'Driving you crazy? Am I?' she whispered, husky and low. 'Like this?'

297

She did not care if he thought she was wanton; she had to feed her need of him and it was a lure that was too strong to resist. Her eyes were glowing with love. There was no argument now between her hurt-saddened eyes and readily smiling mouth.

His chin grazed her smooth cheek but she knew with that slight movement that his mouth was parting, would soon be claiming her lips. In one swift moment, a fiery desire ignited and burned through their bodies. The straps of her swimsuit slipped down her shoulders and her breasts were crushed against him. She felt his fingers biting into the soft flesh of her arms.

'Giles . . . forgive me for last night. I was a fool, frightened of my feelings. They were so strong. So many different feelings were struggling inside me. I know I'm not saying it right, but I'm not frightened any more.'

A wild, unreasoning elation pushed aside the last shreds of common sense. She was tired of being careful and sensible. And she was tired of being a hostage to the past. She might even get hurt again – Giles might love her briefly and then move on – but it was a risk she was prepared to take just for this one moment. Life was made of moments, and this was one that she would treasure.

If it was soon over, then it did not matter. She wanted to be satiated with pleasure, wanted him to love her *now*, to bring her body alive, to make her see stars in the darkness. It was a present to herself and she thought she deserved some happiness. After all these barren months, she wanted Giles to love her, even if it never happened again.

Her hands slid round his back, feeling the ridge of his spine through the thin jacket, pulling him close. The shape of his lips was well-remembered and beloved. Fleetingly she thought of Bruce's boyish kisses, but the memory was so weak that it vanished as if they had never kissed. There was no comparison. This was a man. This was a man who knew how to kiss, who was coaxing her with gentle persuasion into a fever of delight.

Giles was murmuring against her lips, words of love, endearments, small tender names that sent her sailing on a cloud of singular sweetness. His hands were deep in her tangled hair. She would never forget this moment; nothing would ever be so perfect.

'Are you sure, Kira? Is this what you really want?'

Giles had wanted her almost since their first moment of meeting on St Lucia. The lovely curve of her mouth had fascinated him and he had lost himself in her amazing eyes. The fierceness of his longing had been tormenting him for days. He longed to get rid of the last barriers between them, to stroke every inch of her beautiful body, to taste the sweetness of her skin, to become the centre of her being, of her life.

The strength of his feelings had shattered him. It made him fight her with words at every opportunity when all he really wanted to do was to make love to her with all the passion stored inside him. An uncontrollable storm was building up in his hard body.

Long shadows of fringed palm leaves were thrown against the vibrating starlight of the sky. The waves broke softly on the shore in a low, passionate lullaby. The wind fluttered seductively through the heat of their bodies like extra fingers.

He was kissing her with a lingering, pulsing drive that had her thoughts spinning helplessly. His voice was husky with hunger and the words were a melody in her ears. Her abandoned reponse sent them both revolving into a dizzy world where the sky and stars were all mixed up into a crazy, climbing pinnacle of pleasure that neither of them could control.

They lay tangled on the sand, arms and legs entwined. He was slowly slipping the straps from her shoulders, pulling down her wet swimsuit. It was not easy and Kira felt a small bubble of laughter at his efforts. She rolled away to give him space.

'I have to tell you something,' said Kira. Afterwards she could not understand why she had done it. 'I have to be honest with you. It's something you ought to know.'

'No, no, Kira . . . no confessions now. I don't care how many lovers you've had. This is you and me, here and now. The past doesn't matter.'

'It's not about the past. It's the present, about Benjamin Reed.' She hesitated, but she wasn't able to stop.

'Oh, no, not that old man.' He paused and lay back as he had done the night before, breathing heavily. 'Forget him, Kira. He's just a pain, a thorn in my flesh that I have to put up with.'

'And he's my grandfather,' said Kira. 'I think you ought to know.'

The palm leaves wept.

'What did you say?' His voice had gone cold.

'I am Benjamin's granddaughter. Only he doesn't know yet. I haven't told him. I don't know what he would think.'

She heard Giles's slow intake of breath. Her hands began to tremble. She had a glimpse of a terrible pain in his eyes. His face was a mask. What had she done?

'You mean Tamara was your mother?'

Kira was alarmed by the change which had come over Giles. She wished she had not said anything but it had seemed important to be one hundred per cent honest with him. There had been a slight chance he might even be amused.

'Yes,' she said, bewildered. 'Tamara was my mother, his daughter. Does it make any difference?'

Giles exploded, hitting the sand with his fist. 'Does it make any difference, woman! Don't you understand anything? Don't you know?'

'No, I don't,' Kira said, struggling to defend herself. 'I know you and Benjamin don't get on well but that shouldn't change how we feel. Surely it doesn't matter? It's an old, ancient feud between your father and Benjamin and should have been decently buried a long time ago. It has nothing to do with us.'

'It has everything to do with us,' he said, standing up and brushing sand off his jacket. 'Ask Benjamin. Get up, Kira. I'll see you back to your grandfather's house. No doubt he's anxious about your long absence.'

'You can't mean this?' Kira was angry now. She scrambled to her knees, roughly pulling up the straps of her swimsuit. 'Giles, what's the matter? This is ridiculous. You're not being fair to me. You've got to tell me what this is all about.'

'Ask Benjamin,' he repeated. 'Your grandfather knows.'

Locals who watched the weather were suspicious about the conditions on Wednesday, 21 September 1955. Something was happening. Something was not quite right.

Dolly was not aware of the increasing wind for a long time. The previous day had been calm and sunny with a little low cloud, a usual sort of day. A light sea breeze cooled the island. Dolly knew nothing about rising pressure or air movement from the north, and she had not noticed a thick sunset or distant lightning in an overcast sky. The weather was nothing to her.

She rarely listened to weather forecasts on the radio and there had not been any bad storms in her lifetime. The last hurricane had been fifty-seven years before, and she was not interested in history.

She left Tamara at her father's house while she went swimming.

'You will have her, won't you?' she pleaded, the child on her hip. 'Jessy has gone out and I must go swimming. Please . . .'

'"Of course Tamara can stay with me. We'll do some painting, won't we, *ma petite*? I'll get her some brushes and a pinafore.'

'Thanks, Papa.'

Dolly waved as she ran down the lane. Benjamin did not approve of her unconventional ways with her daughter, but Dolly strove for freedom from the ties of motherhood. Being a mother went on so long, every day. The sea called her with an insistent voice, like some witch from the fragrant and salty depths.

She loved her little girl dearly but could not cope with the twenty-four-hour commitment. There was only so much time she could give to Tamara. Part of the day she had to have to herself, to breathe, to think, to be herself. And in case she caught sight of Reuben.

Her passion still burned as fiercely as ever. It was like a knife deep in her ribs. They spoke now, but only distantly. It had taken months before he would even nod or say hello or acknowledge her presence. She had done her best in small, tentative ways to make amends but he was unable to listen, still tormented by her decision to marry Benjamin.

'You kept saying you couldn't marry me,' she reminded him with despair. 'I wanted to be married. I wanted to have my own home, not to live in a falling down wooden shack with my father.'

'You could have waited,' said Reuben, tight-lipped, unable to look at her; her figure had become womanly with motherhood.

'For how long, tell me? Five years, you kept saying. How could I wait that long?'

'It seems to me you married Benjamin for a bathroom,' said Reuben, his voice full of disgust. 'I hope you're making real good use of it, feeling nice and clean. A bath a day will keep your true love away.'

'How can you be so horrid?' Dolly flared.

'Easy. Especially when the girl you've loved for years marries someone else. What did you do? Throw the dice: me or Benjamin? Did Benjamin win you in a dice game?'

When he saw Tamara for the first time, Reuben was shattered. The baby was the image of Dolly, beautiful, dark, wild-looking but with not a shred of Benjamin in her appearance. Reuben could not smother his suspicions. He remembered that ecstatic night at Sugar Hill, when they had made love again and again in the big bed before falling asleep exhausted in each other's arms.

Anger exploded in him and he thumped his fists together, causing pain to shoot through his wrists. If Tamara was his child, his daughter, he had lost more than his beloved Dolly . . . he had lost his family.

Dolly was relieved that Reuben and Benjamin now spoke to each other, if only guardedly. The new plant was a success and even Benjamin was showing some taciturn approval of the new mechanisms.

That morning there had been light showers but only a gentle wind. But the sky was overcast with a low pall of altostratus with soft-looking cumulus clouds. Dolly did not like the darker sky. She wanted sunshine and clear skies, as every other day. There was occasional thunder, but she took no notice.

When the sky lightened over the east and the rain stopped, Dolly decided it was fine to go swimming. She did not connect the lightening of the sky with a change in wind direction.

The sea was relatively calm with any deep swells still far out. She could hear a light surf but was not disturbed by it. Her own special stretch of beach was fairly sheltered.

She did not notice the sea beginning to churn, nor the large waves breaking beyond the reef and sweeping in to the shore to break again. She did not know that the sea at Hastings was washing through the Hotel Royal and that sand was flooding the road. The sea was breaking heavily over the pierhead in Bridgetown.

An unexpected wave reared and broke over her head. She came up, gasping, hair strangled in her mouth.

'What the . . .?' She never finished her exclamation, for when she cleared her eyes she was surprised by the change in the sea's surface. A huge swell was causing problems for the small fishing boats and they were making hurriedly for the shore.

Now she could hear the wind whistling and groaning through the trees, sudden gusts flurrying the sand. Branches began to bend under the strain, leaves rustling and flapping like storms of tired clapping.

Suddenly Dolly was frightened by the speed at which the weather had changed. She did not know that the wind, expected to back from north through west to south over the island, had shifted abnormally from north through east to south. A hurricane was going to hit the southern half of the island instead of passing some fifty miles north of it.

She ran, stumbling through the swirling sand. Rain was pitting the sand like a smattering of Braille. She scooped up her dress and pulled it over her wet swimming costume – Benjamin insisted that she wore one now. She began to hurry inland towards her father's house. Her sandals lay forgotten, soon covered with shifting sand. Everything looked different.

Tamara would be terrified. The little girl never liked the sound that the wind made. Dolly knew that André would be too occupied with securing his precious paintings to give much thought or time to comforting the child.

Her lungs began to labour. She was soon out of breath, alarmed how fast the wind had whipped up. Gusts of fifty miles an hour knocked her off her feet and sent her sprawling.

How could it have changed so quickly? It had been a normal morning, if silently overcast, with a pleasant breeze. Now, only a few hours later, a hurricane was sweeping the island.

Dolly was panting, heaving and coughing, trying to keep her balance, fighting to make progress against the force of the wind. She threw herself from tree to tree, clinging to any branch for support.

'Please God, look after Tamara,' she gasped. 'Don't let her be frightened. My little girl. Look after her, please. Keep her safe.'

The lane was already a mess of broken branches and debris, leaves hurled into the air by sudden gusts. She fell again, rolled by the violence into the dust, unable to breathe. Her hair was streaming, frock soaked and filthy. Her feet were cut and bleeding but she hardly noticed.

The noise was deafening as the hurricane tore across the southern coastal districts of the island. Trees fell, ripped from the ground, roots smashed and wind-lashed. Fences were tossed in gusts, wooden chattel houses shuddered, collapsed, the steeple of St Martin's Church toppled. Small sailed fishing boats sank under the turbulent seas.

Three miles away, a corrugated roof was torn from a chattel and hurled across a field.

Dolly caught sight of a flash of pink cotton. Tamara had worn a pink frock that morning. She was being blown along the ground like a doll.

'Tamara!' Dolly shrieked. Somehow she found the strength to cover the distance, scooping Tamara up, dreading that she might find her child battered and lifeless. She clutched Tamara in her arms. Tamara's face was blotched with tears and dirt but she was still breathing.

'Mama's here, Mama's here,' Dolly crooned, crouching down against the trunk of a tree. They must find shelter. Somehow she had to reach the house.

She tried to look around, to see which way to go, but the landscape had changed so much. Nothing was the same. There was no shelter nearby and the gusts were strengthening. It was a hell of crashing branches and groaning trees, wind howling like a dervish. She covered Tamara's face and pressed the child to her body. Somehow they must get through to André's house. It was constructed of wood, old but strong enough surely to withstand these gusts?

'Mama, make it stop,' Tamara wept, clinging. 'I don't like it.'

'Hush, hush, I will. I will,' said Dolly. 'We

must get back to Grandfather's house. Be a brave girl, now . . .'

They began to crawl along the ground, Dolly half dragging the terrified child with her, hindered by debris and smothered in swirling leaves and sand. The noise was deafening. Tamara was screaming. It was raining again, making the ground slippery and treacherous.

Ahead Dolly saw the shape of a familiar building, one of the outhouses, and hope surged through her. They would get there. They would reach it.

'Not long now, honey,' she shouted hoarsely. 'We're nearly there. You can make it . . . try . . . try . . .'

The corrugated roof had travelled three miles, borne by the devil wind, scything through fields of cane, spinning like a rotor blade.

The sheet of iron rode across Dolly's body, a wheel of death.

They found her some hours later, still protecting the slight form of her shocked and shivering daughter.

Hurricane Janet took thirty-five lives. The animals somehow found shelter and soon returned to their normal habitats.

Eight thousand small houses were destroyed, leaving twenty thousand people homeless. St Michael's was the worst hit. About two hundred larger houses were seriously damaged. Only one church, St Martin's, suffered. Roads were blocked by fallen trees and wreckage. Telephone and electricity supplies were blown down. A few water pipes were damaged by uprooted trees. People wandered about, shocked and stricken, unable to believe what had happened so quickly.

The sea spray blown over the island blistered the leaves and crops. Trees were stripped and broken. Advanced plant cane was broken down, cane blown parallel to the ground surface, eventually back-rooting. Provision crops were completely destroyed. There was going to be a severe shortage of food.

Twenty-three sail-type fishing boats were lost or destroyed, more damaged. Pot boats were lost and hundreds of fishing pots lost. A small motor vessel, a yacht and a schooner were hit in the Careenage. A schooner sank somewhere off Pelican Island. Wreckage strewed the beaches for weeks. The children took it home for souvenirs.

Reuben was shattered by the damage to Sugar Hill plantation. He wandered through the bruised trees and flattened cane, full of sorrow and despair.

He did not know about Dolly yet. When he heard, he lost the last shreds of youth. His spirit shrivelled and died with her.

CHAPTER 14

Breakfast together under the breadfruit tree had become a habit and a sundowner on the veranda a welcome moment of relaxation for Benjamin and Kira after a busy day.

'You know, you don't have to go back to London,' suggested Benjamin, cradling his drink. 'You can stay as long as you like.'

'But I have a living to earn,' Kira replied with a hopeless kind of guilt. She had not told him yet who she was. 'I've no work lined up for the coming months and I've almost finished Giles's research.'

'You could stay and work for me. I need someone young and enthusiastic. Why not stay and help me run my plantation? I'd teach you everything I know. You're a bright, intelligent woman and seem to have an instinct for sugar and a love for Barbados.'

315

The words ran like liquid sugar through her veins. It was what she wanted to hear. She did have an instinct for sugar plantations and their problems. She loved the fields of waving cane. It was as if she had been brought up here on the island and not in a series of squalid bedsits in London. Somehow she had skipped a generation.

'A woman running your plantation?' she laughed. 'Doesn't that go against the grain? I don't know anything about sugar except where to pour it.' Kira kept her voice light. 'Anyway, Giles would have a fit if I started working for you. He's already uptight about me staying here.'

'What does Giles matter? Let the damned man have a fit. I'd like to see it.'

Benjamin chuckled into his long iced rum drink. He called it a Fitt's House Special and he would not give Kira the recipe. She was working on it.

'Giles would make working here difficult for me,' Kira went on, more to herself. The damned man . . . just those words ran round her mind. 'A woman helping to run the Reed Plantation would be like a red rag to a bull. Out of the question!'

Sometimes she wondered if those moments on the sand had ever happened. Could her body ever forget them? Had it been a delirium from near-drowning and shock? Was it so terrible that she was Benjamin Reed's granddaughter? Giles had reacted as if it was a crime.

'You're a very special woman. Think about it, Kira, and let me know. There's no hurry. It's a big decision to make.'

'Blast you, man, what were you thinking, letting her run around alone in a hurricane? And what about Tamara? Didn't you have any thought for either of them?' Reuben's face was contorted with fury.

'I didn't know where she was,' Benjamin groaned. 'She had a mind of her own. You can't blame me.'

'I do blame you. Why didn't you employ a nanny if Tamara was too much for Dolly?' Reuben glared.

'Too expensive. I've a lot of debts . . .'

Reuben could have throttled him. 'You and your debts. This damn fool castle and the money you borrowed from the firm. I'm going to see that you pay back every penny. I won't let you get away with it, Benjamin Reed.'

'Are you threatening me?'

'Take it any way you like, you bastard.'

Reuben took a pace forward, his hands flying to Benjamin's throat. He was seeing red, the red of Dolly's blood.

Benjamin threw him off. Then they were both struggling, fighting for Dolly. But she was dead and neither of them would admit that they would never see her again.

Giles was polite to Kira whenever they met around the island, complimentary about her work, and about as friendly as a cobra. He had put up an invisible wall and Kira could not understand why.

They came face to face at a dance, both guests of another sugar planter. It was held at a local nightspot with a steel band on a small concrete floor, among swaying palms, only yards from the murmuring sea. The music was rhythmic and sexy, the singers making up verse after verse with impromptu words, the drummers putting their souls into the pulsing beat.

The metallic sound was so right out there in the open air, the waves washing gently on the shore, breakers parading far out to sea. The wasted slip of an old moon hung in the sky. Kira let a special kind of peace steal over her.

Giles asked her to dance. Kira accepted without thinking. He moved with the easy rhythm that belonged to a man who had been dancing to music all his life, who belonged to the islands not on any polished Western ballroom dance floor.

The bar was a wooden shack with a thatched palm-leaf roof. The pale moonlight was reflected in the rows of bottles and glasses. The bar was crowded with people.

'I'm glad you didn't dress up,' he said, admiring her gold-threaded blue sarong and bare feet.

'You said not to dress up for a steel band.'

It was a bewitching night, the breeze from the sea full of land scents blowing through her hair, but no longer feeling dangerous. Kira danced in a daze, so pleased to see Giles, feel his hands touching her occasionally to remind her they were dancing together, catching hands one moment then loosing them. They looked at each other as if they had forgotten anyone else existed.

Kira could not stop herself from hoping. Perhaps Giles had now accepted that she was

Ben's granddaughter and realized that it didn't matter. She wanted the situation to go back to how it used to be.

'You said wearing a sarong was perfect for dancing,' said Kira. 'Something cool.'

'So I did,' he said, moving his cheek against her hair, loving the softness, barely able to keep his hands from touching it. 'I was right, wasn't I?'

Kira closed her eyes, starved for his touch. A wave of tenderness rippled through her, mingling with her resentment, not voicing any disappointment. She missed him so much.

'Can we talk some time?' she asked tentatively. 'About us? There's a lot I want to say.'

'Of course,' he murmured.

But the moment was lost. Some more people arrived who knew Giles and they put several tables together and suddenly it was one big noisy party. The intimacy had gone. Giles was laughing with his friends and later he got up to dance with one of the girls, a beautiful slinky black girl in a skimpy silver dress, her hair braided in an intricate design with an exotic flower behind her ear.

Then Lace arrived. Kira recognized her immediately. She was wearing another slip of a dress, all legs and bare shoulders. She came straight over to Kira, eyes flashing.

'I told you it wouldn't last, didn't I? I'm always right where Giles is concerned,' she said, taking Kira's drink from the table, throwing away the straw and drinking long from the glass. What was the matter with the girl?

'Have you left school yet?' asked Kira.

Lace looked surprised. 'Yes. Why?'

'Your manners are positively from the kindergarten. It's a wonder you're let out without a nanny.'

'Has he told you about our mother?'

'Yes, I know she has MS. I'm so sorry.'

'Ah, that much you know . . . so he's dumped you already, has he? I recognize the redundant tone of voice. Don't worry, Russian-named Kira. There are plenty more fish in the sea. Someone else will snap you up. You're quite a catch, I understand.'

Kira felt herself shrinking. She wanted to go home. The leg, which had not troubled her all evening, suddenly began to ache. 'Go and enjoy yourself elsewhere,' she said, getting up. 'I don't need your brand of conversation.'

She found Giles and asked him if he could take her home; she was tired.

'Sure,' he said, searching for his keys. 'I'll drop you off at Fitt's House then come back. The night is young and I haven't seen these friends for months. They've been in the States.'

The States. The women had the gleam and glamour of New York on their skin and in the clothes they wore.

It hurt Kira immeasurably that Giles was going back to the party after he dropped her. He was demonstrating again that he was a free agent. He could do anything he wanted. Barbadians liked to stay up late and sleep during the heat of the day. It was their way of life. The cooler night hours were their leisure and pleasure time.

'Thank you,' she said as he dropped her at the end of the drive to Fitt's House. It was all she could do not to turn and cling to him. Her legs felt stiff as she swung them out of his car and closed the door. She could not look at him.

'See you in my office tomorrow, ten o'clock.'

Kira had forgotten. Her work on the plight of the small farmers and their transport problems was finished. She had written her report. Benjamin had borrowed a word processor with which she was familiar and she had spent the last few evenings putting all her notes and observations into lucid form.

Benjamin was still up, reading *The Advocate*, his glasses perched on the end of his nose. 'You're back from the party early,' he said, sounding pleased.

'I was too tired to dance,' said Kira.

'You've been overdoing it these last few days. You ought to relax more. And perhaps someone ought to take a look at that leg of yours. It doesn't seem right that it's still hurting.'

'They said it would take time.'

'But not this long, surely? There's a very good orthopaedic surgeon visiting Bridgetown this week. Would you let me make an appointment for you?'

'If you like,' Kira said wearily, then remembered her manners. 'Yes, thank you, Ben.'

'Off to bed, then, my girl. Take a drink with you – whatever you want.'

She bent and kissed his leathery cheek. It was the first time she had embraced him. 'You're so kind to me,' she said.

Reuben was still at the factory. It was very late. He worked on auto-pilot these days. He could not remember when he had last slept properly. He had a family now; he'd married, had the perfect planter's wife, Elise, and had two very small children, Giles and Lace. He ought to be happy. But Dolly haunted him and their child, Tamara, was a living reminder. He was being eaten away with regret. He struggled in a mesh of grief and guilt. He was trapped by his old love for Dolly.

He climbed the iron steps to his office then up further to the galleries where the furnaces burned day and night.

He went round checking things which had already been checked. A kind of focused stillness made him concentrate. This was his job, his work, his life. Sugar and more sugar . . . producing calories and alcohol. Surely he should be proud of his work?

For a moment he thought someone else was there. He stopped, listening, his feet scraping on the iron walkway. Strange, but he had a feeling he was not alone. But he dismissed it. It could be a bird or an animal.

He peered into a furnace. There was no need, but the glowing red and gold embers below held a kind of deadly fascination. They were like an entrance to hell.

No one knew exactly what happened. But they found what was left of Reuben Earl the next morning. And it wasn't much.

Kira drove into the yard at Reed and Earl on the dot of ten o'clock, overwhelmed by the sickly-sweet smell of the cane and molasses. She parked the moke next to Giles's car. Her skin now had a deep honey-tan which was shown off to perfection by the short-sleeved blue cotton shirt and skirt she was wearing. She had made up her mind. Today she was going to have it out with Giles. She wanted to know why being Benjamin's granddaughter was such a sin.

As she switched off the engine, Giles came out of his office. His face was expressionless, sleeves rolled to the elbows, arms burnt brown by the sun. He hesitated, then came down the steps to meet her.

'Sorry about the party,' he said. 'I hadn't seen Patsie for years. I went to school with her.'

'I'm not your keeper,' she said, not betraying by a flicker of an eyelash the tidal wave of feeling that the sight of him always produced. 'Anyway, old friends are always special.'

'So are new friends,' he said, opening the door of the moke. He took in the sight of her smooth bare legs and smothered a longing to stroke the long length of them. 'Have you brought your report?'

'Yes. It's all here.' She tapped her briefcase.

'Nice case,' he commented.

'Benjamin gave it to me for my birthday.'

'You've had a birthday?' He sounded surprised.

'Yes. Don't most people?'

'I didn't know the date. We should have had a party.'

'You weren't around.'

He made a sharp, exasperated sound and turned on his heel, taking the steps up to his office two at a time. Kira hurried after him, keeping her eyes off his well-washed jeans and long, muscular legs.

'Briefly, then,' she said, trying to sound cool and efficient. 'There aren't going to be any small sugar farmers in five years' time if you don't help them now. They're turning to vegetables and tourism. Huge tracts of sugar land are being lost. And a whole lot of smallholdings are lying fallow because it's cheaper than losing good money trying to cultivate them.'

'You went out to research lorries and transport,' he said grimly, pouring two glasses of lime juice, adding ice.

'I discovered all sorts of things went hand in hand,' said Kira. 'The small farmer can't grow cane for several reasons, and transporting his crop is only one of his problems. The decline stems from cultivation and reaping, monkeys and fires. He can't undertake the cultivation, fertilization, weeding, and then cut and load the cane in a one-man operation. He buys fertilizer and it's impossible for him to check that it finds its way to his fields. Nor can he be certain that all his cane reaches your factory and is registered in his name. The whole system is eroded with faults.'

She had caught his attention. He was listening, his eyes as hard as granite. His glance darted to his near-empty yard. Kira was momentarily diverted. There were no lorries in the yard. That was strange.

'He can't get labour except at the weekends when it's more expensive and he has to pay more. And he still has to cope with fire bugs, pests and droughts in the same way as a big plantation owner.'

'Are you expecting me to solve all their problems?'

'They think you can. Giles Earl is their hero. It's a wonder they don't subscribe to a statue in the centre of Bridgetown.'

'I like the idea of a statue,' he grinned.

'Surely a big factory like Reed and Earl could organize its own transport system, capable of loading all the smallholders' cane at a uniform rate whether they are five miles or fifty from the factory? Couldn't payment be fertilizer in part, which would ensure they get it? When you close the factory or are on short-work, couldn't you lease the men out to the holdings for that time? I can see a dozen ways of helping.'

'Starting to run Reed and Earl, are you, ma'am? Shall I retire? Go smoke fish down on the East Coast?' Giles was too quiet, bordering on the dangerous.

'Oh, you're impossible,' said Kira, her eyes flashing. She pulled out the bulky file and slapped it on to his desk. 'It's all there, read it when you've got the time, when you're not dancing under the stars with your old – friends.' She had almost said 'flames'. 'Here are the keys of the moke. Thank you for lending it to me.'

She swung away, her eyes blurred. She wanted to get out, to distance herself from his insufferable arrogance. She was getting hurt again and this time she had only herself to blame.

He moved swiftly, stopped her from leaving, his bulk filling the doorway. Her anger and contempt flickered in her eyes but she knew he had only to touch her and she would be lost. His fingers caught her arm in an iron grip. His nostrils were thinned with tension. But even though Kira was alarmed, she saw something else in his eyes that was difficult to understand.

'Where the hell do you think you're going?'

'I'm going to the main road to wait for a bus, any bus, into Bridgetown. The same way that I came here in the first place. First impressions can be very wrong, you know. I once thought you were a really nice man. Now I know better.'

He ignored her rambling explanation. 'Don't you listen to the radio? You shouldn't even be here. You should be safely indoors, preferably down in the stone wine cellar under Fitt's House, that is if the sea doesn't come up and swamp it.'

'If the sea doesn't come up? I don't know what you're talking about.'

'And there's no time to talk now,' he said coldly. 'We haven't got long.'

'What do you mean?'

'Hurricane Hannah. She's heading for the island. It was on the news this morning. I've closed down the plant, sent everyone home, and put out the furnaces. They're evacuating the coastal houses.'

Kira was stunned, her thoughts in confusion. 'Are you serious? I thought Hurricane Hannah was due to hit the coast of America, somewhere like Florida. What about your house on the beach, Copens, and your mother? Heavens, I have to find Benjamin. He's alone.'

'Benjamin can look after himself. He was born here. And my mother lives inland, in the north. With a bit of luck it will miss that area. The hurricane has changed direction. They spotted it at the National Weather Centre at Miami. Earlier it brushed the American coast, then sheared away, gathering force at sea. I don't like the sound of it. The meteorological stations are mystified and Trinidad doesn't know what to make of it. The official hurricane warning systems have been put into operation.'

Giles stopped speaking and lifted his head, listening to something that Kira could not hear. She felt a shiver run down her spine. There was something different in the uncanny silence. The sky looked different too, a leaden grey colour that had nothing to do with normal tropical warm rain.

'I don't like it,' said Giles. 'We'd better get out of here. The factory is none too safe on its foundations since the last torrential rain. I've been arguing with Benjamin for years for money for something more substantial than general maintenance and repair work, but he wouldn't listen to me. This factory was built forty years ago and is on its last legs.' He took her arm. 'You have to come with me, Kira. No arguing.'

He marched her down the steps towards his white Mercedes. 'Get in,' he said. He hit the roof button and the soft top slid into place, self-locking.

'I'll get a bus,' she insisted.

'Don't be stupid. The buses will have stopped by now. You don't want to get caught out there in a hurricane. Haven't you read anything about our weather? I thought everyone knew what happened in August 1831. Sheets of fire . . . meteors falling from the sky, the smell of sulphur, tumultuous seas racing through the streets, whole families buried in the ruins. More than fifteen hundred people died.'

'Do they happen very often?' A small, vicious wind tugged at her skirt and she held it down.

'About once every hundred years on average, with minor ones in between, if such a thing can be calculated. There are more stone and brick buildings now. It's the wooden chattel houses that don't stand a chance. And the land slippage.'

Giles threw the big car in gear and roared out of the yard. He drove fast as if racing the coming wind but he had to slow down on reaching the main highway. The road was packed with families moving inland to safer houses. Cars, carts, bicycles, prams laden with precious belongings . . . the happy, good-natured people dazed by the prospect of a hurricane hitting their island.

The sky was already leaden and overcast. Clouds scurried in dark formations, bruised and menacing.

'Where are we going?'

'Somewhere safe. Sugar Hill.'

He swung off the main highway and took a rough dirt track across a low-lying sugar field. A quarrel of frightened monkeys scampered ahead, fleeing the oncoming violence. The cane had been cut and the golden stubble was dry and brittle.

'One strike of lightning and this'll go up like tinder,' Giles said, his hands clenching the wheel. His face was a mask of stone and Kira could not stop the silence from falling. It was his island, his people, his industry that kept so many people in work . . . and it could all be wiped out in a few hours by Hurricane Hannah.

'Why do they give hurricanes women's names?' she asked more of herself than of him.

'Because women always cause trouble,' said Giles.

'Sexist,' Kira responded with spirit, the word jolted out of her mouth as he took another short cut over an even rougher track. 'I could argue that point for several hours. As soon as this is over, I'll take you out on the money you are going to pay me for my splendid piece of research. I shall get very tight on the best Bajan rum and I'll tell you just what I think of men, British and Barbadian.'

Her fiery speech made Giles laugh briefly, a short, harsh sound, but he was momentarily diverted.

'After this is over?' The wind was already buffeting the car, gusts hitting the doors, the fabric roof flapping noisily like a sail.

'I haven't gone through the last few years of struggling just to be wiped out by a bit of a wind,' she said with more courage than she felt. 'I may get wet and blown about but I'll still be here tomorrow.'

His hand came off the steering wheel and closed over her fingers in a firm, warm grasp. Kira looked down at his strong brown hand and could not believe the aching sweetness of the moment. She glanced up at his face.

The mask had slipped. He was looking at her with an expression of devastating warmth. She smiled, not knowing what to make of his change of mood.

'That's my girl,' he said. 'We'll both be here tomorrow, I promise you. I may lose everything, beach house, factory, plantation, but they mean nothing if I don't have you. I won't make the same mistake as my father. He lost Dolly and regretted it every day of his life.'

Kira was lost for words, longing to respond, but still wary. 'But you've been ignoring me for weeks. I don't understand . . .'

'We'll be at Sugar Hill soon. You'll be safe there and the house was built to stand for centuries. We'll have a few moments to talk, then I must check on the horses.'

Kira let his words wash over her. What did he mean, 'we'll have a few moments to talk'? Did he really mean it? That was all she wanted.

He swung the car off the track, his foot hard down as he drove across a sweeping grass lawn, green as an English bowling pitch. Kira caught a glimpse of a white-columned colonial-style house with tall pillars and verandas and windows that went on forever. It was half hidden by great dark trees, branches creaking and swaying in the wind; flowering bushes that were being stripped of their petals in long streamers.

So this was the famous Sugar Hill, the house in the history books. It looked unreal in the eerie light that was suffusing the whole sky. A long roll of thunder echoed, taking the shadows with it, making the light waver. The house was like a sepia photograph, an elegant old mansion still looking as it might have looked a hundred years ago.

Giles stopped the car in front of the wide flight of white stone steps that led to the front door. He leaned over and took her face in her hands. He kissed her lips with a tenderness that melted her heart. Her arms went round his neck, holding him close.

'Go inside and wait for me,' he said.

'You said we were going to talk.'

He listened, moving slowly to catch every sound.

Kira heard it now, a pulsing murmur in the air that made her throat tighten with sudden fear. An awful blackness was racing across the sky. They stared at it, unable to comprehend that Hannah was so near.

'Sorry, I must look to the horses first.'

'But you will come back?'

'Get in the house, please, Kira.'

Giles wrenched open the door and pushed Kira out of the car. She half fell with the strength behind the thrust. Gravel bit into her hands, stinging the skin. She pulled herself up the steps, stumbling towards the house.

The trees were beginning to move with a frantic whispering, yet the air above was suspended in an tense stillness. They could both hear a roar like a distant train.

'Will you get into the house, for God's sake?' Giles exploded. 'Before it hits here and you get hurt.'

'But what about you? Giles, don't stay outside.'

'Don't worry about me. I'll be round the back. And take your file, unless you want it blown away.'

He tossed the bulky file of her research into her arms. She clutched the papers to her chest, feeling the wind flattening her clothes to her body, her hair streaming and whipping round her face.

There was a sudden crack overhead and darts of fire struck the earth. The sky, still that growling blackness, suddenly lit up with a brilliant flash of whiteness.

'Giles!' Kira screamed.

But he did not hear her. He was battling against the wind, struggling towards the stables.

Hurricane Hannah burst on Barbados with a violence beyond anything Kira had ever seen. The wind came with a savage, roaring fury that battered the wooden townships with a hundred-mile-an-hour force, leaving a trail of destruction as she raced inland.

Roofs ripped off buildings, windows shattered, trees and power lines were uprooted and cane flattened as if by a giant foot. The heavy surf pounded and cracked the coastal roads. Storm waves rose, pushing the water ahead, flooding houses and gardens, overturning cars, washing away beaches.

A huge wave smashed into Copens, taking the ceiling-high sun-windows far across the room, shards of glass flying like silver fish through the water. Books floated on the water, flapping and sodden, plants crashing and swirling down into the mud.

Kira was hurled against the steps, jarring her legs, but she managed to pick herself up and stagger towards the house, lifted by the wind itself. She wrestled with the big brass door handle and it burst open. She fell into the empty hall, her papers scattering in all directions on the polished floor.

She threw herself against the door, shutting it against a blast of wind, finding heavy bolts to draw across. Giles would keep his word. He would see to his horses, then he would be back.

She stood shivering in the cool and lofty hall, a curving staircase leading to the next floor. It was barely furnished, a few side tables with big arrangements of flowers, an intricately carved chest, perhaps from one of Sam Lord's wrecks. Nothing else. The hall did not look lived in, only passed through.

There was a horrendous crash as the wind took out the windows and splinters of glass flew everywhere. She flung up her arms to protect her face, using her arms against the lethal spray. The roar of the hurricane diluted the showering of glass. But it did not drown the sound of cries coming from the outside.

Kira ran to the window, hardly able to see through the curtain of rain and branches and maddened leaves. She caught a glimpse of red between the trees, a slight figure running, floundering around in the debris on what looked like white wedgie sandals, arms flaying wildly.

It was Lace. Kira did not think twice. She wrenched open the front door, the force of the wind taking her breath away. She ran down the flight of steps, pushing her way through the wild air, parrying the flying leaves and branches. It was started to rain more heavily and Kira was soaked in moments.

She reached the distraught young woman and put her arm round her waist for support.

'Come on, Lace. You can make it. Sugar Hill isn't far away.'

'I can't. I can't. I'm exhausted . . .' Lace wept.

'Lean on me. We can do it together.'

'No . . . no . . . help me, help me. Don't leave me. I'm going to die.'

'I'm not leaving you. Don't be silly,' Kira shouted against the wind. 'And I'm certainly not going to let you die. No way. You could run better if you took those stupid shoes off.'

Kira bent down and pulled the sodden lumps of leather off the girl's feet. Her skin was marked with weals from the tight straps.

Lace fell against her and Kira half dragged, half pulled her towards the house. Lace seemed to have no idea what she was doing or where she was going, her arm across her face, protecting herself from the flying debris.

The flight of steps were a problem but Lace at last came to her senses, recognizing home and safety, and made an effort to get through the squall. She crawled up the steps, collapsing with relief on to the floor inside the hall.

Kira pulled the heavy door shut again, leaning against it, collecting her thoughts and breathing heavily.

'I'll get some help,' she said.

'I'm sorry,' Lace gasped. 'I've been so rude to you, twice. I didn't like it because Giles seemed so taken with your company. There was something different about you.'

'It doesn't matter,' said Kira.

'You see, no one matters to him but our mother, even though there's nothing we can do for her. He uses her as a kind of excuse not to get involved.'

'His suit of sorrow,' said Kira.

The door at the back must lead to the kitchens. Kira went to find someone to help them, salvaging pages of her report from the wet floor on the way. They did not seem to be important any more. Many of the small farmers would be out of business by tomorrow, their fields flattened.

'I thought I heard someone moving about,' said a woman standing in the doorway. She was middle-aged, her hair streaked with grey. She took one look at Kira and took her into the kitchen.

'Lace is in the hall, hysterical. She's collapsed,' said Kira, still fighting for breath.

'The rest'll do her good,' the woman said drily. 'I'm Dolores, the housekeeper. Mind your hands. You're cut. I'd better fix them. My, you's in some state, girl.'

Kira looked down at her clothes. She was not only wet through, but blood-splashed, and her skirt was streaked with mud. Her hands were oozing blood. She had not felt the pain but now they were beginning to hurt.

'Giles has gone to check on his horses. I let him go,' said Kira woodenly.

'He'll be all right. He knows what he's doing, miss. We're all back in the kitchen. It's the safest part of Sugar Hill. It's made out of them big old stones and cut out of the hill. It would take more than a hurricane to blow Sugar Hill down. Come along, now.'

'What about Lace?'

'Don't you fret. She knows the way.'

Kira followed the woman in a daze, hands throbbing, along a cold, echoing passage to the back of the house. The kitchen was series of vaulted chambers with alcoves for storing wine, hams, bins of flour and sugar. Fluted columns supported the curved stone roofs as they had for countless decades. A clutch of young girls and boys were huddled together, their eyes wide with fear. But they looked at Kira with a degree of interest.

'Jamie, stir yourself now. Make us some coffee. Sarah get me the tweezers and some hot water. Lizzie, I want clean cotton to tear up. Now who's got the best eyesight? Who's going to help me pick out all these bits of glass?'

'I'll help,' said the smallest boy. 'I can see everything.'

'And can you put sugar in my coffee, please?' said Kira, beginning to shake. 'Then stir it for me?'

'Yes, miss,' he grinned, going off to fetch sugar.

Suddenly a heavy squall hit the house, grey sheets of rain, obliterating any outside view with sheer water. The children screamed. Rain poured in through the broken panes on to the polished wood and ran in a flood through the ground floor. They heard a door banging on its hinges and Giles came into the kitchen, rain streaming off his face and clothes.

'Are you all right?' he asked, taking in the situation immediately.

'Just a few cuts,' said Kira, relieved to see him safe. He looked so strong, nothing could touch him. She wanted to ask him so much but she was too tired to say a word.

'I'll do that,' he said, taking the tweezers from one of the smaller girls. 'Get the magnifying glass.' With infinite care and patience he removed the slivers of glass from the palm of her hand. His hair was plastered to his head and drops of rain fell on to her hand, diluting the blood.

Dolores smiled at Kira. She kept the children busy with little errands. Lace sat quietly in a corner, sipping a glass of rum. There was no power in the house but the cane-burning stove produced the coffee and an oil lamp provided the lights for Kira's clean-up. Giles was meticulous, painstakingly picking out each piece of glass and putting it on a wet rag.

None of the cuts were deep but they were sore, and Dolores produced some soothing ointment. Kira realized how lucky she had been. A foot or two nearer the window and any sliver of glass could have made a fatal impact.

'Kira, I want to talk to you,' he said, picking up his coffee mug. 'It won't take long. But we have to get this straightened out.'

Kira shivered, hardly knowing whether it was fear of the hurricane outside or what Giles might be going to tell her. 'Can't it wait?'

'No. It has to be now.'

He led her down a passageway and into another vaulted cellar. It had once been full of wine but the racks were empty.

'I sold it all some years ago,' he explained wearily. 'I needed the money.'

'What's all this about?' Kira asked. 'I'd rather be in the kitchen; this is a gloomy old place. Look, I can understand your annoyance that night in the windmill. I behaved in a way which would upset any man. And I realize that you're not altogether over the moon about Benjamin being my grandfather. But it doesn't make me a different person. I'm the same Kira Reed you met on the plane from St Lucia.'

Giles took no notice of her desperate words. He stood listening to the raging storm outside. 'You know about the feud, don't you?'

'The feud was between Benjamin and Reuben. Your father and my grandfather. We don't come into it at all.'

'Do I have to spell it out to you?' said Giles, rubbing his eyes. He was bone-tired.

'Yes, you do. I'm not interested in guessing games, Giles. I have to have it in black and white.'

'You know what the feud was about?'

'The new sugar factory, I suppose. Or money.'

'That was only part of it. It was all about Dolly. They both loved Dolly, passionately and in their own ways . . . but the crucial thing was that my father, Reuben, slept with Dolly before the wedding. They were so much in love, they couldn't think straight.'

'They slept together? You mean, they made love?'

'Yes, Kira. Dolly and Reuben.'

CHAPTER 15

'They slept together? Are you sure?'

Giles took her hand and gripped the long, slender fingers. 'Dolly and Reuben were childhood sweethearts. They went to school together, grew up together, swam, played on the beach, went to barbecue parties. Falling in love was the most natural thing on earth.'

'I understand,' said Kira. 'I don't blame them. It's the fact that Dolly then married Benjamin that's so strange.'

'It went round the island that she married him for a bathroom but I don't know how true that is. She was probably very confused. They were so different. My father was sensible, down-to-earth and hard-working.'

And madly good-looking, like you, Kira added mentally.

'Whereas Dolly was . . .' He hesitated.

347

'Wild and untamed, I've heard,' said Kira. 'She was quite a handful, I should imagine. Always rushing down to the sea even when she had a small baby to look after.'

'No one knows how it all happened,' said Giles wryly. 'They were all crazy about each other. Reuben was crazy for Dolly. Benjamin was crazy for Dolly. And Dolly . . . well, perhaps she wasn't sure who or what she wanted.'

'I'm sure she loved Reuben,' said Kira quickly. 'And perhaps she was very fond of Benjamin . . . in her own way.'

'My father was in no position to take on a wife. He was barely twenty and had no money of his own. He had a new factory to get on its feet. There were money problems. There are always money problems in sugar.'

'So Dolly married Benjamin, a man of means, a man much older than herself. I suppose she did it to spite Reuben, to show him that someone wanted to marry her even if he didn't.'

'I don't think even she knew why she did it. She was a creature of impulse, they say.'

He paused, turning Kira's hand over, staring at the delta of lines on her palm. He stroked the pale skin lightly.

'So they slept together,' Kira said gently. The storm was still howling outside but it seemed so quiet in the wine cellar. They were in a cocoon, isolated in time and the stillness of focused thought.

Giles nodded. 'It's common knowledge that Dolly and Reuben spent the night together at Sugar Hill, the night before her wedding. They didn't bother to hide it. Everyone knew somehow, except Benjamin, of course. There were servants and village people. You can't keep secrets on an island this size.'

A coldness came over Kira like a shroud. Suddenly she knew what he was going to say. It was about Dolly, Tamara . . . and herself.

'So Dolly might have been pregnant on her wedding day, but only just,' said Kira, her throat tightening. 'And Tamara's father might have been Reuben, not Benjamin. So where does that leave me?' Kira added with a choked sob. 'Oh, Giles, what does it all mean?'

Giles took her soberly in his arms. It was a gesture of comfort, nothing else. She lay momentarily against his chest, listening to the storm that was almost obliterated by the pounding of her heart.

Then it changed and he was kissing her, tasting her lips, stroking her hair. She was being crushed in his arms, so close that her breath came in ragged gasps. Giles, wet and dirty, bloodied but in one piece, was kissing every inch of her face with a devastating hunger that sent her heart soaring. It was a burning sweetness that held her totally captive.

His strong face was lit by a flickering light from the oil lamp and she touched the firm outline of his jaw in a great wave of tenderness. She loved him. She did not want to lose him, whatever he had to say.

'You see, I shouldn't be doing this. Don't you realize? Oh, Kira, why did you have to be who you are? Reuben did marry eventually, a planter's daughter called Elise, and I am their son. Reuben was my father and everyone believes that he also fathered Tamara. Your mother was my half-sister.'

'Your sister?' Kira almost choked on the words.

'It's a forbidden relationship. I cannot marry my blood-line niece. Leviticus, Chapter 20. "Thou shalt not uncover the nakedness of your mother's sister, nor of your father's sister: for he uncovereth his near kin." Change the sexes, he for she. Thou shalt not uncover the nakedness of your mother's brother . . . me. I am your mother's brother.'

'I don't believe it! I don't! I don't!' Kira clamped her hands over her ears to shut out the awesome commandments and the crescendo of storm noise making the windows rattle and the glass stream with water. 'It can't be true. Someone has got it all wrong. It's just a rumour, after all. No one has proved anything. Forbidden . . . it can't be when I love you so much.'

She wept in his arms and Giles, distraught with his own anguish, did not know what to say. He knew that the island's strong religious roots would not tolerate their union. And there seemed no way he could leave Sugar Hill or the island which had always been his home, the factory and the workers who depended on him. Give up everything for love of a woman, for Kira? And there was his mother, slowly becoming paralysed. He did not know if he could do it.

'Then I understand now why Benjamin refused to help my mother when she was in trouble,' Kira went on, more sadly. 'It was years of bitterness surfacing. He was prepared to look after her when she was a child, for

Dolly's sake, but he washed his hands of Tamara when she was grown up. She had left Barbados and married a Russian dancer, almost on impulse . . . it probably seemed like Dolly hurting him all over again.'

'And you look so like Dolly. Those paintings by Le Plante – they could be you,' said Giles. 'That's why you seemed so familiar.'

'I look like Dolly?'

'The face, the smile, those dimples by your mouth. I think Ben's always been angry and hurt and humiliated, even after Reuben's death. All that gossip about the accident must have hurt him. But there was nothing to substantiate the rumours. There was never any enquiry. It was recorded as accidental death. Everyone knew that Reuben was dead tired, overworked, depressed. He just fell, a momentary lapse that cost him his life.'

'Are you going to tell me what happened?' Kira went even colder. What else had happened? Reuben's death? No one had ever mentioned it.

'Some people think Ben pushed him but I don't even want to think about it. We'll get you back to the kitchen and the cheerful company of Dolores and her brood. My coffee is cold.'

'So is mine,' said Kira, standing up unsteadily. 'But I won't stay, Giles. I think my grandfather needs me, even more now. Fitt's House is very exposed and so near the sea. He'll be getting the worst of the hurricane. I'll call for a taxi, if you don't mind.'

'For heaven's sake, women, don't be a fool. The telephone lines will be down by now. And no taxi driver in his right mind would come out in this even if you could get through. You're not going anywhere.'

'But I am, Giles. I must. He's an old man. I can't let him be alone in this hurricane. He might even die. He's my grandfather and the only family I have.'

She ran out of the room, along the corridor, now awash with water and debris, towards the front door.

'Stop, Kira. Don't go out. It's madness,' he shouted. 'Benjamin's a tough old man. He'll cope.'

'But I must,' she called back. She pulled open the heavy front door and was nearly swept off her feet by the force of the storm. She saw a gust half lift the Mercedes off its wheels and crash it down on the drive, doors swinging open wildly. Debris was being tossed across the drive, palm leaves, branches, broken fencing. A whirlwind of sand enveloped the house.

Kira drew back, tears stinging her eyes, coughing, her mind blank with misery. She could not go out in this. She would not last minutes on her feet.

Hurricane Hannah was in full force. She lashed the island with primitive fury; gusts of over a hundred miles an hour ravaged the southern half. A great storm-wall of seawater raced through the coastal districts. Flashes of jagged lightning lit up the dark, threatening clouds, splitting the sky apart.

Kira crouched against the wall, mesmerized by the scene of destruction, unable to move, unable to think clearly. Somehow she had to get to Benjamin, to tell him that she understood, to tell him that she forgave him.

Giles brushed past her. 'I'll get Benjamin,' he said brusquely. 'Don't worry. You stay here.'

'I'm coming with you,' she said, ducking her head against the wind, holding on to his belt. He turned and said something angrily, but the words were flung away. He tried to shake her off but it was no use. She had found a surge of strength that made her cling on to him. She could do it. Together they could do anything. 'I'm not leaving you.'

She climbed into the car, wrestling with the door to close it. Giles got in, switched on the ignition and the finely tuned engine responded with a low throb. He thrust the car into gear and planted his foot on the accelerator. The engine strained.

'I don't know if the car will make it,' he said grimly. 'But she's big, heavy and powerful. Just so long as a tree doesn't come down on us.'

A root was hurled across the low bonnet, narrowly missing the windscreen. Kira ducked automatically.

'Want to go back? You could sit in the kitchen drinking my best rum.'

'No, I don't want to go back,' said Kira, trying to keep the fear out of her low voice. 'I want to be with you. Don't you realize that? There's no one in the world for me but you. And I don't care who you are.'

She was not sure if Giles heard her. Now that they were out in the hurricane, the noise was deafening. Rain streamed down the windscreen, the wipers unable to cope with the torrent. Giles was driving on instinct, picking his way with caution, knowing that any rash move might land them in a ditch.

'The electronic window button has jammed,' said Giles, more calmly than he felt. 'Can you wind it down manually, and put your head out? Tell me if you can see anything ahead.'

Kira did as she was told. It was like putting her head under a shower. At first she could not see anything and her eyelids were soon glued together with water. But by half shading her eyes, her vision cleared just enough to guide him.

'There's a tree down, about twenty yards ahead, on the left. Some of it is across the road. A bit more to the right . . . steady now, that's it. We're past. Heavens, there's a bicycle coming towards us, on its side . . .'

It was a nightmare drive. They were both drenched with sweat and rain. They were nearing the back lane to Fitt's House when a ferocious gust caught the side of the Mercedes and slewed it across the road and into a stone wall. The bodywork crunched and groaned. The engine whined, protesting, whimpered, then cut out.

'I think she's had it,' said Giles, sitting quite still, clutching the steering wheel. 'Are you all right?'

'I'm OK. Oh Giles, I'm so sorry. Your beautiful car . . .'

'It's only a car,' he said. 'Come on, get out. We can walk from here. Hang on to me and don't let go. What do you weigh? Practically nothing, so you won't be any help as ballast.'

'I'll drag a rock around if you insist,' said Kira, but the words were snatched away.

She closed her eyes and hung on to Giles, letting him take the brunt of the force with his body. They were so near. Surely they could make the last few yards?

The sea was sweeping up the lane, wave-lashed, swirling round their ankles, cold and unpleasant. Palm trees were bent almost double under the savagery of the wind. A striped beach umbrella skittered past like a frantic ballet dancer who had forgotten the routine.

'Nearly there!' Giles shouted.

Kira hardly recognized what was left of the garden and the drive. Giles was helping her climb, one by one, up the front steps, shielding her with his shoulders and arms, clearing a path with his foot.

A man had come to the doorway, holding on to the shattered door, a look of astonishment on

357

his lined face, grizzled hair awry, shoulders weary and hunched.

'Grandfather,' Kira cried out. She was across the last remaining space in moments. She threw her arms round the old man, hugging him with warmth and affection. He couldn't believe what was happening. He almost slumped against her, letting her strong arms hold him.

'Grandfather, Grandfather,' she choked, her hair blowing over her face. 'You're all right? I thought your sugary pink castle would have fallen down with all this dreadful wind and rain. But you're here and Fitt's House is still here . . . I was so worried.'

She could not say any more. Her pulse was beating so fast. She knew Giles was right behind her, probably surprised by her outburst. She did not know whether to laugh or cry.

'There, there, child,' said Benjamin roughly, awkwardly, getting wet. 'Of course I'm all right. So you know, do you? You know that I'm your grandfather? The wicked old man of your childhood, who made your young life so difficult, who could have helped you but didn't because he was plain cussed.'

'And do you know who I am? How long have you known? I'm Tamara's daughter.'

'I've always known,' he said. 'I've known for a long time. But come inside quickly, my dear. The porch, or what's left of it, is no place for a family reunion. You too, Giles. We can't stand out here; we'll be blown away. It's time we sorted all this out.'

He led them to the back of the house, the safest part. The kitchen was solidly built and it was obvious that Benjamin had been sheltering there. A bottle of rum and a copy of *The Advocate* were on the floor beside his rocking chair. The newspaper's pages flew across the room in a gust from the open front door. Giles went back and closed it, pushing a heavy piece of furniture against the splintered wood.

The intense tropical storm was ravaging a path of destruction across the densely populated area of the southern coast, driving inland to violate Sugar Hill plantation, then taking an erratic turn to head out to sea again. They learned later that the path was ten miles wide. The hundred-mile-an-hour wind lost some of its speed overland as it could no longer gather energy from the warm sea's abundant circulation.

Giles put his arm round Kira's shoulder, hips touching her lightly. Kira melted at the touch, relaxing against him.

'Perhaps I should leave you two alone,' Giles said, touched by the obvious affection. 'You have a lot of catching up to do.'

'You can't go out, Giles. It's too dangerous,' said Kira quickly.

'Look who's talking?' Giles teased. 'Who insisted on rushing out in the middle of the hurricane to find her grandfather?'

'Did she, now? I don't deserve it,' said Benjamin. He searched among the shattered contents of a china cupboard for two unbroken glasses. 'They don't match and they're the wrong size . . . but they'll hold a drop of rum to warm you up.'

'We don't match and we're the wrong size,' said Kira, taking the glasses from his shaking hands. 'But we're going to get along very well together. Just you wait and see, Benjamin. Everything is going to be fine from now. So tell me, how did you know it was me?'

'I got a letter from a hospital in London, from a Dr Armstrong, who seemed very concerned, telling me that Kira Reed was coming out to visit Barbados after a road accident, and that she had a grandfather on the island. But he said that you had some problems and were denying my existence.'

'But how did he do that? He didn't know you,' said Kira astounded. 'How did the letter reach you?'

'It was simply addressed to Mr Reed, Barbados. So of course, it came to me first and I knew it was about you. And I didn't blame you for not wanting to know me. When I saw you, over the wall, I knew you were my granddaughter. My dear, there's so much of Dolly and Tamara in you, in the shape of your face, your eyes, your dimpled smile. Tamara was the sweetest little girl and I loved her dearly.'

'But you didn't help her when she needed you,' said Kira, rounding on him, eyes darkened. 'She was desperate. That wasn't fair.'

'I know. I know,' said Benjamin. 'Hate me. It has been on my conscience for years. I was furious that she left me . . . for a male Russian dancer, of all people! I felt humiliated, unwanted, abandoned . . . all over again. All she wanted was my money, it seemed. I'm sorry, Kira. I should have sent money. I didn't realize things were so bad. I turned my back on both of you. I can never forgive myself.'

'But I forgive you, Grandfather,' said Kira, putting her arms around him. 'We can't go on living like this. It doesn't make any sense.

We've a lot of making up to do. I'll never leave you.'

'Not even for this man of substance? My rival in the sugar stakes?' Benjamin looked across to Giles who was leaning on a wall, his hands deep in his pockets.

'No, not even for him. Giles and I are just . . . good friends,' said Kira, somehow trying to make the words sound convincing.

'Very good friends,' said Giles drily.

'He smashed up his car, getting me here,' said Kira. 'It went into a wall.'

'The Mercedes is a write-off,' Giles broke in. 'Ripped tyres, smashed windscreen, crushed bonnet.'

'Thank you for that,' said the old man with dignity. 'But you can afford a new car.'

'Several,' said Giles.

Kira cleared a corner of the kitchen table and sat on it like a teenager. She was suddenly shy of the man who was her grandfather. He spread his hands in a gesture of conciliation. The windows were rattling, the shutters banging wildly.

'Where do we begin, my dear?' said Benjamin. 'I suppose you want to shoot me down for the way I treated your mother? I guess I deserve it.'

Kira took a deep breath. She had rehearsed this moment for years, being able to tell her grandfather exactly what she thought of him, to detail his callous treatment of her mother, to bring home to him the bitter feelings of her childhood.

Benjamin sat waiting for the onslaught, his faded eyes patient and resigned. 'Go on, my dear. I can take it. Right on the chin. Here.'

'I can't,' she whispered. 'It's all disappeared, Benjamin. I don't feel that way any more. The hatred has completely gone and I don't know why.'

Benjamin took a slow sip of his rum and then reached to take hold of her hand. 'You belong to a very old Barbadian family, Kira. The Reeds were among the early English settlers growing tobacco and cotton and then they discovered that sugar was more profitable. The Reed cane fields stretched for miles. We built sugar mills for grinding the cane. We built Fitt's Village for our workers. The genes are very strong, my dear.'

He sighed deeply. Kira waited for him to go on. She was very aware of Giles, watching and waiting.

'When Dolly died in 1955, I had no time or inclination to remarry. Tamara was my joy.

Everything revolved around her. I thought she would inherit everything . . . plantation, house, my share of the plant. Then she met this dancer, a Russian, who knew nothing of sugar.' Benjamin's voice thickened. 'She gave up everything for this man, never a thought for me. They travelled like gypsies over Europe. Tamara wrote when you were born, Kira. Then the letters stopped for years. I didn't even know that Aaronovitch had died.'

'She was too distraught. She fell apart.'

'I understand now.'

'They were so happy,' said Kira. 'They were only together a short time but it was perfect. My mother often told me about those years of happiness and her face would light up and glow.'

'Like Dolly. Her face would glow.' He ran his hands through his grizzled hair, making it stand on end. 'Perhaps she was happy with me, some of the time. My dear, I'm so tired. I can't talk any more but I'm so glad you are here. Your home is always here. Some of Tamara's later letters I didn't even open. I'm so sorry . . . I've been a terrible fool.'

Kira stood, hugging him, hugging away the years of misunderstanding. She could not hate him. He had suffered too much.

'And will you stay with me?' he asked, hesitating. 'Live here at Fitt's House, like a proper family?'

'I will.'

'Thank you, my dear.' Benjamin shook his head. 'I don't deserve this. I don't deserve your kindness.'

He found an old stretched out-of-shape sweatshirt from somewhere that fitted Giles, but at least it was dry. Giles pulled on a waterproof sailing jacket that was hanging behind a door.

'You're not going out again?' said Kira, aghast.

'I've some pensioners living down the road. They used to work for me. I'm going out to check on them,' he said, trying to fasten the jacket but the edges wouldn't meet. 'The storm is playing out. It's moving eastwards. We've had the worst.'

'But what about us?' Kira protested, catching him up at the doorway.

He took hold of both her arms and held her at a distance. He was searching her face as if looking for a likeness to Reuben.

'I've told you, Kira. There is no "us", nor will there ever be. We have to learn to live without each other.'

'But what's going to happen?' she wept.

'You will get over this and in a year or two you'll meet someone new and fall in love all over again. And all this will seem like some strange Caribbean dream, a little bit of magic. It won't be so simple for me. I shan't find anyone else and I won't be looking. You're all I have ever wanted and there isn't another woman in the world like you.'

'Don't say that! I don't want to find someone new. I only want you,' Kira cried.

'Then you will end up being alone, an old maid.'

As Giles spoke, Kira had the strangest feeling. She heard the words . . . 'old maid, old maid . . .' echoing in the wind, only spoken by a woman, a woman of long ago.

'Can't we be friends, really good friends?' she said brokenly.

'I don't know if I could stand it, seeing you, but not having you.'

He bent and kissed her fiercely, his lips hard and demanding. The wind howled in her ears and it was if all the devils in Barbadian folklore had been let loose to cause mischief.

'Goodbye, my darling. Never forget that I love you.'

Then he was gone and Kira stood stunned and desolate as the storm swallowed him. Her life was being torn apart again, the tender roots wrenched from the soil and thrown into the air.

They could rebuild the chattel houses, but could she rebuild her life?

CHAPTER 16

The island was devastated after Hurricane
Hannah. Copens was flooded by the high
seas. The Reed and Earl sugar plant lost its
roof and thousands of dollars of stored cane
were damaged. Sugar Hill survived the onslaught, apart from a few broken windows,
but the grounds were flattened, trees uprooted
and tossed about like sticks. André Le Plante's
house was too dilapidated to withstand the
storm and many of his paintings were ruined.

Kira made herself useful around Fitt's House,
tidying up, unable to work until the roads were
cleared. She managed to check that Jessy and
Dolores were all right. Jessy said that Moonshine
was back on the beaches, though many of the
tourists had gone home on the first planes available.

It gave Kira time to think. If Giles was right
and Tamara was indeed Reuben's daughter,

then that could be the strongest reason why Benjamin had refused to help. He had been prepared to bring Tamara up as a child, accepted her as his daughter, but the island gossip must have been humiliating. At some point he would have decided enough was enough.

She could not speak to Benjamin about it, afraid of broaching the subject, of causing more hurt. He wanted her as a granddaughter and that was what she wanted too. But why? Perhaps it was simply because she reminded him of Dolly and he wanted a living reminder.

'We shall have to live on breadfruit,' said Benjamin, collecting the fallen fruit.

'Wonderful as it is, breadfruit doesn't make a drink. I'd like some tea and coffee and fresh milk.'

'We got plenty of limes.'

Kira walked into Bridgetown to shop for food. It was not that they were short of food, but a lot of the supplies in the kitchen had been spoilt, burst open or broken. Some of the shops might be open.

She was appalled by the damage she saw on the way, particularly the rows of wooden chattel houses. Carpenters were already at work, repairing doors, windows, replacing roofs.

A leggy girl bumped into her round a corner, not looking where she was going. She was swinging an empty bag and was clearly at a loose end. It was Lace, in shorts and a sleeveless T-shirt.

'Don't bother going around,' she said. 'Half the shops in Bridgetown are closed for repairs. My car was wrecked in the storm, total write-off, and there are no parties to speak of. It's hopeless.'

They were in Trafalgar Square, near the bronze statue of Nelson. It had survived the storm. Lace's mouth was turned down, her clothes unpressed as the electricity to Sugar Hill was still cut off. It looked as if she hadn't bothered to wash or comb her hair either.

'Giles has found someone else,' she told Kira, a glimmer of amusement coming into her eyes. 'Remember Patsie? They've been going out quite a lot recently. She's one of the international set, so clever and smart, bags of money.'

'How nice,' said Kira. 'You know, Lace, I always enjoy meeting you. You're such good company. But I wonder why you set out to upset me every time. Is it a form of infantile insecurity, do you think? Some personality flaw?'

371

Lace looked taken aback. 'I don't know what you mean! I like to keep up to date with the news, who's going out with who. And what my brother does is always of supreme interest. There's nothing else to do on this damned island.'

Kira felt sorry for the girl. 'It seems that you really need something to do, some occupation that you would enjoy. Isn't there anything you like doing? Couldn't Giles give you a job? If everything he does is of such supreme interest . . .'

'Heavens, no. Work with my brother? Perish the thought. He does nothing but tell me off.'

'With reason. Hasn't it ever occurred to you that your flighty ways and irresponsible chatter might irritate him? He works very hard and perhaps you take it all for granted, do nothing but spend his money. Do you ever go and visit your mother?'

'I hate illness.'

'That says a lot about you.'

Lace flashed her eyes with contempt. 'Oh, dear, you are upset, aren't you? Has big brother really got under your skin? Better forget him, Kira. He's lost interest in you. Your time, brief as it was, is over.'

Kira nearly called her 'auntie' but she swallowed the word. The taunt would have been wasted.

'You need a job. You're frittering your life away. You'll be screwed up, your mind atrophied and old before your time, Lace. Find something to do. You like clothes, don't you? Open a boutique. Sell dresses, design dresses, anything . . . there are lots of good dressmakers around who would make up your designs.'

'I don't need your advice,' said Lace, flouncing off. 'I have no intention of wasting my time working.'

'Why don't you open a second-hand dress agency, then you could get rid of all your old clothes?' Kira suggested lightly. Lace pretended not to hear. 'After all, some of them must be out of date. You could call it Lace Work.'

Kira watched her go, tottering on unsuitably strappy shoes despite the pot-holes in the pavement, and wondered who could help her. Perhaps she would fall in love and make a happy marriage. But Lace did not seem the homemaking type. She would probably flit from affair to affair.

The roads were not cleared for public transport so it meant walking back as well, or else cadging a lift from Land Rovers that were managing to make a few trips. Kira had been lucky to get a part-way lift coming into town. Now a crowded Land Rover was going as far as André Le Plante's house.

'Done make a real mess of that old place,' said the driver, welcoming her aboard the crowded vehicle. She sat tightly on a bench seat next to buxom housewives also out looking for food.

Kira was sad to see the damage that the hurricane had inflicted on the old house. It looked shrouded in sorrow, windows shattered, veranda torn apart, doors off their hinges, several walls down. It would need a lot of repairing.

No one seemed to notice her as she wandered around. The carefully preserved artefacts from the artist's life were strewn over the ground, caught in trees, hanging from branches. She started to retrieve them, putting them in baskets. Kira found a pair of brocade evening shoes in the debris and wondered who they had belonged to. She had a feeling that Dolly had rarely worn shoes.

'Who do these shoes belong to?' Kira asked one of the women custodians, who did not seem to know where to start with clearing up.

'I dunno, miss. I ain't ever seen them before. Perhaps his daughter wore them but they look mighty old.'

'Would you like me to help you? I know a little about the family,' said Kira. Dolly was certainly her grandmother, even if she did not know who was her grandfather.

'Why, sure, mizz. That would be really nice of you. I don't know what to do. I shall have to be talking to the authorities of the museum. Such a terrible storm. You're Mizz Reed, ain't you, staying along at Fitt's House?'

'Dolly was my grandmother,' said Kira.

'You don't say? Well, I never. Then you're right welcome here. Your grandmother, you say? I can make some coffee for us. I've brought a little oil stove with me.'

Kira walked back after helping with some of the clearing up at André Le Plante's house. She promised to return another day, to sort out the baskets of items they'd found. His paintings were lined around to dry out, but some were ruined beyond renovation. She could not find the one of Dolly running across the sand, the first painting she had seen all those weeks ago.

Kira thought of Lace's latest gossip. Giles had every right to go out with whom he pleased. And if he had known Patsie since schooldays, what could be more natural?

She tried not to think of him, kept herself busy. Gradually the island went back to normal. Electricity and telephones were reconnected. Food began to appear in the shops. The airport reopened.

Giles phoned once, a short, sharp conversation just to see if she was all right.

'We're fine,' she said, her voice strangled. She waited for a personal word that did not come.

'That's all right, then,' he said, ringing off.

Jessy found Kira working in the garden, sweeping up branches into a huge pile with a broom. Jessy had brought out coffee and home-made biscuits, aware that Kira had not stopped for breakfast.

'Just like your grandmother, you are,' said Jessy, putting the tray down on a cleared step. 'Never had no time to eat. She thought food wasn't important. Thought she could exist on air.'

'I don't want Benjamin slipping on this lot,' said Kira, clearing the rest of the steps. 'He's so anxious to find out the extent of the damage to the plant. And only some of the phones are back.'

'I guess it's taking time to repair the lines, counting their losses. And the cane's flattened. It's all right for the big planters who are insured, but the small farmer can't afford no insurance.'

'Giles will help, if he can,' said Kira. 'He won't let the small farmers go under.'

'Sure, Mr Giles will help, but he don't have a bottomless purse. I hear his beach house, Copens, took it pretty bad, real smashed up. You're real taken up with Mr Giles, ain't you? I see'd it on your face.'

'Yes, I'm real taken up with Mr Giles,' said Kira, making light of it. 'But Lace says he's going out with Patsie now.'

'Don't you take no notice of that silly girl. She done make up half of what she says. Ain't you sure about Mr Giles, then? He's the finest man on the island. No one been able to snap him up till you come along. The girls all tried, of course, but he had so much on his hands, especially his mother getting ill after Reuben died. Dolores looked after her for years, but it got too much for her in the end.'

'How did Reuben die?'

'Oh, it were terrible, mizz. The island went into shock. Such a dreadful end for a great man. No one knows how it happened. Most folk think it was an accident, that he was dead tired and fell, but there's others, less kindly, who think he was pushed.'

'How appalling. What do you think really happened? Did someone hate Reuben so much that they would want to kill him?' Kira thought she knew the answer. Benjamin hated Rueben, but she could not believe that her grandfather would take such an awful revenge.

'Well, maybe, but I knows it wasn't Mr Benjamin because he was here, nursing a sprained ankle and in a mighty bad temper with it. And he was too much a gentleman, even if he was raw jealous of Mr Reuben and Dolly. He'd fallen over some left-out tool in the yard and there was no way he could have climbed the steps up to the furnaces. He was hobbling about on a stick for days.'

'Does Mr Giles know this?' Kira asked quietly.

'I don't rightly know. He was only a small boy when it happened and Lace just a toddler. You know, you and Mr Giles would make an ideal couple, right for each other, both so clever and hard-working, looking out for sugar and the island.'

'Mr Giles doesn't think so,' said Kira, turning away so that Jessy could not see her face. She did not want to talk about Giles any more. It was over and nothing could be done about it. As Lace had said, she had had her time.

Kira tried to light a bonfire but the wood was still too wet to burn. Steam was rising off the sodden land as an apologetic sun rose in the sky. The breadfruit tree was badly damaged, despite Benjamin's pruning, but its roots were secure and it would survive. Benjamin said he was going to put a plaque on the tree, commemorating their meeting, and ordering that the tree should never be cut down. She smiled at the thought.

'Is it all that old rumour and gossip that's stopping you and Mr Giles from getting together?' said Jessy, collecting the empty mug and tray. She went indoors to fetch more matches. 'That stuff won't burn yet, you know.'

'I know,' said Kira, suddenly tired of the effort.

'The island won't let that old gossip go, yet it's so far back in time. Then especially when Reuben done get himself killed. As if he couldn't stand living any longer without his Dolly.'

Kira felt a headache coming on. She was more tired than she knew, and tired of loving people who didn't love her back. The trauma of the hurricane had taken its toll, then all the physical work since. She wanted Jessy to go on talking, yet she also wanted her to go away. 'You mean he may have killed himself? You know about Reuben and Dolly, then . . .?'

'Lordie, yes, mizz. Everybody knew. It was no secret. Those two thought nobody knew, but the whole island knew of them meeting on the beach. Secret? It weren't no secret, lordie, no!' Jessy went into a peal of laughter that denied the tragedy of the romance.

Kira was afraid of what Jessy might be going to say. Her heart suddenly lost its rhythm.

'They were mad for each other and it showed. Especially Miss Dolly. She were just reckless in love. Nothing could stop her, yet she done go marry Mr Benjamin all the same, daft thing.'

'They say that before her wedding, she and Reuben . . .' Kira began cautiously, not sure how much Jessy would divulge. 'That she and Reuben spent the night together . . .'

'Sure, they spent the night together at Sugar Hill. Nobody know what went on, but it don't take too much guessing. They sure weren't playing dominoes or drinking cocoa.'

'If that's so, then Tamara, my mother, could have been Reuben's child. That's the crunch,

Jessy. She might not have known it but she could have been pregnant when she went to her wedding.'

There, Kira had said it aloud. It was out in the open, black and white. Tamara could have been Reuben's child.

'Rightly so, she could have been,' said Jessy, a disapproving tone entering her voice for the first time. 'But she wasn't. I dressed Miss Dolly for her wedding in that old ramshackle house of her father's. I went up because she had no mother or bridesmaid to help her. When I got there, she was mortal upset.'

'What do you mean?'

'There was blood running down her legs and she thought she was dying. She didn't have no regular times of the month for her flow and she didn't know what it meant. No mother to tell her and a father with his head in a paint pot. So I told her and fixed her up and she was terrified it was going to show through her wedding dress and everyone would see. She was so ashamed but I told her it was natural and nothing to be ashamed of. No, Dolly weren't pregnant on her wedding day. Just inconvenienced.'

Kira knew Jessy was telling the truth and the relief was overwhelming. She felt suddenly carefree and amazingly happy. She could hardly wait to find Giles and tell him the truth, to throw herself into his arms and make him love her again. But she did not know where he was or if his love for her had survived. He had gone away, that day of Hurricane Hannah, and she had not seen him since; she was not sure of anything.

'Poor Dolly,' said Kira. 'What a dreadful thing to happen on your wedding day – but not the end of the world if the man really loves you.'

'And Mr Benjamin loved her badly, so you see, he's your true granddaddy. Tamara was his baby girl.'

'But he was never sure?'

'No, how could he be? Because Dolly never told him or let him anywhere near her bed for days. Like she said, she was ashamed.'

'Couldn't you ever tell him what you've just told me?' Kira asked. 'It might have helped.'

'Lordie, no, I wouldn't talk to a gentleman about such intimate feminine things.' Jessy was shocked at the idea. 'It's women's talk. 'Sides, it wouldn't be nice, Mr Benjamin being my employer and all.'

Kira sighed. If only Jessy had overcome her scruples all those years ago. But she wasn't to know that the knowledge would have made such a difference to so many people's lives. Tamara would not have died, thousands of miles away, in poverty; Benjamin and Reuben might have been able to work together more amicably; Kira would have had a family when she'd most needed one.

But Kira did not blame Jessy. It was her upbringing, her sense of her place, of what was right and wrong to talk about. Nothing could change the past but Kira could now change the future.

Kira wiped her hands hastily on her old jeans. 'I've suddenly remembered something else I must do,' she said, hurrying away. 'Thank you for the coffee.'

She did not stop to tidy herself but hurried down the lane and towards the beach. It was unrecognizable, strewn with flotsam and jetsam torn from the ocean's depths in the storm. The beach had completely changed in appearance, even if this morning the sea was as peaceful as if Hannah had never happened.

She would have no scruples about telling Giles. It was too important. She was sure now about their rightness for each other. She loved him. A seed was growing out of the darkness and it would blossom in the sun.

Giles was at Copens. She knew he would be there. Something had told her, drawn her to his villa like a magnet, not aware of the pull. She hesitated in what had once been a lovely garden, wondering how he would greet her.

But she need not have worried. He flung his arms round her and held her tightly. Not kissing her, holding himself away from her mouth, but the closeness telling her everything she wanted to know. The moment was golden and still. They clung like survivors after a disaster.

'Darling, darling . . . are you all right? That stupid phone call, I'm sorry.' He had not shaved for days and a dark stubble covered his jaw. His clothes were old and crumpled but he still looked every inch the man she adored. He was so strong and the intensity in his eyes made her bones weaken.

'I'm fine. I've been clearing up. Fitt's House and Dolly's old home, the painter's museum.'

'So I've heard. News still travels fast. And now you've come to help me. Here's a broom.'

He was sweeping out the sand and the glass from the rooms. The sea had done a lot of damage, furniture sodden and chairs broken. But a sturdy cane fire was flickering and burning in the open fireplace to dry out the rooms.

'I've never used that grate before.' Giles grinned. 'It was put in purely for decoration.'

'A fire in Barbados,' said Kira. 'Whatever next? You'll be filling hot water bottles for the bed.'

'Talking about beds,' he said huskily, 'it's a little damp but still intact. Would you care to try it for size?' His voice hovered on uncertainty.

'It doesn't have to be just for size,' said Kira, now not knowing how she was going to tell him. 'I've been talking to Jessy.'

'And can that lady talk!'

'But not always the right things or to the right person. I have to tell you something about your father's death, which only Jessy knew. However Reuben died, it was nothing to do with Benjamin. He's innocent of any criminal intention.'

'I never thought . . . it was all rumour. All those tongues wagging. But no one ever knew the truth.'

'Forget it, my darling. The truth is in the past and not for us, for you and me, to carry as a burden. And also, for us, the truth about Dolly's wedding . . . about why Tamara was Benjamin's true daughter, with no doubt about it. Physical proof. No doubt at all.' She was getting incoherent.

She heard his sharp intake of breath. Giles put his arms around her and she lay with her face against his chest, not moving. 'Do you mean that? There's no doubt about it?'

'Absolutely, one hundred per cent. We are not related in any way at all, except by the bonds of their love. Truly, Dolly loved Reuben and they made love that night, but she didn't give him a child. Never, ever. On the morning of her wedding, she began a period and Jessy found her, crying, not knowing what it meant. She knew nothing, poor girl.'

'Those sad lovers,' said Giles lifting her up in his arms and carrying her through to the bedroom. There was another fire burning in the grate, a gaping hole in one wall, and through it she could see and hear the murmuring sea. 'Their happiness was so short-lived. Ours will be different, Kira darling. Ours will go on forever.'

His lips touched her soft skin and she felt her senses being aroused. Her hands betrayed the passion which had been dormant for so long. She felt the warmth of his body through the material of his shirt, breathing in the musky scent of his skin.

He drew her so gently to him, his arm supporting her, slow and silent. She seemed to be carried along in some delicious and heady emotion, his kisses touching her cheek, his warm breath on her face.

'I love you, my darling. Yes, I love you.' His voice wrapped her in lightness and she ached for more.

She moved closer to him, asking him without words to take off her clothes. He drew the T-shirt over her head and unfastened her bra. With a small cry, she let his mouth touch her breasts, the surging so soft like a wild bird fluttering. She drew him nearer, moving together, loving him, amazed at their perfect harmony. She let him take what he wanted, bear over her, hard and fierce.

But he was still careful, so tender, caressing her bare flesh, mindful of her tiny cuts and bruises. Her breath caught on a sob as his thumb brushed her nipples, and there was no mistaking their growing, frenzied desire. His fingers went to the soft moistness between her thighs.

Kira could not deny this love. It came to her with a clarity that was electrifying. What was happening to her? This maddening, transcendent desire was beyond any coherent thought and she did not care. Touching and caressing, they were together. He was her destiny. Together they had won the right to love each other.

She could hear the sea washing the whiteness of the beach, see shafts of sunlight lanced across the ceiling. This was her island and she would never leave it.

She came to him with an eagerness as strong as his own. She glowed with her overpowering love for him and had a vision of a love that would last forever. It would take them together anywhere, like untouched souls. It would be a paradise indeed.

Hurricane Hannah veered towards the sea, as capricious as ever. Her power was waning and she needed to feed on the energy from the temperature of the underlying ocean. The island had survived her battering. Hannah took her savage winds into the vast Atlantic, eventually to blow herself into oblivion and be lost among the wind pattern of the upper hemisphere.

THE EXCITING NEW NAME
IN WOMEN'S FICTION!

PLEASE HELP ME TO HELP YOU!

Dear *Scarlet* Reader,

As Editor of *Scarlet* Books I want to make sure that the
books I offer you every month are up to the high standards
Scarlet readers expect. And to do that I need to know a
little more about you and your reading likes and dislikes. So
please spare a few minutes to fill in the short questionnaire
on the following pages and send it to me.

Looking forward to hearing from you,

Sally Cooper

Editor-in-Chief, *Scarlet*

QUESTIONNAIRE

Please tick the appropriate boxes to indicate your answers

1 Where did you get this Scarlet title?
Bought in supermarket ☐
Bought at my local bookstore ☐ Bought at chain bookstore ☐
Bought at book exchange or used bookstore ☐
Borrowed from a friend ☐
Other (please indicate) _____

2 Did you enjoy reading it?
A lot ☐   A little ☐   Not at all ☐

3 What did you particularly like about this book?
Believable characters ☐   Easy to read ☐
Good value for money ☐   Enjoyable locations ☐
Interesting story ☐   Modern setting ☐
Other _____

4 What did you particularly dislike about this book?
_____

5 Would you buy another Scarlet book?
Yes ☐   No ☐

6 What other kinds of book do you enjoy reading?
Horror ☐   Puzzle books ☐   Historical fiction ☐
General fiction ☐   Crime/Detective ☐   Cookery ☐
Other (please indicate) _____

7 Which magazines do you enjoy reading?
1. _____
2. _____
3. _____

And now a little about you –
8 How old are you?
Under 25 ☐   25–34 ☐   35–44 ☐
45–54 ☐   55–64 ☐   over 65 ☐

cont.

9 What is your marital status?
   Single ☐   Married/living with partner ☐
   Widowed ☐   Separated/divorced ☐

10 What is your current occupation?
   Employed full-time ☐   Employed part-time ☐
   Student ☐   Housewife full-time ☐
   Unemployed ☐   Retired ☐

11 Do you have children? If so, how many and how old are they?
   _____
   _____

12 What is your annual household income?
   under $15,000 ☐ or £10,000 ☐
   $15–25,000 ☐ or £10–20,000 ☐
   $25–35,000 ☐ or £20–30,000 ☐
   $35–50,000 ☐ or £30–40,000 ☐
   over $50,000 ☐ or £40,000 ☐

Miss/Mrs/Ms _____
Address _____
   _____
   _____

Thank you for completing this questionnaire. Now tear it out – put
it in an envelope and send it, before 31 January 1998, to:

Sally Cooper, Editor-in-Chief

USA/Can. address
SCARLET c/o London Bridge
85 River Rock Drive
Suite 202
Buffalo
NY 14207
USA

UK address/No stamp required
SCARLET
FREEPOST LON 3335
LONDON W8 4BR
*Please use block capitals for
address*

SWSED/7/97

Scarlet **titles coming next month:**

THE MARRIAGE CONTRACT Alexandra Jones

Olivia's decided: she's not a person any more . . . she's a wife! She's a partner who's suddenly *not* a full partner because of a contract and a wedding ring. Well it's time her husband, Stuart, wised up, for Olivia's determined to be his equal . . . in *every* way from now on!

SECRET SINS Tina Leonard

When they were children, Kiran and Steve were best friends, but they drifted apart as they grew up. Now they meet again and Kiran realizes how much she's missed Steve . . . and how much she loves him. But before they can look to the future, she and Steve must unravel a mystery from the past . . .

A GAMBLING MAN Jean Saunders

Judy Hale has secured the job of a lifetime . . . working in glamorous Las Vegas! Trouble is, Judy disapproves of gambling *and* of Blake Adams, her new boss. Then Judy has to turn to Blake for help, and finds herself gambling on marriage!

THE ERRANT BRIDE Stacy Brown

What can be worse than being stranded on a dark road in the dead of night? Karina believes it's being rescued by a mysterious stranger, whom she ends up sharing a bed with! But better *or* worse is to come, when Karina finds herself married to Alex, her dark stranger.